# The Unabridged Life of Missy Kinkaid

Kirsten Pursell

The Unabridged Life of Missy Kinkaid
By Kirsten Pursell

*Dedicated to the three women who made me:*
*My mom, because she has super powers*
*My daughters, Quinne and Britt, because they are the epitome of*
*bad ass women*

# The Scarlet Letter

<br>

Dear Missy,

We have a date! Beau and I are getting hitched (that's what they say in the South, no?). I suppose I could have shared the news the next time we meet for coffee, a walk, or a glass of wine. I would cry if I said these words out loud, though, so I sit here trying desperately not to weep as I put them to paper.

Where would I be without you? I would have found my way to Sullivan's Island. Driving here from California was easy. But I don't know that I could have navigated the small-town dynamics without your sage insight and less-than-subtle humor. You were the first person to take me in, defend me, support me, and understand me. Your non-judgmental understanding has been a lifeline for me.

You've been my compass in moments when I was most lost. You helped me navigate the craziness of Ben. You appreciated the beauty and youth of him when you learned he helped me sow my wild oats. Had I only known I would fall in love with his father! And you laughed out loud with me (not at me) when Abby tried to sabotage my future with Beau by trying to expose that. And then cried with me when I thought I had lost him. No one warned me that small-town drama is real!

I came to Sullivan's Island to start fresh. I didn't have a horrible divorce, as you know. They don't all have to be. And you know that too. I did not expect to fall in love. But it was easy with Beau (thank you for not asking him out just to spite Abby). He let me be me. It's so cliché, but when you least expect life to happen, it does. Same for love. I keep wishing you'd walk with your eyes closed so you'll crash into someone worthy of the beauty that is you, my friend.

I know your story has not been simple either. It's what made it so easy to connect with you. Sisters from other mothers, from opposite coasts, with drastically different beginnings, who met at a dank public library to discuss books with divorced women. Long live Scarlet's Harlots!

When I look back at my time here, I see the threads of you everywhere. You have been my rock. Cheering me on, laughing until we cry, and dragging me to book club even when I wanted to wallow instead. If friendship has been my foundation, you are a solid, unwavering presence. You've never once made it about you.

I know you have your story too. You've been this spark of joy that makes the rest of us believe maybe, just maybe, life isn't done surprising us. But I also know you are so much more than what we see on the outside. You have a story that is deep and complicated, equally heartbreaking and inspiring.

I guess that's why, as I step toward my future with Beau, I feel so strongly about writing you first. Marriage feels less like "arriving" and more like another chapter in a bigger book. You are, without a doubt, one of the central characters in mine. Beau may be the love story, but you were Porn Star martinis and red wine when the morally rigid, slightly toxic book clubbers wanted to count me out.

So when I stride down that aisle racing to be with Beau, know this: Part of me will carry all the versions of Scarlet you know well—the broken one, the laughing one, the leery one, the happily-in-love one. The other part of me will carry gratitude for you and the beautiful, often compli-cated, but totally amazing women who helped make this my home.

Thank you for your friendship. Thank you for helping me to find myself. Know that when I say, "we have a date," part of the joy is knowing you'll be there, sharing in my happiness.

Cheers,
Scarlet

*Before I send out any of these invites, I'd love to hear your opinion. That we can do in person. Over wine, of course.🤍

# Chapter 1

## *Clean-Up on Aisle Twenty-Three*

Missy stares at the cereal boxes and swears they are mocking her. Each one is plastered with the face of a man she once knew. Her ex-husband is front and center, offering his familiar condescending smirk. Has she really known that many men in her life? Or are they simply the faces of the men who've made an impression, fleeting glances at a bar, a nudge at a club? How did Shaun Cassidy make the cut? He was just a childhood crush, a poster on her wall. And maybe a practiced pillow kiss or two.

And why is she even in the cereal aisle? She detests cereal, the reminder of a childhood chastised for eating Apple Jacks and Cap'n Crunch instead of muesli. Her southern belle of a mother barely nibbled to get nutrients in her body, but Missy is full-figured. She deprived herself of nothing in her rebellion against a mother who attempted to control her.

Missy feels the tears start to roll down her face. She looks up at the drab, lentiginous ceiling, knowing God must be on the other side of the speakers playing muffled elevator music, watching her. "What the fuck, God? Now? Really?" She grabs a tissue from her handbag, wondering why her feet are frozen in place. She wants to run out of the store but cannot. Instead, she sits herself down in the aisle, facing the cereal boxes that taunt her, and lets herself cry, then wail.

She doesn't care about the other shoppers staring at her, walking around her like she's a leper. Missy needs this moment. It has been fifty-four years in the making. Her angry, bitter, righteous mother is dead. She should be celebrating. The woman has been nothing but a thorn in her side, passing judgment, attempting to make her doubt herself. Missy, the epitome of confidence, would not let herself be brought down in the face of her mother's evil.

But sitting sobbing in the middle of aisle twenty-three, Missy realizes her mother didn't know better. She was evil because the voices in her head made her that way. She had not been a strong presence in Missy's life because she'd spent most of it locked away at a home for the mentally ill. Missy had persevered because her mother wasn't there to beat her down every day; instead, she did it in small doses when Missy went to visit. Her father was every bit the doting dad, showering Missy with the love and affection her mother could not afford. She finds herself struggling to reconcile that both her parents are now dead and the ghosts of her lovers past are staring at her from cereal boxes. She swears it's a message from above, beyond the ceiling that, she has decided, is in desperate need of repair.

When she's certain this wave of her nervous breakdown is done, Missy blows her nose twice, wipes away any residual snot, and smooths her pants leg as she gets up. She catches a Millennial staring at her, confused. Missy smugly says, "Menopause. Just you wait." Then she pulls the oversize black Gucci sunglasses from her bag and gently places them on her face, pulling a few loose strands of her red hair forward. She has regained her composure. For good measure, she intentionally swipes at several boxes of cereal and lets them fall to the floor as she walks past. "I can't remember all of you," she whispers as if they can hear her.

She has come to the grocery store for wine, cheese, and crackers. She might throw in some grapes for good measure, she thinks as she exits the cereal aisle. And some almonds because they're healthy and delicious. She likes the idea of charcuterie boards; she just can't commit to the art of them. Her version is a wooden cutting board where she mostly randomly throws all the ingredients in the middle, then spreads them out.

It's her night to host her close friends, Scarlet and Amber. They'd playfully named themselves "Scarlet's Harlots," the "unwronged" women of the Sullivan's Island Divorced Women's Book Club. When Scarlet arrived in town after her divorce, she discovered that not all women share the same story; some women, in fact, can be closed-minded and judgmental. But she and Missy had found each other, discovering not only a similarity in age but aligned stories, and Scarlet had quickly become Missy's closest confidante. It was Scarlet who had reminded her to fully embrace her place in Sullivan's Island.

Missy is glad that Scarlet has found happiness with Beau, and she looks forward to their wedding in the coming months. Beau, the retired firefighter who loves to swim as much as Scarlet does; who loves her even after learning of her relationship with his son, Ben, when she first came to town; who stood by her side despite his ex-wife, Abby, attempting to sabotage their relationship. They're perfect for each other.

Amber, though a good decade younger than Scarlet and Missy, is an old soul with hilarious stories from her previous glamorous life. As a contestant on *The Bachelor*, her world became a whirlwind of high society, dating rich men, marrying one of the richest, and then divorcing him because he was a boring dud. She is a youthful reminder that someone who appears perfect is not impervious to pain.

Missy strolls along the wine shelves, mulling over her choices. Scarlet and Missy both like chilled reds, but of course, Margo, her cousin, will also be there and she prefers white. She had been her best friend once, too. Missy isn't always sure why she's included in Scarlet's Harlots, whether out of guilt or because she's family. Missy stopped fighting the demon of past betrayal long ago, and neither Scarlet nor Amber questioned it. Four harlots felt right.

Despite her initial fears that Margo might report their conversations back to the other members of the book club, she has not let Missy down yet. Whenever the four of them get together, Margo is on the periphery, but even so, Missy knows being part of the club makes Margo feel like she is included in something that isn't blatantly bitter, angry, or vindictive. The irony of that is not lost on her since Margo's personification of those petty emotions is Oscar-worthy.

Missy struggles to hold her chosen three bottles of wine, cursing under her breath that she forgot to grab a cart on the way in. She looks up and finds her gaze met by the partially deflated Mylar balloons doing a tired dance above her. She bobs her head in heightened irritation, then mumbles, "This is your fault," as if her dead mother might hear her and apologize for distracting Missy with her death.

"Excuse me, ma'am, you look like you could use a cart. Take mine. I'm just getting started." Missy looks at the kind stranger who's spoken up, an older gentleman she does not recognize. She gratefully puts her items in the basket and thanks him.

"I'm in a bit of fog today," she says. "Thank you for coming to my rescue."

She begins to walk away when he calls after her, "Are you Charlotte Kinkaid's daughter?" She feels her face drain of its color. She sees the imaginary puddle of anxiety pool on the tiled floor beneath her, challenging her not to slip in it. She turns to look at him, her despair apparent on her face.

"Do I know you?" she finally asks.

He smiles at her, reaching out his hand. Missy shakes it gently as he speaks. "I'm Malcomb Horner. I knew your mother once. I heard that she passed. I'm sorry." She wonders how he found out so quickly. Charlotte died only two days ago. She wonders why her mother didn't wait a week and die on Missy's birthday. That would have been fitting, she thinks.

It occurs to Missy that the only people who will remember her mother are her mother's late peers, octogenarians and beyond. Her father, Dex, had made sure the world believed Charlotte Kinkaid vanished as soon as he institutionalized her. The story Dex told, albeit painfully and religiously, was almost verbatim: Charlotte packed her things while he and Missy were off visiting family, left a note saying she didn't want to be found, and disappeared. When asked if he looked for her, he would always nod with a lost look in his eyes. "She was gone and could not be found," he would say. It was a form of the truth. Soon, folks stopped asking him questions, instead quietly wondering what really happened to Charlotte Kinkaid, followed by a mumbled prayer for Missy. Prayer was the answer to everything in South Carolina.

"How'd you know her, Mr. Horner?"

"Malcomb, please." He takes the cap off his head and begins fidgeting with it, turning it in small increments with shaking fingers. Even though she is in a hurry, Missy recognizes he has something to share and puts her haste aside.

"Did you know her well, Malcomb?" she asks softly, her interest piqued. She has not met many people in the small town of Sullivan's Island who knew her mother outside of her immediate family. And if they did, they did not speak of Charlotte Kinkaid. She was the sort of skeleton in a closet you were reminded to keep locked away.

Her memories of her mother are fragmented and often unkind. Missy would look at pictures of Charlotte from when she was younger, a true southern belle. She'd inherited her trademark bright-red hair and her father's distinctive emerald eyes, a striking combination of traits.

Charlotte had been imposing, standing at nearly six feet tall. Missy is grateful she didn't inherit that gene. She finds her five-foot-eight height perfect. Charlotte was thin, too thin by most standards. Family members would whisper in concern about how emaciated Charlotte always looked. They stayed silent in those moments when she was accused of being a drug addict. It was, after all, the sixties, an era synonymous with drug abuse and ultra-thin models like Twiggy. Perhaps, Missy has wondered in her later years, when she tries to assimilate all the pieces of her mother's story, it was less shameful to be a drug addict than an anorexic. Missy remembers when Karen Carpenter died, reading about her struggles with the disease. She always thought her mother's image could have easily replaced that of Karen Carpenter.

Missy has always been confident in her body: a little curvy, a little booby, a little hippy, with a tiny muffin top that won't go away no matter how hard she tries. After her two children, Mackenzie and Kinkaid, were born, she found them a convenient excuse for the little bit of middle she had. It was almost as if children gave her license to wear that middle proudly.

It was Missy's dad, Dex, who reminded her what a beautiful girl, then woman, she had become. He would pick up on her dismay after visits with her mother, knowing that Charlotte would have criticized Missy for not being thinner, more in her image. Charlotte was cruel like that. "She doesn't know better, honey. She doesn't understand those things. Her view of the world has been distorted by the voices in her head," Dex would explain. "You need to know I love you and think you are perfect, the most beautiful of them all." In those moments, Missy felt like Snow White, knowing that her mother would look in her mirror and ask who's the fairest of them all and be met with her father's words: "Missy is." She knew that wasn't how the fairy tale went, but she liked her version better.

Malcomb watches Missy intently. He sees Charlotte in her, and he sees Dex, too. He sees her sadness, and he sees her resolve. "I suppose I'm one of the last ones standing," he says with a chuckle.

"I don't think I've ever seen you around here, Malcomb. You weren't friends with my dad," Missy observes.

He laughs at that. "Only because he was jealous," he replies. "Although, I suppose, I'm the one who was jealous in the end. Your mother was my first crush. Oh, I was so sweet on her."

"Charlotte and Dex in a little love triangle," she says, amused. The smile leaves Malcomb's face. She quickly adds, "I'm joking! I'm sorry."

"Oh, no, no. There was no triangle. No time for that. I got drafted and was off to Vietnam. I tell myself if it wasn't for that damn war, Charlotte would have been my girl."

"You might have dodged a bullet there," she kids. "You do know she spent nearly fifty years in a home for the insane, don't you?"

"I do. I would stop in once a year when I was in the area." He looks up at her as if gauging her reaction to this news. "I was in DC for most of my career, after the war and college and all, but we kept in touch. Then when she disappeared, I visited your father, and he told me. That man was devastated. And I knew he truly loved her. You were lucky to have him, Missy."

"I know. I miss him every day. And now they're both gone." Missy feels the potential for more tears, so she looks at her watch to mitigate the moisture, then seamlessly reverts to the happy woman everyone knows her to be. "Malcomb, I'm so glad I ran into you and that you shared a sweet story of my mother. My memories are not always so kind, actually more tortured than anything, but you softened them a little. Thank you." Missy embraces the man, hugging him while he awkwardly tries to figure out what to do with his arms, unaccustomed as he is to such open displays of affection.

Missy grabs her cart, hurries to the snack food aisle, and throws in several varieties of chips. Then, she beelines to the cheese aisle, randomly grabbing four different shades of cheese. She passes the produce section on the way to checkout, picking the first bunch of red grapes she sees and the walnuts that are on display above them. She wanted almonds, but today she won't be bothered with the usual.

She finds her mind wandering back to Malcomb and what he has shared. She wishes she had known his version of Charlotte. How different her life might have been if she had had a mother to help her navigate men and the complications that came with them.

Instead, she is left wondering if she might not be losing her mind just a little, too. *Who sees faces on cereal boxes if you aren't going crazy?* she wonders.

"I'm not crazy like you," she mutters under her breath within earshot of the cashier, who looks only slightly offended by the clearly confused woman buying groceries.

# Chapter 2

## *Baby, You're a Firework*

Melissa Jean "Missy" Kinkaid was born two weeks early, on a swelteringly hot July Fourth weekend. Charlotte's water broke in the early evening hours of July 3. The baby wasted no time in arriving; she announced herself several hours later, at 11:57 p.m.

She'd come into the world screaming and yelling as if her hair was on fire. Her parents would often laugh at the idea of it since, of course, she'd made her entrance with a head full of fiery red fuzz. At the time, Dex had shrugged his shoulders in joyous acquiescence. Charlotte had laughed and said, "Told you the baby would have red hair. Those Mulligan Irish genes are mighty." Dex loved Charlotte's red tresses and had secretly wished his child would inherit her hair.

"She's a little firecracker," the doctor wisecracked. He held the tiny, alien creature up, covered as she was in the thick, creamy, white goop of the womb. "She's going to be a handful," he said as he lay the baby on Charlotte's chest.

To some extent, he was right. Melissa was a mischievous girl. She was curious about the world around her. She bombarded her parents with endless questions as soon as she was able to string the words together. "Now, missy, you need to be careful," they told her in kind, or, "Look now, missy, don't be so sassy." Melissa was shortened to "Missy" as soon as Dex and Charlotte realized it would just be easier to call her that; it was like killing two birds with one stone.

Missy had perfect white skin, which stood in stark contrast to her hair and emerald-green eyes. She would spend her summers covered from head to toe in sunscreen. Charlotte would lather it on Missy's fair skin, hoping to ward off a sunburn. Charlotte refused to set foot on the sand if the sun was out. She would have preferred Missy to do the same. But Missy was not to be stopped and spent hours in the hot sun, splashing in the water with her friends, while Charlotte attempted to scold her from the deck of their beachfront home to come inside. "In a minute," Missy would yell, showing up an hour later with perfect pink lines outlining where her swimsuit had been.

"You're going to end up a freckled mess if you keep up in the sun like that, young lady."

"Freckles are the sun's kisses. I love being kissed," Missy would say and giggle.

Her mother's expression remained unchanged. "No man will want those freckles," she'd say.

Missy never knew if she meant to be hurtful or helpful with those words. She was five and did not understand.

"The sun gives me all the kisses I need, Mommy." She sometimes gave Charlotte a giant kiss after saying the words. "And I give you kisses."

Charlotte was not an affectionate woman. Period. She was awkward in embrace. She did not know how to console with touch or words. Her cold exterior showcased the conflicted woman she was on the inside. As Missy got older, she wondered how her father had ever fallen in love with her. He was the opposite of

Charlotte. He was warm and affectionate. If he could put his arms around someone to console them, say a jovial hello, or just because, Dex did.

Even as a small child, Missy would watch in adoration her father's ability to connect with others, show love, and offer support. It was in stark contrast to her mother. Yet Dex stood firmly by Charlotte's side. Missy would watch as her dad stared adoringly at her mother, wondering what it was he saw that she did not. Occasionally, Missy would observe her mother reach ever so slightly for her father's hand, and he would squeeze it tightly. Their affection confused Missy.

Decades later, when her father's health began to fade and he was still relatively lucid, they had a conversation that left her broken in pieces. "I loved her so much," he confessed. "I loved her so much that I had to put her away. At least then I could still see her, parts of her, even though I knew she was mostly lost. I tried to love others, but the only woman I could ever love was you. She was my heart, and you were the rest. I died a little every day without her."

"Tell me about her, Daddy. Tell me why you loved her so much," Missy begged to know the story. She had tried many times over the years to get her father to share it with her, but he would just tell her it was too difficult for him to talk about. She was surprised when he began to speak.

"Oh, that Charlotte Goodwin sure was a looker. All the guys were in love with her. She picked me, though. Said it was the sparkle in my eye. She was quiet but so smart. We could talk about the world, wonder how hippies got their name, how many more of our friends would die in Vietnam. It was an awful time in the world," he said.

Missy wanted to tell her father it was an equally awful time in the world these days, too. Just different. But he would not have been clear enough to remember.

They were just twenty-two when they got married, and Missy was born five years later. As she got older, she had often wondered why she didn't have siblings. Her father would say that she was all they had needed, but at death's door, Dex admitted pregnancy had been difficult for Charlotte. "I think losing the babies made her go mad. I said we didn't have to keep trying, but she wanted a baby so badly. It was all she ever wanted. Then we finally had you. And..." Dex lost his train of thought, but Missy knew the end of the sentence: *I was born and she went crazy.* And the word *babies* hung in the air.

"We finally had our beautiful baby," he said finally. "You. Our little girl. That was all she ever wanted. But you cried. She screamed. You screamed. She went silent. She shut down. She would disappear sometimes for days. She stopped eating, worried she would be fat, that I wouldn't love her. She was skinny as a toothpick. There was hardly anything left of her to love."

He closed his eyes. It broke Missy's heart to think that she had played a role in her mother's madness. Logically, she knew this wasn't possible. Babies don't have that ability. She was a mother to two strong-willed children. She had not gone crazy.

"No, no. Stop, Charlotte. Don't hurt her." Missy watched as her father struggled.

"Daddy, it's okay," she said, gently touching his arm. His eyes shot open.

"She didn't mean to hurt you. I saved you. And I knew then that it wouldn't get better. I took her to a psych—psychia..." The word failed him.

"Psychiatric," Missy slowly finished the word for him.

"Yes, that. A hospital. They used all sorts of words I didn't understand. All I knew was that I went there with her and I came home without her."

She looked at her father as a tear streamed down his face. He had done that for her. He had chosen his daughter. He loved

Missy, never once making her believe she was anything less than his singular purpose. When she would catch him staring at her growing up, she realized now that he was looking for pieces of Charlotte in her.

"Daddy, you were the best father. I was so lucky to grow up with you. There was never a day I didn't feel loved or like I was your princess. If you could have, you would have brought her home. Thank you for protecting me and loving me." It was Missy who wiped away a tear this time.

Her father had died five years before her mother did, his death perfectly timed with her divorce from Cal. Dex had always cast a leery eye Cal's way. There was something about the way he treated his daughter that Dex did not like. Missy had always been a daddy's girl. She'd dismissed his concerns when she and Cal first began dating, saying, "I'll always be your princess, Daddy. Your love is special." Dex didn't think so, but he was not going to stand in the way of his strong-willed daughter.

Missy would rarely show outward signs of dissatisfaction. She'd smile widely, especially when she thought someone was watching. In later years, as she began to unravel, her father would pull her aside and ask her if things were okay. He sensed she was not being forthright with him and persisted in his questioning until, of course, he was no longer able to see things as they were in his declining health. Inside, Missy was glad he hadn't witnessed how Cal treated her during the divorce. Dex would have been appalled.

When Dex died, he left Missy the house and a decent amount of money, enough to support a modest lifestyle. Cal had gotten off easy in the divorce, and her spousal support was minimal at best. As a contractor, he was able to manipulate the numbers, show losses even if he had gains. Missy wasn't going to fight him; she just wanted out. All that mattered to her was that Macky and Kaid would be taken care of.

Cal has always been a good father to the kids. Macky and Kaid are both adults now, have graduated from college, and are working in Charleston. Missy had hoped they'd go farther away, experience a world that was bigger than South Carolina, but she also appreciates that they stayed close, an easy visit for them and her, and that she can fill her voids with dates with them.

Missy made monthly trips to her mother more out of guilt than a desire to spend time with her. She did not feel she owed her mother anything. She had been a sweet child. She had tried to show her mother affection. She wondered when it was that her father had saved her. Shouldn't she have remembered something like that? It saddened her to think that her mother had hated her so much. Charlotte was cruel in her comments at times, focusing on Missy's weight or her freckled skin. Every visit was a repeat of the one before. Charlotte had no concept of time. She would perk up when Missy came, if only to say, "Oh, it's you. Where's your father? I need to tell Dex that they keep overcooking the chicken. He should be able to fix that. He fixes everything."

Missy would remind her that he was dead, that he would no longer captain the fight for better chicken. Every time Missy reminded her of this, Charlotte's face would drain of color, and tears would begin to uncontrollably flow. "Dex, no," was all Missy could hear her mumbling.

Her father, she realized, was like a box of Cap'n Crunch cereal. It was his face she saw under the bright blue captain's hat. He had led the ship, but it wasn't smooth sailing.

# Chapter 3

## *Confession of a Non-Virgin*

Missy makes it home with twenty minutes to spare. She throws the wine in the fridge and grabs a wooden charcuterie board from the large stack she has in the kitchen. She looks forward to the day friends and guests stop bringing them as gifts or leaving them behind. Her collection is large, and she no longer entertains as frequently as she once did. She relishes her alone time in her childhood home. It felt like forever before she started to appreciate the big, old space, but now, she chooses a night in, binge-watching shows or reading a book, and doesn't feel she owes anyone an explanation. It took a lifetime of guilt to get there.

As a mom, she found herself feeling guilty for doing any of those things. She knew it was silly, but she never wanted Cal to think she wasn't carrying her weight. Even he would defend her when she'd say she was "just a mom." He didn't know if she was reading or watching TV when he was at work and she had a short break in between kid runs and errands. There were days when she longed for the corporate world, with its rigid schedule and strict standards of execution. Parenting was a crapshoot half the time, with outcomes unpredictable at best.

Missy had dedicated her life to raising her children. The once-successful advertising manager at a large agency in Charleston gave up promotions, glamorous commercial shoots, and travel to move back to Sullivan's Island with Cal. He hated the big city even if it was the primary source of his income. They purchased a small home and remodeled it to fit their growing family. Missy loved their home. Unfortunately, it was a casualty of the divorce. With both kids in college, they no longer had children living there full-time, he argued. Neither of them needed something so big. Had her father died two weeks earlier, when they had closed on the sale of their house, she would have considered buying Cal out. Timing was everything, she conceded as she reluctantly moved choice pieces of furniture, boxes of the kids' lives, and her belongings into her childhood home.

She wasn't sure she should keep her father's big house after he died. It wasn't her style, but the more time she spent there in the days after her divorce, the more she appreciated that it felt like a place where she belonged. She spent some of the money she inherited making modifications to the kitchen, her bedroom, and the main living areas. The rest, she maintained, would not be lived in anyway. Those rooms got new paint, light window coverings, and throw rugs. She preferred a more modern look, something for which she gave Cal credit. As a contractor, he had an eye for architecture, specializing in modern remodels of many traditional Southern homes. She hired his nemesis to do the remodel.

Missy finishes tidying up the living room, setting out the bottles of wine next to four neatly placed wineglasses. The charcuterie board looks more like Pollock on an off day than Pinterest perfection, but these women are her dear friends. She doesn't need to impress them.

The four women tried to meet weekly to catch up on life

outside of their monthly book club meetings. Those gatherings lingered, sparking leftover conversations and the inevitable swirl of innuendo. But mostly, they talked about life. No one's feelings were hurt if someone couldn't make it or had to cancel altogether. W(h)ine night with Scarlet's Harlots was their time to embrace life's imperfections.

She is elated to find she has minutes to spare, so she sits on the white, three-seat sofa and closes her eyes, letting out a large exhale. The memory of Malcomb's face flashes like hazard lights in front of her. She tries to focus on seeing her friends, forgetting Malcomb, but he is front and center, gnawing at her.

It is true that her mother just died. She is supposed to feel sad. But seeing Malcomb makes her feel more disappointed than anything. Her mother had been there her whole life. In spirit, at least. Her words—sharp, bitter, cold—are a constant in Missy's psyche. Her mother lived to be eighty-one. Now she's dead, and Missy realizes she didn't even know her. She knows she had to be saved from her, if you believed a dying old man. She knows her father would not make that up. She wants to feel sad. She wants to feel the weight of losing her mother, but she feels nothing except relief.

Her friends do not know. She isn't even sure if Margo knows. She hasn't told her. It has been years since Margo even asked about Missy's mother. Missy never spoke of her, and most people assumed Charlotte had died long ago. If they mourned her death, they did it decades ago. Missy never corrected them when they spoke of her in the past tense.

* * *

Scarlet, Amber, and Margo arrive together, each giving Missy a hug. Scarlet hugs Missy last, then holds up a bottle of wine. "Just in case," she says with a mischievous grin. Generally, a safe bet.

Missy does not know what overcomes her, but in that moment, she begins to cry. She looks at her three friends, fans her hand in front of her face as if it might stop the tears, and then closes the giant front door. She stands facing it briefly, seeking comfort in its sturdy oaken panels, and then turns slowly toward the other women.

She takes a deep breath, then speaks. "She's gone. Yet I feel her presence more than I ever have." Scarlet and Amber look at each other, but Margo knows in that moment what she means. She puts her arms around Missy.

"I'm sorry, Missy. It's been a long time coming," she says.

They walk to the living room as Margo proceeds to explain that Missy's mother had been institutionalized most of her life and that most people had just assumed she was long dead. Scarlet has never heard Missy mention her mother before. She just assumed that, like her, Missy's parents were both gone. "I just figured most of us in our fifties are orphans," she says.

"Well, I've been a half orphan most of my life," Missy explains. "Motherless, at least. My dad was awesome."

"It's something we've always shared, huh, Missy? Charlotte and Adeline Goodwin were absent at best. But, hey, we turned out okay," Margo proclaims.

The women all choose not to comment on that. They all know it's not true, especially not in Margo's case.

Amber and Scarlet sit together on the love seat opposite the giant glass doors that opened toward the water. Margo claims the armchair. Missy wants to be annoyed—Margo knows it is her favorite seat. She likes to think of it as her throne. Instead, she pours three glasses of red and one of white. She doesn't ask. She hands them their drinks, lifts her own in a casual "cheers," and takes a long gulp.

"Thanks," Missy says. "I didn't think I'd react like this. I've had a couple of days to process—it's not like I didn't see it coming

—but then I ran into this man at the grocery store who knew her. A sweet old man named Malcomb." She dabs her nose on her sleeve before grabbing a napkin to dry the tears. She starts to giggle. "He was in a love triangle with my mom and dad."

"What?" all three women say in unison.

"So it was, like, the early sixties, but still. He was sweet on her. Apparently, a lot of the men of her time were. It's hard for me to imagine, but it also makes Mom a little more human. She's always been this cold, sterile woman to me. It was as if I were never a part of her. But I swear, since she died, she's been everywhere."

"Subconscious rising," Amber offers. "There's a whole bunch of stuff about that." They look at her, confused, but even in their lack of understanding, the term makes sense.

"So, you think she and this Malcomb ever had a thing?" Margo asks.

"No. It didn't sound like it, but he visited her over the years. And he knew she was dead when he spoke to me today. It's really kind of weird to have a crush on someone like that your whole life. I didn't ask if he'd ever married or had a family. I was too frazzled." She wants to tell them that moments before she met Malcomb, she had a nervous breakdown in the cereal aisle, but she refrains. She's already sounding a little nutty, strains of Charlotte echoing within her.

"Do any of you still have contact with your first crush?" Scarlet wonders aloud. She reminds them of Carter and how he reappeared in her life at a time when she was most vulnerable. She shudders to think how much she let herself feel for him, to be reminded of a crush, and then to come so close to being with him again. "I was stunned when he showed up here after breaking my heart," she says. "God, I don't even want to imagine what would have happened had I not met Beau."

"Things like that happen for a reason," Amber says, continuing on her New Age refrain. "I totally believe it. I know it can sound foo-foo-like, but we wouldn't be friends if our worlds didn't simultaneously combust, bringing us together."

Amber's youthful energy might grate if it weren't so genuine in delivery. Ten plus years of marriage hadn't left a bitter taste in her mouth, like it had with Margo. They had all experienced empty marriages, though, so maybe that was the tie that bound them.

"Yes, we were like a multi-vehicle crash waiting to be cleaned up," Missy jokes.

A half hour later, with a bottle of wine downed and only grape stems and cheese crumbs left on the charcuterie board, they open a second bottle of red. They're a thirsty lot tonight. Only the white remains half-full, which Missy figures puts Margo a few ounces ahead of the rest of them.

"Okay, let's lighten this up," Scarlet says and cocks her hip to one side. "Malcomb: Charlotte was his first love. And for your dad, we'll assume he was hers, too. Maybe, maybe not. It seems there's a lot to Charlotte we'll never know." A sly grin spread across her face. "But I just can't help but wonder who might have been her first time..."

The thought of this makes them all smile - except for Missy, who has just seen a ghost.

A sudden wind sweeps through the living room. No one seems to notice but Missy. She looks around and swears she sees Charlotte in the kitchen, waggling her finger at her in disapproval for speculating. Missy squeezes her eyes shut, and just like that, Charlotte is gone.

"Feels a little like a high school sleepover. Who kissed who?" Missy says. She's shocked to feel this okay discussing her mother and father's romantic lives, but the Cab Franc does the trick. That, and she never liked when her mother waggled her finger at her.

"Except it's, 'Who did you lose your virginity to?'" Scarlet continues.

Amber smiles widely. "Andy Murray. Not the tennis player,

but, oh man. I was seventeen. Senior summer. He was so hot. Dumb as all get out, but I didn't care. We had a lot of fun together."

"Do you know what happened to Andy?" Margo asks.

"He married a supermodel, who was also dumb. They made dumb babies together. But they're super cute. And super happy."

Missy sizes her up, but Amber genuinely seems happy for them.

"You know this, why?" Margo presses.

"I've Insta-stalked him. Duh." Amber giggles. "Also, he reached out when he saw I was on *The Bachelor*."

Amber sometimes says things that make the other women wish for an evening dedicated entirely to her relaying stories of her life with the rich and famous, but Amber, knowing how not to outstay her welcome, shares only enough to keep it interesting.

"My first time turned into my boyfriend for a few months," Scarlet says. "The summer before college. He was a foreign exchange student from Sweden. Anders Johansson. He was so cute. We were both clueless, but we figured it out. Well, at least he did. I'm not sure I knew what an orgasm was then."

They all smile at that revelation.

Missy remembers her first time, too: Mike Chambers. She had just turned sixteen. Boys were top of mind all the time, but she wasn't interested in most of the boys who liked her. They were too young, clueless, not in control of their bodies, let alone mature enough to handle her. Missy had always been very self-aware. Even if she'd only kissed a handful of boys, she felt in control, like she knew what she was doing.

So when Mike Chambers came home from college after his freshman year looking fine and all grown-up, Missy couldn't help but find herself smitten. When he asked her to see a movie and then made out with her from the title card to the end credits, she thought she might just be in love for the first time. Two weeks later, Mike and Missy consummated their relationship. Missy's first time gave her confidence. Not because she'd had sex with a cute boy, but because her body relished it. "It didn't hurt. It was fun. We laughed. He came. We went again. My body enjoyed it. That probably wasn't normal for a virgin. But I did." She smiles as she reflects. "Even so, I don't think I'd figured out the orgasm thing yet."

Of course, none of them had at that age. Only men came ready to go. They all agree it's too easy for them. They don't need books or tutorials. Their penises just know.

"Did you date after?" Amber asks, circling back to Missy.

"Not for very long. I think he was the first boy I loved."

Margo squirms as Missy says this, which shifts the group's attention to her.

"And your first, Margo?"

She turns red at Amber's question.

"Seriously, you're embarrassed by that at this age?" Missy asks. "It was Russell, your husband."

"It wasn't, though," Margo defensively blurts out.

Missy looks surprised. "But you told me that's who it was! Remember? Years ago. At a girls' night out."

"Yes, I remember what I told you," she says, then adds, with a shrug, "but I lied."

"Why? Did you think I'd judge you for sleeping with more than one man?" Missy asks.

"No. It's not that. I thought you'd be mad at me because…" She fidgets, looking as if she is fighting back a tear. "Because I slept with Mike that summer, too. After you two broke up."

Missy is dumbfounded, then irritated. "See? This is why we always said Margo took our scraps. Jesus, Margo! You started with Mike and ended with Cal, right after I asked him for a divorce. Doesn't it bother you at all to be constantly walking in my footsteps, taking my leftovers?"

Margo is both stunned and speechless. She mechanically gets up from the couch, walks to the kitchen, downs the remaining wine in her glass, and then puts it down. She turns toward the group. Amber and Scarlet are still, while Missy fumes.

"Leftovers?" she seethes. "Yes, Missy. Let's talk about that. I have always felt like I'm the consolation prize—well, except I've never felt like a prize. You're the prize. Everyone always loved you more. You were prettier. You were taller. You were smarter. Your dad loved you while mine abandoned me. Your mom was hidden from sight, but mine stayed on full display. I did not have the option to run and hide even if I wanted to. My whole life has been in your shadow. It sucks. And never ever did you stop to think that maybe I didn't do it, that I didn't pursue Cal. Or Mike. That they came to me."

At this point, Margo is crying, doing her best to get the words out, words she has clearly been practicing in bits and pieces over time, in front of her mirror or while stuck in traffic. "The worst part is knowing they only came to me to spite you. And only God knows why, but I let them. Maybe because I knew it would hurt you if you ever found out."

Margo wipes her nose with her shoulder. She abruptly turns to leave, knocking the wineglass to the kitchen floor. It shatters loudly, leaving shards everywhere; only the stem remains relatively intact. "Fuck," she says, startling herself as Margo is not one to cuss.

Missy does not move. She watches as the world around her shifts into slow motion. She sees Mike's face on the cereal box: Cheerios. *Why Cheerios?* she wonders, then comprehends. Because he was simple and basic, the starter cereal. She watches motionless as the glass falls from the counter. Margo cussing. Scarlet and Amber running to the kitchen. Amber tries to console Margo, but she shoves her out of the way as she heads to the door. The door slams, shaking the house as it closes, bringing Missy back to the present. She looks blankly at Scarlet and Amber, then sits down on the sofa.

Missy speaks slowly and deliberately. "What the fuck just happened?"

Amber finishes cleaning the broken glass while Scarlet makes her way to Missy's side. Scarlet answers her question with a simple: "A lot."

Missy spends the rest of the evening trying to process how she and Margo have reached this point. She thought she had always been supportive of her cousin, included her even after what she did with Cal and, unbeknownst to Missy, Mike. She knows her cousin had it harder than she did, pretending to be okay in a world that was often unstable and imploding around her. They had shared a special bond since childhood. They were practically sisters. She had to find a way to remember that.

When Missy goes to bed that night, she wonders how she would have reacted as a teenager to learning that Margo had slept with Mike. Would she have been as angry as she had been when Margo slept with Cal during the divorce? Or would she have taken pity on Margo? As a woman, Margo would know what she was doing. As a girl, she had no clue, modeling herself after Missy, who equally had no clue but wore it better.

Life had not been kind to Margo. Some of it was of her own making; other parts, the sad reality of growing up in a dysfunctional family. It is not lost on Missy that the roles could have easily been reversed. She thinks of that often, especially in those moments when she tries to show Margo some grace, but she is tired of always being the one to have to show mercy. Margo never apologized for sleeping with Cal. And clearly not Mike.

As Missy goes to turn out the light, she sees tomorrow's book club read on her nightstand. She rolls her eyes; she's nowhere close to finishing the book. She grabs her phone. "Hey, Siri, summarize *Hello Beautiful* for me." She knows it's cheating, but she is too bothered to comprehend. Besides, from what she's read so far, she senses a sad ending.

When she finally turns out the light, a small tear has formed in the corner of her eye. It trickles down her cheek. Siri has confirmed it for her. The book is true to life in many ways. And it makes her ache.

# Chapter 4

## *The Crazy That Makes Us*

Missy and Margo are just six months apart in age. Born Margaret Eloise Harper, Margo was the only child of Charlotte's sister, Adeline, and the former heir apparent to a giant furniture company, Vance Harper. While Missy was born in the heat of summer, Margo was born six months later, in the dead of winter—on the coldest day on record, in fact. The contrasts between the cousins were stark even from the beginning.

Margaret was shortened to Margo thanks to her father. He was usually too inebriated to say Margaret, stopping after "Marg" and then slurring, "Marg—Oh, it's just too long." He stopped saying the *It's just too long* part, and she became simply Margo. She preferred it to the stiff and formal-sounding Margaret, which was then reserved for moments she knew meant she was in trouble. Margo was the one thing her father gave her that she remembered fondly. She thought it would be a funny story to tell her children someday.

Vance Harper's time as Margo's father was short-lived. He gambled his furniture fortune away, drank his kidneys to death, and died when Margo was a teenager. Margo doesn't remember crying or being upset when he died. She only remembers her mother dropping her off at Missy's house so she could go play in the Caribbean with her new boyfriend. Needless to say, Margo's issues with acceptance were deeply rooted in her backstory: two emotionally unavailable parents who barely acknowledged her existence.

Missy and Margo had been the best of friends as children. They played dolls together, went on bike rides, read teen magazines, and pined over the likes of Shaun Cassidy and the Bee Gees. While Missy flourished in her teenage years, developing ample breasts, long legs, and an attitude that matched her fiery red hair, Margo suffered from severe acne, a penchant for too much sauce with her chicken fingers, and an uneasy air that made her seem slightly on edge most of the time. Her hair was a nondescript shade of brown. Missy was tall and voluptuous while Margo barely surpassed five feet and was considered chubby. They acted and looked like polar opposites but were thick as thieves. Missy liked her then. She knew Margo was her loyal confidante and staunch supporter. She flew under the radar while Missy stood atop it, directing traffic.

It wasn't until they got into high school that Missy recognized Margo was trying too hard. If she saw Missy flip her hair or do her flirty laugh, Margo would make every effort to replicate it. While Margo thought she was being cute like Missy, the rest of the school saw it as trying too hard to be something she was not. What worked for Missy did not translate for Margo. While the other kids laughed behind Margo's back, Missy found herself in the increasingly awkward position of defending her cousin. "She is so not you," they would tell Missy. "She just looks stupid," they'd chide. No one, including Missy, had the heart to tell Margo to stop.

When Missy started kissing boys behind the bleachers during school or at the drive-in after football games, it was Margo who watched and waited. When Missy had her fun, which usually meant a French kiss and maybe a hand on her boob, she'd giggle and say she couldn't go any farther than that. "I mean, I do have my dignity," she would say with a wink. Margo would then swoop in to console the boy left behind, saying, "She's such a tease." Most of the boys would look at Margo with a disgusted face and walk away, but on occasion, one would decide to kiss her. It never involved tongue, and there was never any boob. "She's flat as a board," she heard a boy say once. She would curse Missy in those moments, wondering why she got the perfect genes when Margo clearly got only the leftovers.

The girls attended different colleges but met up for sleepovers during breaks. Even so, their relationship had become stifled and fragmented after high school. It was clear that Missy was thriving in her new environment. She joined a sorority as one must at a big school like the University of South Carolina. She attended football games, drank too much, and slept with frat boys with names like Victor, Donahue, and Scooter. She did this one time each after she had had too much to drink. The second time, sober, she needed to prove to herself their chemistry wasn't just drunken attraction clouding her judgment. While she found them all uniquely attractive, once they took her out on a proper date and showed their human side, they revealed themselves to be self-absorbed and boring.

The fourth frat boy she would meet was a tall, well-built, slightly cocky, but humorous former high school linebacker named Calvin Sutton. He was two years ahead in school but needed five years to graduate. When Macky and Kaid later asked why he didn't finish college in four years like their mom, he said there were just too many distractions. They'd jokingly ask back, "But wasn't Mom just as distracted by you?"

He would snidely remark, "Your mother came after the fun. I was already more serious when I met her."

Missy would hold her breath in those exchanges, wanting to explode at his narcissism. After rethinking her impulse, she'd just smile instead.

Missy knows Cal only graduated because she made him focus. Cal was easily distracted, had several things going on at once, and needed a little guidance and prodding. She gave herself more praise than he ever would for helping him graduate and start on his career track. In a show of resolve, Missy refused to marry him until he'd proven his financial worth and stability. She did, however, sleep with him during those years. In hindsight, she wondered if that was the only time she ever felt really connected to him. Or had time distorted the nicer memories of their courtship? She couldn't be sure anymore.

Margo, on the other hand, attended a small liberal arts college that few folks had heard of. It would be easier not to judge her that way, she had thought, or to compare her to Missy, which she knew everyone did. She blamed her lack of involvement on being too busy with studying to have time for extracurricular activities. Her only friends were her two roommates, Amy and Steph. Even then, Amy and Steph were active in sports, which Margo had no appreciation for.

So when she met Russell Jones at the one bar night she went to, she was convinced that he was her true love, her soul mate, and the future father of her children. She pursued him with reckless abandon. At first, he did not appear interested, but when he learned that her daddy was once wealthy, he just assumed it meant that Margo was rich, too.

They married the day after college graduation. Margo insisted they wait to have sex until they were married. Her one time with Mike had been less than noteworthy, and she was convinced she was a born-again virgin who would give herself only on her wedding night. (One time with Mike would not define her virginity. Her shop had been closed since then. Her vagina probably didn't know the difference.) Russell assumed she was a virgin, and Margo never gave him reason to believe otherwise.

Russell, meanwhile, had plenty of experience with women during college. Margo was surprised by his knowledge of where to touch and what to do. Sadly, he was not as keen on her lack of knowledge. He had thought he might be able to train a virgin to do what he wanted in bed, but Margo was stiff and cold and relatively lifeless between the sheets.

Years later, she would learn that he had been having affairs with several women to satisfy his desires. He had once even hit on Missy, who promptly laughed in his face. When she told Margo this had happened, Margo naturally defended her husband and accused Missy of trying to stir up trouble and ruin their marriage.

Margo had desperately wanted children, someone to love who would love her back. Unlike her parents had been with her, her children would be the center of the universe. But the universe continued to play a cruel trick on Margo by denying her the children she so desperately wanted. Russell had become frustrated by the process. He felt that if they could not have children naturally, then they shouldn't have any at all. Margo was devastated. After a decade together, she knew that Russell didn't love her. He would never say he didn't, but he also never said he did.

Just as much as Margo was convinced he was her true love and soulmate, she was equally convinced they should divorce. She was only thirty-two then. Maybe she could find another man and have a child with him. That she might adopt had never occurred to her.

Margo had one talent that made her shine, but she did not see it. She was a brilliant artist, capable of transforming colors and shapes into beautiful works of art. Missy's home had several of her pieces, and her cousin had encouraged her to branch out and start her own business.

Russell had belittled Margo's efforts to create art; instead, he'd encouraged (read: forced) her to take an office job at her father's former factory. Margo had a one percent stake in the company. Her mother had another one percent, which she took out in an advance against future earnings. Adeline made sure to spend every cent she had from her dead husband while Margo had downplayed her stake to Russell. It wouldn't have mattered, but somehow it felt like the one thing she had over him. She would tell Missy, "One percent of nothing is still nothing, right? Just didn't feel right telling him I was worth nothing."

"Margo, when will you see that you are so much more than nothing?" Missy would ask her in those moments.

"All I know how to do is disappoint people," she said often. "I can't have a baby. I have to work at my daddy's old factory, the one that he broke. It's like sitting there with a ghost looking over your shoulder, waiting for you to mess up so it can laugh at what an idiot you are."

Missy wondered how much Adeline had told Margo that she was worthless in those years after Vance had died. She sensed it was frequent. She had hoped that once angry alcoholic Vance was dead, Adeline might see her daughter in a different light. When Margo left Russell, she cried in Missy's lap. "You know Adeline used to tell me I was why Daddy died. She blamed me. She said I disappointed him."

Missy's heart had sunk to hear those words. While they lived several blocks apart, she imagined their homes side by side as children and teenagers. Her own dad would tell her every day how much he loved her and how beautiful she was, that she deserved the world, and he would help her make her dreams come true. Years later, of course, she learned she could have had a story not unlike Margo's.

Missy tried to be sympathetic. She knew it was not easy to grow up with a mentally unstable parent. Hers had been removed from the home, but she still felt the weight of Charlotte's words and actions, how they sometimes infected her. Margo lived with the evil, though she did not share this while they were growing up. Maybe Missy didn't see her cousin's pain, or perhaps she did. All she knew was that she did not want to hold herself responsible for Margo's happiness.

Much to Missy's surprise, Margo would rise from the divorce, like a phoenix from ashes. It was almost as if she had been emancipated, set free from Russell's controlling web. To his disappointment, Russell had to pay her a small amount of alimony. It was evident that the judge did not like his cocky attitude and condescending manner toward Margo. It was the one time in her life Margo did not resent someone taking pity on her.

Margo dreaded having to tell her mother that she was getting divorced. She knew her mother would chastise her, tell her it was typical for her to fail, expecting nothing less of her. After all, she never gave her a grandchild. Not that Margo would have trusted Adeline with her child. She would have protected it fiercely.

All the same, she reluctantly reached out to her mother, asking her if she could come over for coffee and to catch up. "You must have some big news to share if you want to catch up," Adeline said in a snarky voice.

"Can't I just come spend some time with you? I have the morning off," she lied.

When Margo knocked on the door that morning, she did not hear her mother's voice saying, "The door is open, come in," as she always did. Margo knew she didn't need to knock or wait to be invited in, but she did it anyway. It was part of their routine.

She peeked through the windows with the cracked molding, pieces of paint sticking to her fingers. She tried the door and found it locked. A sense of inexplicable calm came over her. She put her key in the door, called out "Mom?" and "Adeline?" but there was no answer. She looked around for signs of life. The coffeepot stood empty. Last night's dishes still sat by the sink. She called out again.

She walked to the back bedroom, where she knew her mother

slept. It was the smallest room in the three-bedroom house, making it an unlikely choice for the main bedroom. She never understood why Adeline preferred the small space at the back. But that morning when she walked in, she saw the beautiful morning light shining through the windows and understood. Her mother hated curtains. It was the one thing they had in common: They both loved light. Ironic, really, since most people thought Margo's and Adeline's personalities were anything but shining.

The morning light shone perfectly on Adeline's dead body, almost like she was an angel. The irony was not lost on Margo. She slowly walked over to her mother, reaching out for her hand, and felt it was cold against hers. It was the first time Margo looked at her mother and felt peace. She was gone. Her words would no longer hurt her. Margo wanted to feel sad. She thought she should cry, but she could not.

She went to the kitchen and made coffee, waiting as it brewed. She poured two cups and brought them both back to her dead mother's room. She put Adeline's cup down, then sat on the edge of the bed.

She thought about how pretty her mother looked in that moment. There was no anger in her face. Her muscles weren't clenched. No biting words were waiting to attack Margo. "I'm getting divorced, Mom," she finally said to her. "Oh, what's that? You hated him all along? You knew I could do better? Oh, Mom. I'm so glad you understand."

This would be how Margo remembered it. It would be the one thing Adeline ever gave her. Even if she was dead.

Margo had been spared her mother's humiliation. She had been spared the pain of her mother's chagrin at having failed her marriage. Adeline had spent all her money but left Margo the house. Margo's one percent added up to enough money for her to pay the remaining mortgage on the house, something she had learned had been refinanced seven times over the years.

She was grateful she had a home. While it was in disrepair, she would work tirelessly to make it a home for herself. At this point in her life, she was resolved that being alone was safer than being with a man. Vance and Russell had taught her men were no good; Dex Kinkaid and Cal Sutton were the exceptions to the rules. Missy was, of course, the only woman who would get both a great dad and a good husband.

"Why did you get the only two good men in the world?" she would wonder out loud through sobs to Missy.

Missy had barely been a decade into her own marriage and knee-deep in the realities of motherhood. She had not yet been afforded a glimpse of the real Cal. Or she quickly turned a blind eye if she was. "There are more than two good men in the world," Missy would insist. "There has to be."

At Missy's encouragement, after she moved in, Margo converted her mother's old bedroom into an art studio. There was magic in the light, and Margo couldn't bring herself to sleep in the room where her mother died. She would channel Adeline's spirit into her love of art. She would take the peace that came from her death and live.

Missy was her first customer, buying her first three pieces. Together, they built an Etsy page for Margo. Missy felt just as excited about helping her cousin express herself in a manner that was finally, uniquely her. Missy's enthusiasm was contagious, and Margo began to drink the Kool-Aid, too. She went to art shows and even developed a social media presence. She popped a bottle of champagne when she amassed a whole four hundred followers. Hardly viral, but enough to suggest people were interested. There was reason to celebrate.

As the years passed, Margo excelled as an artist, but her bitterness toward men and the happiness others found in the company of their spouses, significant others, and children would take expression in snide comments, rude actions, and blatant disregard for anyone not taking pity on Margo, the young spinster of Sullivan's Island.

It has been twenty years since she divorced. She is no longer the young spinster. Just a spinster. Margo wishes for love. Sometimes she even prays for it. She silently curses Missy for her courage to find love again and cheers when she fails. She did this with snide observations. "Finally, not everything is perfect for you."

"Perfect?" Missy would ask in those moments. "How the fuck has my life been perfect? My mom is certified nuts. I am divorced. I have had my heart broken."

Margo said nothing in return.

"You know, Margo, when will you ever figure out that your life isn't all shit? Maybe you should start asking yourself how much you're to blame instead of blaming everyone else." How many times over the years had Missy said some variation of those words to her cousin, hoping to break through to her?

# Chapter 5

## *Let Dysfunction Reign Among Us*

Summers on Sullivan's Island mean tourists are everywhere. It means locals take long vacations to escape the crowds. And it means the Divorced Women's Book Club takes a one-month hiatus. But with June behind them and July fireworks on the horizon, the women are eager to see each other again, catch up on local gossip (assuming their group chat hasn't already covered it), and discuss their latest read, *Hello Beautiful*. A story about dysfunctional family dynamics is perfect for their group. There isn't a member among them who doesn't have some level of dysfunction among the skeletons in their closets.

Although Missy makes several attempts throughout the day to contact Margo after the revelation and, dare she say, betrayal, Margo does not return her calls or answer her messages. She sighs and sets down her phone after her latest attempt at reaching out is left on *read*. Missy and Margo have hit a new bump in their relationship, a severe jolt that will leave no one unscathed.

Margo has put it all out there in one dramatic display of confession. It hurts Missy on a level she did not anticipate. She loves Margo. She is more like a sister than a cousin. She has never really forgiven Margo for sleeping with Cal, but after the evening's revelations, she's taking new assessment of their relationship. She has never considered Margo the victim; that Cal had used her.

As the women begin to pull into the library's parking lot for book club, a heightened anticipation fills the air. It is the first time they will all be together since the start of summer. Amber is making Sullivan's Island her semi-permanent home, living with her parents and feeling like a child, relishing the simplicity of it all.

"I know it sounds glamorous, but it was exhausting to always have to be on," she would say about having been a media darling. Missy and Scarlet would wonder how she managed all those years in the spotlight, being on television, the target of paparazzi, and then leaving her husband. Knowing Amber as they have come to know her, they know she is good at pretending, but she prefers unfiltered honesty—not to mention days without makeup and perfect hair.

"Did either of you hear from Margo today?" Missy asks as they walk into the library. "I tried calling and texting her, but she just left me on read."

"I texted her. Asked her if she was okay. She gave me a thumbs-up," Scarlet says.

"Same," Amber adds. "I'm glad I'm not the only one she ignored."

Scarlet, Missy, and Amber settle into their seats on the periphery of the group, forming their united front as Scarlet's Harlots. Of course, no one else calls them that. The requirement for membership in their secret society is being the opposite of a woman scorned. They were the ones who had pulled the trigger on their marriages, who had cheated, who had asked for the divorce—scarlet letters practically stitched to their chests. Dahlia technically qualified, too, but she kept her allegiance quiet. She preferred to stay neutral, especially if it meant staying in every-one's good graces as the Realtor of choice. So the Harlots stayed a trio, bound by their defiance and their own brand of unapologetic infamy.

Shortly after unofficially branding themselves Scarlet's Harlots, they clinked champagne glasses to celebrate. "To the three Harlots," Scarlet had said. "I don't know what I would have done if you two weren't by my side. Missy always. And you, Amber, are such a fun reminder of being young. So glad you showed up when you did. To we women who brandish the scarlet letter."

"Cheers," they said, then sipped their champagne.

"All we need is a tree house to hang out in. Then we'd really be a secret society," Missy added. They giggled at the prospect.

In the year and a half since Scarlet moved to Sullivan's Island, followed several months later by Amber, the formation of the Harlots cemented their roles in each other's lives. Scarlet, Missy, and Amber all needed each other. They found strength and unity in their little club.

And then there is Margo, the fourth member. Not an official Harlot. She doesn't know there's a name for the group, but she senses enough to realize she's left out of certain moments. She does not wish to be expelled or excommunicated, so she feigns ignorance.

"Although," Missy said out loud once, "she did scorn me by being with Cal. But scorning one of your own shouldn't count."

As they take their seats, they are afforded a perfect view of the others as they jockey for center seating in what is generally viewed by Scarlet's Harlots as their monthly pity party—this time with two months of grievances coming in between.

There are now an even dozen of them. The women scorned outweigh the anti-women scorned eight to four.

Audrey enters the room, followed by Margo. Audrey is a large woman, easy to hide behind. Margo avoids looking toward the Harlots, who are averting their glances. Inside, Margo knows it took all the courage and self-preservation she could muster to attend tonight's book club. If she hadn't come, there would have been more questions than if she had gone and silently sat apart from the group.

Margo is embarrassed by what happened the night before. She has spent her adult life compiling a mental list of grievances to assault Missy with. She has hoped someday to tell her cousin all the things that have consumed her throughout her life. How she's hated being her shadow. How she hates that she can't figure out how to be her own person without Missy. But how she also loves Missy because she's the one person who has always been there for her. Who reminds her that she had talent. Who enthusiastically encourages her. But it's hard not to resent her, too. And to have to admit that she—What did Missy say? *Took their scraps*—hurts her to the core. Have they really thought that about her all those years? Or is Missy just trying to hurt her?

After she stormed out of Missy's house, Margo spent the night in tears. She looked at the few photos she had of her and Missy growing up. Missy was always beaming in their photos together, especially the ones where she was looking at Margo. Even if she was looking down on her, she knew it was their height discrepancy that caused it. She looked at her wedding pictures, Missy proudly standing by her side as her maid of honor. And then there was the picture Margo took of Missy holding the first piece of art she'd bought from her. She looked so proud of Margo.

Margo had gone to bed feeling worse than when she'd arrived home a wreck from the disastrous confrontation at Missy's. Missy had been loyal and, until that night, had never used her words to hurt her. She was silent in the months after she learned Cal and Margo had been together. It wasn't even an affair; they were divorcing. It was betrayal, Margo knew. At the time, it felt good to hurt Missy, to know she finally had something over her. It wouldn't be till later that she recognized Cal had the same intention: to inflict pain upon Missy.

Margo had unleashed decades of pent-up anger on her cousin. Missy could not have seen it coming, and now Margo isn't sure how to move forward in their relationship. If they even can.

Margo sits to the side of the Harlots, finding a spot next to Abby. She wants to roll her eyes at them. She had hoped someday she'd be afforded a chair in their inner circle. She knows today will not be that day. Today, she wants to avoid all interaction with Missy.

Margo knows she does not have the same priority in their group. She thinks about her place in it and wants to believe they have room for her. She believes that Scarlet and Amber don't just pretend to like her or be her friend because Missy told them to. They are grown women and can make their own decisions. They always seem sincere, and both of them reached out to see how she was; both reacted with support when she imploded last night, taking that wineglass down with her.

She knows there have been many occasions when she has been included, but she assumes Missy acts primarily out of obligation. She knows her cousin pities her. She includes her despite what she has done, dismissing it under the caveat that Margo has always been a follower and Missy has been her anointed one. She has assumed all these things, but looking at the pictures, truly reading into them, Margo begins to wonder if she has been wrong about Missy.

Audrey calls the book club to order. All twelve members are present as they begin their first post-hiatus session. Audrey holds up her copy of *Hello Beautiful*. "Isn't this cover fabulous? I mean, I feel like we could just discuss how representative of the book it is. Just heartbreaking."

Audrey's enthusiasm can be overwhelming at times.

Audrey is an extraordinarily plain-looking woman; her bright blue eyes are her most expressive quality. Tall, broad, and slightly chubby, Audrey chooses to wear clothes that are loose-fitting and not the least bit flattering. She might have been attractive once, but time has not been kind to her. Her face wears the burden of raising her four children on her own after her husband never returned from a business trip. Herb had left her and their brood for a man.

Over the years, she asked herself if she could see it. And she could. Herb was feminine in every way and strikingly handsome, if not beautiful. He had perfect features. When Audrey first brought him home, no one could understand the attraction. Audrey was ordinary. There was nothing special about her, not even her personality. But Audrey and Herb had sex. They had sex exactly ten times. Four of those times had created children. Audrey adored Herb and didn't dare to ask him why they weren't having more sex. She considered herself lucky to be with a man who looked like he did. Forget that he never complimented her. Sex was fast and furious. It served a purpose.

Audrey might have been more critical of her poor decision-making in the years after Herb left, but she did not have time for that. Herb had left her when their youngest, Celeste, was just two years old and their oldest, Declan, was seven. Audrey did not have time for anything but them. Herb had come from money and basically bought her out. He was absent from the kids' lives, but he did send money every month, affording Audrey and the children a comfortable life. Audrey had been grateful for that, but she would have preferred a husband who loved her and their children. When the kids asked about their father, Audrey would lie. She wasn't sure why she did, but she told them she had asked him to leave because she had feared for their safety in his presence; she had asked Herb to go for them. In her eyes, it would make her children love her even more.

Audrey has been a good mom. So good, in fact, that all four children, now in their mid- to late twenties, still live at home under the careful supervision of Momma Audrey. Audrey has no desire to find another man. The prospect frightens her. She had been wrong once, and the pain of losing Herb is something that stirs painfully close to the surface. Her children are all she has to protect her from the self-destructive thoughts that came with Herb's rejection. She is fierce and protective of her family. No one messes with Audrey when it comes to them.

Book club, however, is another beast.

The women in the group are initially excited about the book. They discuss the characters and the decisions they made. Every character's choices are an exercise in seeing opposing perspectives. Missy wants to hate the mother in the book for being so critical and judgmental, but then again, she thinks that at least their mother was present.

Margo wants to hate the sisters for not seeing the value they all brought to each other. She hates that they didn't stay together as a family. "Family is everything," she blurts out. "It was selfish of her to take it away."

Missy hears the pain in Margo's voice as she speaks. Is she trying to say more? To send her a message? In all their years, Margo has never once apologized to Missy. As children, when things would get tense, Missy was the first to acquiesce, offering an apology even when it was not warranted. She had an innate sense of Margo's struggles.

For her part, Margo has learned to play the victim. At least, she has with Missy. She loves her cousin dearly. For all the ways she loved and adored Missy, Margo found more ways to resent her as the years went on. If it wasn't watching Missy decide between B- and C-cup bras, it was watching her decide between size 4 and 6 pants. When they went out to eat, Missy was disciplined enough to drink Diet Coke whereas Margo struggled to choose between a chocolate or strawberry shake. And that was just when they were growing up. Margo's list of reasons to resent her cousin was long.

Missy's patience was constantly tested, but her loyalty was true. Margo was her blood. She was more a part of her than her own mother had been.

The mood changes swiftly over the course of book club. Dysfunctional family drama feels too close to home for many of the women.

"When I chose this book, I thought it would be a fun discussion about sisters and relationships with family," Audrey bleats. "I didn't think we'd end up with so much darkness."

Missy rolls her eyes at those words. "What part of the word 'dysfunctional' makes you think there will be a healthy discussion with positive outcomes?" she snips at Audrey.

Audrey is taken aback by her comment.

"It's not like you chose *Free Willy* and we discussed what happened to the whale," Missy adds.

Amber looks at Scarlet and mouths, "Is that even a book?"

Scarlet shrugs. "I liked the movie, though," she says with a smile.

A frazzled Audrey looks at her watch. "That's probably a good place to end it for today." The women nod in agreement. As they pack up their belongings, Dahlia announces, "Drinks at Poe's. After this, we could all use one."

The women take their time leaving the library and heading in groups of two or three toward Poe's. Missy is not in the mood to go to the bar, but Scarlet and Amber have persuaded her that she needs to join them, that it would be good for her.

As they begin their walk, Margo hurries past them.

"Margo, wait," Amber calls out.

If you listened loud enough, you could hear Margo exhale like a bull ready to charge a conquistador. She stops in her tracks and, without turning around, waits for the Harlots to catch up.

"What?" she says.

"'What?' Are you shitting me?" Missy is livid. "I tried to call you. I texted you. You left me on read. I was worried about you, Margo. That was shitty of you."

"Shitty of me. Seriously?" she says, holding back tears on the brink of release.

"I didn't do anything. You're the one—"

"What?" Margo interrupts. "I'm the one who slept with your leftovers? I'm the one who picked up the broken pieces you left behind? I'm the one no one wanted? Go on and pity me, Missy."

"I have never, ever pitied you, Margo." Missy's voice trembles with fury, but beneath it runs the crack of something deeper, almost broken. Scarlet and Amber exchange uneasy glances, both uncomfortable as accidental spectators. "I have been steadfast by your side our entire lives. Even after Cal. You hurt me so deeply when you did that. And never did you ask me how I was after the divorce. Never."

"Because you'd already moved on with your boy toy," Margo yells through a sob.

"My boy toy? Do you mean fucking Spencer? Do you know why I even needed him? No. You have absolutely no fucking clue because you never asked me. Ever. Our whole lives, I've looked out for you, taken care of you, been your friend. You just found ways to push me away, to resent me. I'm over it. Seriously."

With that, Missy turns around and heads toward her car. She starts the ignition, turns the radio to full volume, and screams at the top of her lungs. Once. Twice. Three times. Each one louder, burning her throat. Her fists slam the wheel. Pain stings her hands, but she doesn't stop.

She drives numb behind the wheel. Lights blur. Streets vanish. She does not remember stopping at any lights. Or stop signs. She pulls into her driveway and the safe space her empty home offers her. One without judgment. If only it were true.

As she walks towards the front door, she sees Charlotte's pale figure, her silhouette blurred, her hands crossed over her chest shaking her head in disgust. *Why is it every time I feel like a fuck up, she's there?* she wonders, holding back the tears on the precipice of eruption. "Go away. This isn't about you," she says as if talking to a ghost were completely normal.

In the quiet of her home, she weeps. She cries at the realization that her own cousin doesn't know her. Not really. There are parts of her own story she hasn't shared with her. She kept the emptiness of her marriage to herself. She mourned her father's death alone. She is haunted by her mother's passing, feeling her presence in death more than in life. Her burden to carry again. Alone.

Missy has always been there for Margo. A shoulder, a sounding board, a safety net. She wonders if Charlotte's presence is a sign telling her that Margo is all she has left. Missy's awash in forced self-reflection, and Margo is front and center.

## Chapter 6

———————

### *Noodle Necklaces and Brown Paper Bags*

Missy and Margo had a tradition of celebrating each other's birthdays the day before their actual birthdays. It had begun when they were young girls and felt like a secret language. Margo would come to Missy on her birthday; Missy would go to Margo on hers. They would hide in each other's closets, giggling while they tore the newspaper wrapping off their handmade gifts to each other.

When they were little, they made things for each other: homemade cards, noodle necklaces, macrame anklets and bracelets. Missy made everything in blue for Margo. Margo made everything in pink for Missy.

As they grew older, Margo would paint pictures of them together, capturing a memorable moment from the previous year. Missy would write a poem for her cousin. Happy poems, she said, like those written by Shel Silverstein; not sad ones, like those of Emily Dickinson.

When they became teenagers, making each other things began to feel silly. They agreed they could buy each other something from

50

the five-and-dime, and they would have to guess the meaning behind the gift. One year, Missy bought Margo a soda. Margo knew right away: "Oh my gosh, because I had gas that one day! That was so embarrassing." But they laughed until they almost peed their pants. For Missy's seventeenth birthday, Margo gave her a glow stick. Remembering that gift still makes Missy weepy. "It's because you are my light," Margo had said. Missy thinks that might have been the last time Margo said something genuinely nice to her.

The tradition continued throughout college. They both had birthdays during breaks. Even after they had married, they would sneak away to talk about their husbands. Margo would talk about futile attempts to get pregnant while watching in envy as Missy's belly grew—twice.

They barely managed to celebrate when they turned thirty. Margo's marriage was already painstakingly difficult. She was embarrassed that she couldn't get pregnant. Missy was knee-deep in Band-Aids, carpools, and PTA. Their tradition became an hour-long meeting in the park while Macky and Kaid played and the women secretly drank wine from brown paper bags. They found they had less to talk about. Or, at least, they had less to talk about that either of them felt comfortable discussing.

"How's your Etsy shop?" Missy would ask.

"Good. I have two new prints up," Margo would reply. "I've sold a few. Anything new with you?"

"Life is busy." Missy almost always said *with kids*, but she would remember and refrain at the last moment. "Cal works a lot." There were awkward pauses that sometimes felt like an eternity. "Oh! Macky won an art prize. I thought she would call you to tell you." Missy could see that Margo was hurt; even her niece had forgotten her. "She's eight, Margo. She's got a lot going on." Inside, Margo would think that Missy could have called or texted even as Missy thought the same thing to herself.

On Margo's fortieth birthday, she invited Missy to join her in Turks and Caicos. "I want to learn to scuba dive," she declared.

"You hate water," Missy replied.

"I don't hate water." But she did. They had grown up with an ocean at their doorstep. Summers on the beach. Winter bonfires with high school friends. First dates. Breakups. They all happened on the beach. Missy loved the beach and did her best to protect her overly pale complexion from getting more freckled, her mother's words still occasionally echoing in her ears. But Margo's complexion soaked up the sun, giving her a pretty shade of brown in the summer months. Missy hated that Margo was devoid of freckles.

"You have the lucky skin, you know," Missy would tell Margo.

"It's a small consolation prize for everything else you got," she would say, as if joking, but Missy knew she was not.

Missy couldn't leave her family for Margo's birthday celebration. Her kids were young. They needed her to take them to soccer practice. Or swim team. Or to their friends' houses. And Cal couldn't help. He worked long days, leaving early and getting home late. Her dad could help, sure, but it felt like too much to ask of him.

"But you should go. It'd be good for you," Missy encouraged.

"Fine. I need to get out of here. I don't want to do a fortieth birthday party and have to invite people, then have them feel sorry for me because I'm still single," Margo finally confessed.

"No one feels sorry for you." They didn't. Margo was too bitter for anyone to pity. "Plus, you hate me. Or at least, you act like you do," Missy said, half joking.

"I don't hate you," Margo paused. "Only sometimes. But you're right. I need to do this for me." That year, they celebrated three days early, with wine in a paper bag at the park under ominous clouds that threatened rain. She would be in balmy, warm Turks and Caicos for her real birthday. Margo was relieved by the thought.

In the eight years since her divorce, Margo had learned to travel independently to art shows and conventions. She had become quite good at selling her work, mainly because it spoke for itself, but when asked, she morphed into a different person. Missy actually liked that version of Margo. She was confident. She was articulate. She didn't stand in anyone's shadow, least of all Missy's. When they were together, Missy tried to step aside, remove the shadow, but it was often Margo who moved in sync with her, like she wasn't quite ready to shine brightly on her own.

Margo arrived at the small boutique hotel in Turks and Caicos on a Thursday afternoon. Scuba lessons started the following morning. She was picked up by a driver named Norman, who would double as her scuba instructor. He was a local boy, not even a man yet. He had grown up on the island and was happy and smiling the entire time.

Norman instructed her in the pool first. Then, they went on a small shore dive. On Saturday and Sunday, she completed two dives a day to earn her certification. Margo was proud of herself. She didn't panic when she saw three sharks swim by. She squealed as she swam next to turtles and marveled at the multitude of tropical Caribbean fish that moved through the water as if she didn't exist. It was a perfect world. If all water was like this, she would never get out. The waters off Sullivan's Island were not crystal blue with sixty-foot visibility.

Sunday night, she celebrated her accomplishment and her fortieth birthday. She went to the bar of her hotel and ordered a bottle of the most expensive chardonnay. A red felt too heavy, and she was feeling light, airy, on top of the world. The bartender asked if she wanted it brought up to her room. She looked around at the hotel bar, which felt full of life.

"No. I'll take it here. And an order of prawns and some French fries. With ranch if you have that." *What the hell?* she thought. *I've earned this.*

The bartender uncorked the bottle and poured her a small tasting. She swirled it in her glass, smelled it, then sipped. She pretended she knew what she was doing. She'd seen it done on TV. God knows, she didn't have good role models. Her father guzzled liquor like water. Russell preferred beer. Dex drank bourbon. But this was what they did on TV, so she felt sophisticated.

"This is delightful," she said to the bartender. He poured enough to fill a third of her glass. "It's my birthday. Fill it halfway, please."

He smiled at her and poured a few more ounces in her glass. "Happy birthday. Is it a big one?"

"One does not ask a lady that." She couldn't even finish the sentence before she began to giggle at the white-gloved pretense. "I'm forty."

He whistled playfully. "Well, I would have guessed thirty-five. Cheers to you, lovely lady." He winked at her and walked away.

Margo was feeling good about herself. She'd conquered her fear of the ocean. She'd swum with sharks, turtles, and other large, mysterious creatures of the sea. She felt pretty in her flowy, flowered dress with its bouquet of reds, yellows, and greens. Her skin was sun-kissed the perfect shade of brown. *I did get lucky there,* she thinks. Weight would always be her nemesis, but she liked the joys of food more than she cared to worry about her waistline. Her hair had lightened from the water and sun. It didn't feel so mousy anymore. *Maybe this decade won't be so bad after all,* she thought to herself and smiled.

She was halfway through her first glass when a handsome man sat a seat removed from her. His skin was darker, but his features were distinctly European in nature. Maybe he was British Indian. She wasn't a world traveler, she reminded herself and felt a sudden sense of ignorance. This man was tall, but most people were taller than she was. He smiled at her as he took his seat. His teeth were remarkably white against his darker skin. She felt herself tingle inside. It had been a long time since she had tingled.

As the man looked on, the bartender placed a large plate of prawns, fries, and ranch dressing in front of her. Margo felt embarrassed. She didn't know what overcame her, but she asked if he wanted to share. He smiled and said, "That would be amazing," in a beautiful English accent. She pushed the plate between them. He moved over a chair and sat next to her. He looked even younger then, even more attractive.

"Wine?" she asked, motioning toward the bottle.

He smiled, so the bartender put a glass in front of him. The handsome man put out his hand. "I'm Will."

"I'm Margo."

"Nice to meet you, Margo. You have a beautiful smile."

She could feel her grin deepen. No one had ever said that to her before, but she had always thought it was one of her better features.

Margo and Will found they had a lot in common. He was an artist in London. His wife had just asked for a divorce, he said, and he needed to get away. He made Margo laugh. He made her smile. He made her feel. They finished the first bottle of wine. Then another.

When Margo woke the next morning, she found Will lying naked in her bed. She ran to the bathroom to throw up. Naked. She stopped in front of the full-length mirror, taking in her nude body, with tan lines outlining her torso like the lines of her swimsuit. She smiled at herself, then tried to remember what had happened. Did they have sex? God, it had been forever since she'd had sex, since she had been naked with a man. Did she still know how to please them? Was it good sex? Did she even know what good sex was? But it had to have been good for her. After all, Will was a beautiful man.

She brushed her teeth, quickly finger-combed her hair, threw on a robe, and walked back toward the bedroom. Will was standing naked on the balcony, looking out over the Caribbean's turquoise waters. He turned and smiled when he heard her. He looked even better in the light of day, not under the influence of alcohol. He walked his surprisingly thin naked body toward her.

"I have to piss," he said, "and then I'd like to continue where we left off last night."

Margo smiled at him, but as he retreated into the bathroom, her smile melted into worry lines. Oh God, what did that mean? Did he remember and she didn't? Was that just an expression?

He came back, and his intentions were on full display, so Margo just went with it. She had never "shagged" so much in her life. He explored every part of her, and she found herself exploring parts of him she didn't know were explorable. They ordered room service—twice. They drank a bottle of Dom Perignon. They talked about art. She said she mainly painted. He said he specialized in charcoal. It was a perfect day.

By evening, she was exhausted and totally, completely satiated. She hadn't known she could be so vocal in bed. She liked the uninhibited sex with Will. Every part of her was sore in the best possible way. She told herself she needed to get in better shape if she wanted to keep this sort of thing up once she got home.

Margo had an early morning flight the next day, so she and Will said goodbye with a sweet kiss. She asked for his full name and promised to look him up when she returned home. Margo wanted no more. For the first time in her life, she felt utterly content.

Six weeks later, Margo realized she had missed her period. A pregnancy test was positive. Margo was excited. She was scared. She thought, *Where's the irony in this?* She looked up the artist. Will Folger. There he was. She began to scroll through his Instagram page, and that's when her heart began to capsize. Will Folger was a father to three beautiful daughters. And his wife was smiling by his side in every photo.

Will Folger was not divorced. Will Folger was not getting divorced. Will Folger was a happy husband and father. That's what the pictures said, at least. Margo didn't feel bitter. If she were honest with herself, she felt a sense of relief. This child would be hers and hers alone.

Margo wanted to tell Missy she was pregnant. Of all people, Missy would judge her least. Of all people, Missy was her only people. But she couldn't tell her. Not yet. She wanted to wait the requisite number of months, the safe ones. The ones she had ignored before, when the first couple of false positives left her and Russell gutted with disappointment.. As the next several weeks passed, Margo began looking at baby clothes, thinking of baby names. She liked Alexandra for a girl and Beckett for a boy. She imagined saying, "What the heck, Beck?" to a little boy's mischievous antics, a little boy with her eyes and Will's smile. It had a fun ring to it. She stood in the doorway of her guest room, thinking about how she would decorate it. She would find out if the baby was a boy or a girl, and the room would be done accordingly.

Ten weeks into her pregnancy, Margo lost the baby. She swore she could feel it start to squish around inside her. And when she looked in the toilet at the mass of blood and tissues from her uterus, she thought she could make out the small shape of a tiny human the size of a strawberry.

"I would have loved you so much, my sweet baby," she whispered before she flushed the toilet and her dreams.

She had decided it was a little girl. She wanted a girl so she could give her everything she never had. She called Missy, who dropped everything to be with her cousin.

"Jesus, Margo, why didn't you say anything?" Those were the first words that left Missy's mouth when she entered Margo's house and wrapped her up in her arms.

Inside, Margo knew. She had never said anything because she never truly believed it would happen. She never believed she would have a child of her own to love.

"I had a feeling," was all she could mumble into Missy's shoulder. It smelled of Bath & Body Works Warm Vanilla Sugar lotion and Spring Meadow Tide.

That night, Missy left to tend to her children. Cal had poker with his buddies, and Margo forbade her from telling him. She preferred to be alone rather than have anyone other than Missy know about her loss. It tore Missy apart to see her cousin in such pain, and it pissed her off even more that she herself was trapped in a marriage to a man as selfish as Cal.

When she shut the front door behind Missy, Margo walked to her bedroom and sobbed. She hated that she had let herself hope, but it felt good to share her secret.

Months later, she shared the story of Will with Missy. Missy saw how Margo lit up as she recounted their time together. She wished her cousin would find happiness. And it saddened her that in a moment when Margo allowed herself to have hope, it was ripped from her womb.

# Chapter 7

## *Personal Delivery for a Dancing Queen*

Zander Hancock leaves downtown Charleston in the late morning on an already sweltering July day. The air is thick with heat and salt as the streets of downtown give way to Highway 17, the city thinning into stretches of marsh and oak trees draped with Spanish moss.

The road climbs onto the Arthur Ravenel Jr. Bridge, its white cables cutting against the bright, blue sky. From the top, the harbor sprawls out—Fort Sumter invisible in the distance, shrimp boats inching along the Cooper River below. The pace feels slow.

On the other side, tidal creeks and spartina grass shimmer in the sun, the pungent smell of pluff mud ever present. The drive narrows toward Sullivan's Island, carrying him across Breach Inlet, where the water sunlight dances across the water ahead. Moments later, the island opens up—quiet streets lined with weathered porches, sandy drives, and the Atlantic glimmering just beyond the dunes.

Zander had heard stories from Dex about the house—the one he had proudly restored when Missy was a child. Now, as he turns into the long driveway, he isn't sure what to expect. The home rises before him, stately and timeless, the kind of place that could have graced the cover of a magazine.

Zander pulls into the circular driveway, parking beside a bright red convertible with the top up. He understands the appeal – a car built for sun and open air – but in the summer heat it has to be miserable. He locks his own car, though he doubts it's necessary, heads up the steps toward the door.

Zander knocks on her front door. The enormity of it tells him he should probably ring the doorbell, but that seems like an imposition. The woman has recently lost her mother, and, given the contents of the file he possesses, he guesses his visit will be unexpected. He cannot explain why he decided to make the drive to Sullivan's Island. He tells himself he was tired of the pretentious colonial office in downtown Charleston.

He had also been fond of Dex. Zander enjoyed his stories about the early days in business - how he had started a small shipping container company, then later, after becoming Missy's primary caretaker, sold his shares, invested wisely, and ensured she was provided for both emotionally and financially. His devotion to his daughter was unwavering, and it had left a strong impression on Zander.

Zander Hancock is not a Southerner. He grew up on Long Island, New York, close enough to the big city yet far enough away to feel he had a relatively sheltered childhood. He found his way South when he attended law school at Duke. His parents had beamed with pride when their public school boy aced the SATs and received an acceptance letter to Yale as an undergrad. Even back then, Zander was more pragmatic, attending the State University of New York at Stony Brook instead. His parents were simultaneously relieved and saddened. At least they had the paper proving he'd been accepted. Years later, his mother presented him with an album of pictures and articles she had saved over the course of his younger years, including the Yale acceptance letter. It did not include the one for Stony Brook.

Attending law school at a prestigious university had always been his endgame. His father hated lawyers. He liked his dad, so he wasn't always sure what had driven him toward law.

"Maybe it's because of him," he once told his mother.

"That makes no sense," she squawked in the thick Long Island accent she never got rid of.

"Dad's the hardest, strongest, most humble man I know. Maybe men like him deserve to have lawyers on their side. You know, stand up to the man for them," he explained.

But in the end, he hadn't become that kind of lawyer. He'd gone into corporate law instead - defending the very men his father had spent his life standing up to.

Nonetheless, Zander graduated in the middle of his class, passed the bar on the first try, and landed a job at a prestigious law firm in Charleston before he even graduated. He couldn't explain what kept him in the South. After all, he had offers in New York City, Chicago, and Boston.

But, really, he did know. It came in the form of a woman with curly, black hair named Lucy. Lucy was more New York than he'd ever been, growing up in the Bronx, claiming to have known Jennifer Lopez before she was Jenny from the Block. He liked her Puerto Rican sass. They embarked on a fiery romance in their last year of law school. She'd been offered a job as an immigration attorney in Charleston, and he followed her with his tail wagging between his knees.

Zander and Lucy had lived together for three years, their careers flourishing, when he finally decided it was time to propose. She said yes, and they married a year later with two hundred of their closest friends—and many of her Puerto Rican relatives—in attendance. Zander felt himself the luckiest man to have married her.

On the night of Lucy's fortieth birthday, Zander found himself the unluckiest man. Lucy was killed as they walked out of dinner at a restaurant downtown. A teenager texting lost control of his car and veered onto the sidewalk, pinning her under the vehicle and killing her instantly. Zander was helpless. He cradled Lucy's head in his lap until the paramedics came and took her away.

Zander spent the next ten years living in the modest home they had bought. He could have afforded pretty much anything by now, but he found it challenging to move beyond the tragedy of that night. He saw therapists. He contemplated taking his own life. He wondered how he was supposed to live without her. They had not wanted children, recognizing that their jobs were their children, coddled, loved, and adored. They once rescued a dog but promptly returned it when they realized the demands even it caused.

After a year of mourning, he woke up one day, understanding Lucy would have wanted him to keep living, to do the things he loved to do. She would have told him to find a new love, that he was worth loving. He would have told her the same thing. He knew that. But it was one thing to recognize it and another to execute it. He tried dating. Friends would set him up. He tried the apps. He kept looking for Lucy, unable to find her in the multitude of cringeworthy, sexy photos women posted there. He told his best friend, Trace, that if he was meant to meet someone, it would happen organically. Trace laughed and said, "Good luck with that, man. Apps *are* organic these days." Zander hoped he was wrong. Trace had been on at least twenty dates in the past two months and had yet to find something organically.

Now at fifty years old, graying around the edges but with a full head of nicely trimmed hair, Zander Hancock stands at the door of a woman he does not know to share news that may not be well received. He knocks loudly, then pushes his glasses firmly onto his face.

He had always preferred glasses to contacts, and as he got older, he felt they made him look more distinguished. When he looked at himself in the mirror in the mornings, he acknowledged that the wrinkles around his blue eyes and on his forehead also gave him a more distinguished appearance. He hasn't aged horribly, he thinks, even though the last ten years of his life feel like a movie playing in slow motion, waves of pain cycling through in moments of loneliness left by the void of Lucy's death. He has marched on, though, finding ways to be happy most of the time. He stays fit and active. His love of tennis has morphed into a love of pickleball, something he reluctantly found himself drawn to. He plays in several leagues. And he has Enzo, his rescue dog. Despite his one-time feelings about dogs, he would readily admit Enzo has saved him more than once over the years.

Knocking feels more personal than a doorbell to him, less of an intrusion or statement that something is looming. He knocks louder a second time. He can hear someone moving inside and peers through the side glass panes of the door. He sees the back of her, moving like she is dancing, oblivious to the knock at the front door. He tries the doorbell this time, then rings a second time when he notices her taking her earbuds out. She turns, smiles, and mouths, "Sorry," as she scurries toward the door.

Missy had gone to bed sad but woken up determined to take back her life. Margo would not impede her happiness. She would be present, and she'd start by cleaning. Dusting and sweeping were metaphors for wiping away the past and making room for the present. She had been so happy, but losing her mom and watching her relationship with Margo become fractured felt like she'd slipped and fallen on Crisco, making it hard to get traction to stand again.

She'd been through a lot in her life, but she knew she was an innately happy, glass-half-full, enthusiastic, vibrant woman. It's why she chose herself when Cal tried to repress her. She stands firmly by her friends, even by Margo, though that has been challenged lately. She is a cheerleader of life. She just needs a reminder to take care of herself, too. Prioritizing her happiness would be her new forward.

And she would dance. She puts on her favorite eighties music, shuffling it with a Spotify list Macky sent her recently. She loves that her daughter thinks she's cool enough to share music with. Music has always been a refuge for Missy, who finds comfort in lyrics, beats, and rhythms. She doesn't love exercise, but she loves to dance, which is why she enjoys the occasional Zumba class—when she remembers to sign up for it.

A barefoot Missy flings open the door. "Hi. I'm sorry. I wasn't expecting anyone."

Zander doesn't know what to make of this woman with the wild red hair, other than that he hasn't felt a flutter in his belly in a very long time.

He takes a deep breath and announces himself. "I'm Zander Hancock, senior partner at Murphy, Cline, and Barrett." He puts out his hand, and Missy returns hers, recognizing the name.

"My dad's attorneys?" she says as she reads the business card he hands her.

"Yes. Some things came up with the passing of your mother. Condolences, by the way," he offers.

Missy recognizes her ignorance on the matter of her mother's death. It did not even occur to her that there would have been a will or something that required attention that her father hadn't already taken care of. Missy naively believed that, when her father passed away, all legal matters had been taken care of. He had taken care of everything else, after all. He had arranged with St. Dymphna's Sanatorium to have Charlotte cremated upon death. He had never consulted Missy on any of it. Another thing, oddly, she was grateful for.

She did not consider that her mother, living a secret life locked up in St. Dymphna's Sanatorium for those deemed mentally insane, could have consequences. Alas, that would have been too easy.

She opens the door and lets Zander Hancock into her home. He follows her to the kitchen. Although the house is enormous, most of it appears closed off, as if only a small part is occupied. She senses him taking it in.

"Daddy left me the house when he died," she explains. "Not going to lie, it was perfectly timed with my divorce. But it's huge. And pretentious. And I kind of like pretending it's smaller. Makes it easier to take care of."

He can't believe the way his ears perk up at the word "divorce." "And you live here alone?" *Where did that come from?* he wonders.

"Couldn't bring myself to sell it and downsize. Someday, maybe." She notices the way he looks at her. It isn't out of pity. Well, she knows no one would pity a woman living in a mansion. Except for the part where she lives by herself. Even then, there's something that says he can see through her. He isn't just looking at her; he's trying to figure her out. It's been a long time since she's felt that, allowed that, wanted that. She stops herself at wanting and pulls herself back into the conversation.

"So, what unexpected curveball did my mother throw at me from the grave? I should have expected she wouldn't just go in peace," she says with an unapologetic laugh.

Zander likes her sassy, matter-of-fact attitude. Too often, clients feign sadness when inside they're relieved by a loved one's passing. He knew bits and pieces of the Kinkaid story Dex has shared with him over the years. He adored his daughter, spoke highly of her and his grandchildren. But Dex had failed to mention how uniquely beautiful Missy was. How could he forget to describe her fiery red hair? Those vibrant emerald eyes? Her big laugh?

"We tried to get in touch with you by mail"—Missy looks toward a massive stack of envelopes piled up on the living room table and hopes he won't notice—"but when you didn't respond, I took the initiative to come over. I really liked your dad."

"Me, too," she says, flashing her bright smile. "I think I might have missed that letter." She walks to the living room, picks up the stack of mail, and flips through a few envelopes before getting to the simple business envelope from the attorney. She waves it at him. "Should I bother to open it?" she says with a mischievous glance. "I'm sorry. I've had a lot going on." She looks at the stack again. "I'm sure there's other stuff in there I should get to. But, really, who uses the mail anymore? Couldn't you have just emailed or called?"

To which, Zander replies, "We did."

Embarrassed, she says, "So if I look at my emails and listen to my voicemails, I'd probably not be surprised by your visit?"

"Probably not," he says and can't suppress a grin.

"Then I won't look," she proudly proclaims.

He likes her straightforward, no-nonsense attitude. It has been a long time since he'd noticed a woman with fierce qualities, comfortable in her skin, owning her shortcomings.

Zander opens his attaché case and pulls out a large, legal-size envelope. He hands it to her. "I was instructed by your father to give this to you upon your mother's death. As you know, his estate continued to cover her care costs. And our fees, of course, to manage it." He gives her a check. "This is what was left after our fees and the final costs at the home. The burial costs were also already covered." Missy had been in such a fog that she had never even considered those parts of her mother's death. She is relieved it is taken care of but embarrassed to admit her brain hasn't processed that part yet. Not having her mother present for most of her life made even her death feel unreal.

"He was pretty spot-on with his calculations," Zander is saying. "Sorry it couldn't be more."

Missy smiles down at the check. "I wasn't expecting anything, so it's all good, right?"

"Of course. And now that she has passed away, our services can come to an end."

"So no curveball? Just the end of the contract with you?" Missy says, relieved. It's then she feels a slight pang of panic inside herself and feels the color leave her face. It never dawned on her that she might lose her home or small inheritance. She would not have put it past Charlotte to do one last thing to make her life a living hell.

"No curveball," Zander reassures her. "Cash is a gift, right? Just need you to sign that our services have ended."

Missy feels the warmth flow back into her face. She signs the contract, which he then returns to his briefcase. He pushes the original manila envelope toward her.

"I do not know the contents, but he was very clear that you should only get this when your mother had passed away."

Missy picks up the envelope and carefully opens it. Inside, she finds a card with her name on the front written in her mother's handwriting. She feels herself begin to tremble and puts it aside. "I'll read this later," she says. He smiles a warm, knowing smile. "Thank you for bringing this."

There is an awkward moment of silence between them. Neither of them wants their interaction to end, but both are unsure what should happen next.

Zander musters the courage to speak first.

"You know, we'd be happy to take you on as a client. Legacy rate, of course," he offers.

"Legacy rate? Wow. That sounds important."

He chuckles. "Your dad was one of our longest-standing clients. He and the first Mr. Barrett were good friends."

Missy does not have an attorney for her estate. She has a living trust to ensure things are passed on to her children. After her divorce, she had hoped she would never need an attorney again. "Do I *need* an attorney?" she asks.

"I'd be happy to take a look at your affairs and make sure they're in order. And then you can decide."

"So pro bono? Like I'm a charity case?"

He laughs the most natural, easy laugh that Missy has ever heard. It is a beautiful sound that fills her living room.

"You are a fireball, aren't you?" he says through his mirth.

"Maybe."

*Oh my god*, she thinks. *I am flirting with this man. What the hell has come over me?*

She wants to tell him how much she likes his laugh. How it makes her feel a warmth inside she hasn't felt in a very long time.

He smiles and grabs his briefcase while berating himself: *You idiot. She's flirting with you, she might become a client, and you don't know what to do next.*

"You have my number," he says, grasping for whatever professionalism he has left. "Reach out when you're ready to have me look things over." He walks himself to the front door, and Missy follows closely. She finds herself checking him out from behind. He looks good even from that side.

He opens the door and puts out his hand. "It was a pleasure to meet you, Mrs. Sutton."

She laughs. "God, no one's called me that in five years. It's Missy. I dropped Sutton in favor of Kinkaid. I always preferred that name anyway."

Zander walks out the front door, and Missy closes it behind him. She finds herself smiling, realizing she is just a little bit smitten by him. On the outside of the door, Zander has the same smile on his face, equally smitten by Missy.

*Don't be a fool twice*, his inner voice tells him. He feels uncharacteristically impulsive. He stops, turns around, and strides up to the door. Just as he is about to knock, Missy flings the door open. They both giggle like teenagers, recognizing they are thinking the same thing. They simultaneously speak. Then they stop, motioning for the other to go first.

"Ladies first," Zander says.

"No, you," she says.

"Okay then." He fidgets like a schoolboy, which makes Missy smile. "I'm suddenly nervous," he admits.

"Yes," Missy jumps in.

"Yes?" Zander asks, ever the lawyer, seeking clarification.

"Yes, let's get a drink or whatever you were going to ask me."

He feels relieved. Missy feels bold. They are both happy in that moment.

"I'll text you. Maybe drinks at sunset?" he says.

"Those are my favorite kind of drinks," she replies, almost demure.

He starts to walk away, but pauses, turning back. "I hope whatever's in that envelope is good news for you."

"Me, too."

The silence stretches, not uncomfortable so much as charged. His phone rings, breaking the moment. He gestures apologetically. She nods, though her eyes linger on him a beat longer than necessary. As he answers, his grin widens, his voice trembling with excitement—but it's the look he gives her before turning away that stays with her.

# Chapter 8

## *The Edge of Crazy*

Missy closes the door for a second time. She is proud of herself for trusting her instincts. For not being afraid. It felt right. And it's been a long time since it felt right.

The smile fades from her face, though, as she sees the envelope on the table. She looks at the clock. Too early in the day for a glass of wine. She has waited a lifetime to get something personal from her mother. Even when she was a small child, Dex signed the birthday and Christmas cards from them. Dex chose the gifts. Charlotte would watch as Missy opened them with a glazed, lost look in her eyes as if she couldn't process all the fuss over her daughter. Missy had tried not to look at Charlotte in those moments, but she always did. Somehow, it was Charlotte's forced smile that etched itself into her memory, representing some of the happiest memories she held of her mother.

By Missy's sixth birthday, Charlotte was no longer present. Dex had told his daughter that Mommy was very sick and needed to go to a special place to get better. Missy wanted to be sad that she was gone, but something inside her told her that she was safer without her. Missy remembered that feeling her whole life. Why did she need to be protected from her mother? Wasn't her mother supposed to protect her?

Missy sits at the table and stares at her mother's handwriting. It looks unsteady, like she had been trembling when she wrote it. The envelope is addressed to Melissa Jean Kinkaid. "That's weird, Mom. Even for you," Missy says.

She feels it then. A shift in the room, a shadow at her shoulder. The hairs on her neck stand just like when Charlotte would say, "A tight squeeze, a cool breeze, now you have the shiveries." Then she feels the bony fingers – cold and clammy- tighten around her throat. She gasps as the memory floods back.

The necklace. She had asked her mother to clasp it once. Charlotte's heavy sigh, her irritation sharp. Missy had erased that moment, burying it deep in the hollows of her psyche. But the truth was darker: Charlotte's hands weren't fastening. They were tightening. Choking. Squeezing. Taking her breath.

She turns, but the room is empty. There is no ghost. Just her own mind, unearthing what had been buried for decades. *How could a mother do that to her child?* she thinks. *What had I done to deserve it? And why the fuck is she haunting me now, when I've earned the right to forget?* She refuses to cry, instead agonizing over what the contents of the letter might hold.

Missy takes a deep breath, recognizing the irony. She composes herself, returning her attention to the letter.

Missy feels her heart begin to race as she turns the envelope over and opens it. She wonders if her mother had bothered to use her own saliva to lick it closed or if she had taken a sponge or wash-cloth and run it over the adhesive. She tries to imagine her mother in those moments. Had she ever seen Charlotte genuinely smile? She had. Once. In the wedding picture Dex kept by the side of his bed. The one before Missy ever existed.

Missy pulls the letter out. It has been folded into quarters. The paper is a thick, cream-colored linen with writing on one side. After she carefully unfolds it, she feels disappointed to find only a few lines of writing. "What did you expect?" she mutters under her breath, knowing the answer. This is already more than she ever expected. But, in the days since her mother passed away, she has been finding her presence in unexpected ways.

The letter was dated one month after Charlotte was institutionalized. It had been written on her sixth birthday.

*Dear Missy,*

*Today is your birthday. I am writing this for you. I know I am not well. I know I have not been kind. I know I did not love you like a mother should love a daughter. I did not know how to do that. But I wanted to. I really, really wanted to. I never wanted to hurt you. You are safe now. Your father says you are a happy girl. He will love you for both of us.*

*Your Mother*

Missy reads the letter over and over again. Each time, the tears flow more freely. Twelve simple sentences on an old piece of paper in her mother's writing. Twelve sentences that somehow explain a lifetime of questions.

Missy gets up and finds the old wedding photo of her parents. Charlotte was stunning and eloquent. She was the same height as Dex in the photo. They were both beaming as if they were the happiest people in the world. Missy had never seen that smile on her mother, but she knew her father's smile well. It was the smile he gave her all her life, the one that said, *You are the most beautiful, most important person in my world.*

She looks up at the heavens, recognizing that Dex and Charlotte are smiling at each other again. "He did, Mom," she says. "He really, really did."

An unexpected peace comes over Missy. Her mother had never given her anything positive in life, but she had given her a gift in death. Missy will cherish that letter forever. She wishes she had had it for the last five decades of her life, and she wonders why it had to wait until Charlotte died. She'll never know, but that doesn't matter. She has it now.

Missy wipes her tears and blows her nose, laughing at the quacking sound it makes as she does.

Her phone pings. Her heart skips a beat when she opens the message.

*Hey, it's Zander. Drinks tomorrow?*

She does not hesitate to respond. If there are rules on how long to wait to answer, she doesn't care. If she had learned anything from her mother's letter, it's that life is short. She should live in the moment.

*Yes.*

* * *

When Zander said drinks, she assumed he meant in a small bar or a dinner place where they could watch the sunset from the bar. When he shows up in shorts, a casual polo, and flip-flops, she feels confused. She has curled her hair, applied just a little makeup, and is wearing a colorful sundress with a cute pair of navy espadrilles. Her surprise is evident when she opens the door.

"Did I forget to mention drinks on the beach?" He gives her a boyish grin.

"You did. But hold tight." Much to his surprise, she closes the door on him, leaving him standing out front, scratching his head. Two minutes later, she swings open the door wearing a pair of khaki capris with a cream-colored, flowing blouse and a pair of slides.

He smiles at her, and she feels herself melt a little.

"You look amazing," he says.

"For the record, I love that other outfit, so we're going to have to have a second date." Even Missy is stunned by her forth-rightness.

Zander drives them down Atlantic and pulls into the country club lot. Missy lingers in her seat, confused, while he grabs a picnic basket and blanket from the back.

With his arms full, he nods towards the path. "Come on. It's just a short walk."

Missy almost giggles. *Since when did dating involve sneaking down to the beach?*

"You're a member here?" she asks.

He looks genuinely confused. "You have to be a member to use the beach?" Then he winks. "Don't worry. I know a guy." His easy humor disarms her, and she can't help but smile.

He kicks off his flipflops; she slips out of her espadrilles. She feels like a little girl. The sand still feels warm under their feet. He stops at the end of the trail. The sun begins to dip, softening into a gentle descent.

"Drinks at sunset, as promised," he says. He feels nervous. She notices – and thinks it's adorable.

Missy and Zander sit on the blanket that he had brought. They snack on crackers and cheese and drink a lovely bottle of red wine from plastic goblets. They laugh. They talk. They take long moments to look at each other. When the sun has winked good-night, leaving only its soft afterglow, Zander tells Missy about Lucy. The story breaks her heart. Then Zander says to Missy, "Tell me about Cal."

She rolls her eyes. "Not too soon?"

"No. You say his name, and I know there's so much more."

"Where does one begin the story of Cal?" she says, bemused.

"The beginning is always a good place." She smiles at him as he says it.

Missy gives Zander the abbreviated version. She leaves the difficult parts out, the parts she isn't ready to share yet. She likes him. She will be guarded. Someday she knows she'll have to share the story of Travis and how he was the real reason she lost her flame and why her heart wore a protective shield.

"Things with Cal started sweet. We met in college," she says.

Calvin Amadeus Sutton looked as strong and confident as his name implied. She remembered how he entered the lecture hall of their international marketing seminar. He looked tall. She'd later learn he was "exactly six feet, two inches and five-eighths." She thought it was cute that he knew his exact height. He seemed surprised she did not. She said, "Five-eight-ish." Worked for her. She was tall for a woman, she felt. It seemed to matter more to men. He was built, too, like he played football. When she playfully squeezed his bicep, she asked, "Do you play football?" It might have been the only time Missy remembered seeing him blush.

"I did in high school, but I decided to focus on college instead of playing." It implied he had options to play college ball. After getting to know Cal, though, she recognized that he only looked athletic. He was much better at passive activities, ones that required no stamina or endurance, that took all day, like fishing and golfing.

Missy liked his confidence, and he often complimented her in the early years. He would always say how pretty a dress looked on her, that he liked those heels, that her hair looked "fancy" when she wore it in a high bun. He told her she had a nice ass, that her boobs fit perfectly in his hands. As the years went on, he would pat her ass like he owned it, and he would do it in front of others. Missy did not like this. When she told him as much, he doubled down on how often he would make public displays of touching her inappropriately.

"What? You're my wife," he'd reply.

"Exactly. I am your wife. Not a piece of meat," she would snarl like a pit bull.

He would retract briefly before saying, "When did you become so uptight?"

*When did you become such an ass?* she'd think, knowing that the better response was: "It makes people think less of you."

Cal hated that response because he genuinely believed he was all that.

Cal had been a master of deception. He made the world believe that he could do no wrong. It was rare that she saw a soft side of him outside of the bedroom. There he could be tender, at least in the early years.

She had seen signs of his arrogance, his growing narcissistic ways in the early days of their marriage. It was as if marriage had given him license to become an asshole, but she was busy with work, too. It became easy to shrug off the alarm bells in her head. And then she got pregnant.

First came Mackenzie and, barely a year later, Kinkaid. She stopped working, but it made sense. Cal's contracting business had taken off. They built their dream home. They were a picture-perfect, postcard-ready family. She enjoyed watching Cal with the kids. He loved them, but it was as if Cal only had a limited supply of love to give. She would always prioritize him giving the kids love. That much she knew. As for herself, she took it when he gave it, which was sparingly and which mainly involved intercourse. He always loved her then; it was his way of saying I love you, which she understood to mean he loved that he had a place to put it.

"He wasn't overly ambitious," she says to Zander, "but I encouraged him, supported him, and he started his own business. He did really well. I was proud of him. In the beginning, he was very loving, but as the years went on, he became cold and predictable. I chalked it up to having kids. And the stress of his business. But he started being mean and condescending. I think his father had been a narcissist. He'd hidden it well. But then..."

Missy stopped briefly. She was embarrassed to admit she had not been strong enough in those years to leave. "I think we stayed together for the kids. At least, I did. I'm not sure he ever saw it. He never really talked about it. Hard to be in a marriage when you're the only one who has issues." Zander touches her shoulder sweetly.

"I think Cal loved me the best he knew how. Or would let himself. I never asked if he had an affair." Parts of her knew Cal would not. He had a wife who served him, took care of him, and pleasured him when asked. She challenged him just enough. "In the end, we had both lost interest in each other. The big difference was that I was not okay with it, and he was. So I asked for a divorce." She keeps it simple. Too much information, too much detail might leave Zander frightened. He was a widower. He had his own tragedy, but he had adored Lucy until the moment she died. Missy had stopped adoring Cal long before they divorced.

Missy finishes sharing the parts of her story she thinks might matter with Zander. "I was alone for the first time since I was twenty-one. It was scary, but it was also really exciting." She looks at him, checks for his reaction. "Is that horrible?"

He shakes his head. And then she realizes Zander did not have the choice to be alone. "I'm sorry. That was insensitive."

He looks at her. "Life happens. I've had a lot of time to reflect. I think people deserve to be happy, and sometimes you have to have heartache to appreciate what that might look like." He stares out over the water. "Even if it feels like some cruel trick has been played on you. It's how I've been able to reconcile it in my mind."

Missy stares at his profile. His long, thick eyelashes match his brows. His nose is perfectly straight, his lips full in silhouette, and his chin is strong but not angular. She especially likes his ears, though she finds the thought strange. All the same—"You have perfect ears," she says to him. He turns to her and smiles.

"Can I kiss you?" he asks.

"Yes, please," she replies.

Zander turns to her, leans in, and gently places his lips on hers, feeling them, warm, soft, moist as they eagerly await his. It's a sweet kiss. Gentle. When he pulls away, he runs his thumb over her bottom lip.

"You have perfect lips," he says. This time, she leans in and kisses him.

# Chapter 9

## *Walking on Sunshine*

Missy feels like she has been walking on clouds since meeting Zander. Even though things are moving slowly, he's a nice distraction. She doesn't want to think about Margo. She has avoided any possibility of seeing her, instead spending her days filling a notebook with potential children's stories, reflections of Macky and Kaid growing up, the happy snippets of her own childhood. She chooses not to write down the parts that feel dark. She has managed to tuck those away for most of her life. Her mother's death is like taking a hammer to a piggy bank: all that wealth, only in pennies. It isn't worth the effort to open it when the return will be so small.

Zander works in Charleston but finds himself visiting Missy whenever he can. And she makes more visits to visit the kids than she did before. Macky is overjoyed that Missy is seeing someone; Kaid doesn't care one way or another.

"You're such a boy," Macky chides him on the rare occasion that the three of them meet. Then she turns to her mother. "You're so secretive, Mom. When do we get to meet him?"

Missy oddly likes having something that is hers alone. Zander has become her perfect secret. Even she finds it hard to believe she's kept him to herself for a month. She prefers not to worry about what others think. She doesn't worry that Dex might be disappointed because Zander was his attorney, creating a conflict of interest, or about Margo calling him a boy toy because he's younger. Not much, of course, but still.

She wishes she could tell Margo. She's always the first person she wants to share things with, and Missy hates the feeling of keeping secrets between them.

She wants to share with Scarlet, knowing she would be honest, but Scarlet and Beau only recently returned from a two-week vacation. With their nuptials rapidly approaching and Scarlet's excitement mounting, Missy doesn't want to take away from that.

"It's silly I'm so excited for this, right?" Scarlet asks.

"It's a wedding. If you weren't excited, I'd be worried," Missy offers.

Scarlet admits she likes not having to worry about what her mother will think. Did she pick the right venue? Why a fall wedding? Will her dress be too sexy or inappropriate?

"God, she asked that when I was twenty-five. I can only imagine what she would think I needed to wear in my late fifties," she quips. They laugh, but it's a sad laugh once they realize how much they miss their mothers, each in their own way. Missy does not share that her mother has haunted her since she died, feeling oddly more observed by her now than she ever did when she was alive.

The opportunity to share the news about Zander passes. Missy knows she wants to hold on to her secret just a little longer, even though it isn't really a secret. They have nothing to hide. She'll share her good news soon enough. When she does spill the tea, it will be a veritable flood that requires wine and a long, uninterrupted evening with her best friends. She makes a mental note to invite Scarlet and Amber for drinks. They're past due for one. Margo is still persona non grata. This is Missy's happiness, and she does not feel the need to share it with Margo, even though she's the first person she thought to tell after meeting Zander.

Zander and Missy did not have sex until their fifth date. Two weeks wasn't an eternity, she knew, but it felt like forever before they finally gave in to pleasure. Missy wasn't sure if there was something he didn't like about her because he turned her on from the moment she first met him. Or were there new rules about when to have sex with a man? Rules had never been her strength. She chalked her impatience up to deprivation. Each time she left him, she was hornier than the time before.

Over the years, she had gotten good at satisfying herself. Cal had forgotten her needs often enough, and the alone years had only sharpened her libido. She liked sex. She liked orgasms. Sometimes, it was just easier alone, she had learned.

But she yearned for Zander. Maybe it was part of his plan, she thought. What did they call it? Delayed gratification? That was it. But all she could think was that she would climax faster, and so would he. And she was right. The first time they had sex, it was over in three minutes. He apologized profusely, to which she joked, "I still got it." He laughed hysterically, grateful that she could turn his premature ejaculation into a joke. That was the last time Zander Hancock prematurely ejaculated when they had sex.

Missy is grateful her body doesn't disappoint her. She is postmenopausal, thank God, and she knows she is lucky. She never stood with her head inside the freezer, hoping it would cool her down. She never sweated so much that her sheets were soaked. She only ever experienced mild hot flashes that would overwhelm her body for seconds. She called them "not-flashes." They lasted for six months and were gone. But she knows she could be dry.

"Maybe that's the part of you that gets sucked out in the sweat," she mused at one of the Harlots' wine nights.

"Your vaginal fluids?" Scarlet asked.

"Yes. It can be so dry sometimes."

Amber looked at them both, mouth agape, eyes wide open in disbelief.

"Yes, Amber. You have much to look forward to," Missy said matter-of-factly.

Amber cheerfully responded, "Lubes are all the rage these days. Even if you don't need them, you need them. Flavors. Warmth. Tingly sensations."

This time, it was Scarlet and Missy wondering how they had missed out on all the fun. And how easy sex would have been post-babies, post-requisite-date-night-with-your-husband-sex-when-all-you-want-to-do-is-sleep.

"Beau still turns me on. He still gets it up. There is no blue pill. Sometimes I wonder which one of us will need an aid first."

Amber crinkled her nose and said, "TMI."

To which Missy added, "Goals."

Missy ordered some lube online just in case. She hoped her body would be so ready for Zander that she wouldn't need it, but she wanted to be prepared. The tube of lube remains unopened in her bedside drawer.

There are many aspects of being with Zander that she appreciates. She loves how his baby blue eyes dance when she moves on top of him, how his hands gently rest on her hips or caress her breasts with just the right intensity. Sometimes she wishes he had three hands because she wanted to spread the magic out, but then she thinks herself selfish. It has been a long time since she felt so alive in bed.

After sex, they lie in bed, twisted in the sheets. He likes playing with her hair, coiling it around his fingers. She likes the smattering of dark hair on his chest. When she moves her hand to cover her belly roll, he gently takes it away and then moves his mouth over the area as if it were a national treasure. Missy has always been confident in bed, aware that she's good at pleasing a man. She has learned to be comfortable with her body. She doesn't know why she suddenly feels any need to cover up her tummy. She knows Zander loves it. She squelches the thought that it's her mother interfering where she shouldn't.

Zander tells her how fascinated he is by her positivity. Her energy captivates him. He senses she is sometimes guarded and knows there is more to her story than she has shared so far.

"I can be a lot," she admits when pressed. "And I've been hurt." She nuzzles his neck, her long hair brushing lightly against his skin. "I promise, I'll share the parts of my story that make me me, but not all at once. Gotta keep the mystery alive just a little," she toys.

"I will simply say that after my divorce, I had found my fire again, only to have it extinguished. I've been working hard to get it back," she explains.

"You mean this isn't you on full flame?" he jokes.

"A tempered flame," she counters. "At least when it comes to love."

"That's interesting," he says, though there's a hint of confusion. "I can't imagine you on full flame."

"Sex and love are two different things," she explains. "You definitely make my fire burn. And maybe it's fair to say we aren't to love yet." Though deep down, she feels that part flickering too – slower, steadier. "But when it comes to the people I love - my children, my friends – Scarlet, Amber, God, even Margo – I'm an inferno if you mess with them."

Zander laughs softly but raises his hands in mock surrender. "Warning heeded." Then, more nervous, "I can't wait to meet them."

Missy realizes it's time to tell her friends about Zander. He's too good to keep secret any longer. He does not come with baggage, at least not a complete set, unlike her. He's more like a piece of carry-on luggage. No need to check it at the gate. She has done her internet sleuthing. She has scoured his social media. She has learned he is virtually nonexistent save for his bio on the Murphy, Cline, and Barrett website, which offers no new information about him.

She hates to admit she looked up Lucy Hancock, too, and wonders how sick and morbid it is to stalk a dead woman. She only finds a sweetly written obituary with hundreds of comments on how tragic and sad it was to lose a shining light in the prime of her life. Missy quickly closed the tab and decided it wasn't healthy for her to spend any more time on a ghost. But the air shifts as she does, a chill brushing down her spine. She swears she feels a hand, soft but deliberate, pat her back. Charlotte. Not scolding this time, not berating—but there, watching. Seemingly always watching.

* * *

The weeks between the altercation with Margo at the last book club meeting fly by thanks to Zander. She is excited, almost giddy, to tell Scarlet and Amber about him. She texts them before book club: "It's been crazy lately. I have fun news to share."

Scarlet and Amber stand in the library parking lot, anxiously anticipating Missy's arrival. Missy walks toward them, grinning from ear to ear, unable to contain her smile.

Amber leans into Scarlet, loud enough for Missy to hear, "Missy's been fucked."

"You think?" Scarlet isn't sure. She thought for sure Missy would have shared that with her. Unless it was just a fuck. But this isn't a *just a fuck* look. This borders on deep like, lust, possibly even love, she thinks.

"So, y'all, I have met someone," she says, emerald eyes glittering as she joins them. "It's new, but I can feel the parts of my heart I closed off opening a little again. And, yes, I have been fucked."

They laugh, and Missy tells them the abbreviated version of Zander as they walk into the library, all the while keeping a close eye to make sure no one else is listening.

# Chapter 10

## *Mutiny in the Public Library*

Missy struggles to read their next book, *Eleanor Oliphant Is Completely Fine*. Mostly, she struggles because she finds herself wondering how much of this story could have been about her. She wasn't a social misfit. She didn't imagine herself with a rock star. She had friends. But her mother haunted her most of her life, just as Eleanor's did.

"Most of us had dysfunction growing up. And then we all had it in divorce," Audrey leads the discussion with that.

Amber raises her hand as if she needs Audrey's permission to speak. "I would like to propose we move away from dysfunctional stories for a while. This is two in a row. And it's kind of exhausting to be honest."

Audrey's irritation is evident. She looks around the silent room. Only Scarlet is nodding in agreement. "Of course, you'd agree, Scarlet."

Scarlet is caught off guard. Clearly, she didn't think she would be the only one thinking Amber was right. She looks at Missy, who appears to be zoned out, somewhere far away, like an exotic beach with Zander. Margo's eyes dart as she looks at her. Abby smugly crosses her arms over her chest. Scarlet hates that Abby can still get under her skin. Scarlet makes it a point to talk with her hands, showing off the engagement ring Abby's ex-husband gave her. Abby sneers.

"She's not wrong. I mean, I think we all do a lot of reflecting at this age anyway. Maybe it would be fun to do a cozy mystery or some of that weird romantasy stuff." Abby scoffs at Scarlet's suggestion. "Or even go back to the classics, like Steinbeck or Hemingway."

Audrey snaps. "Okay. I get it. Too much drama. Used to be too much divorce. Now too much dysfunction. Someone else should just take this over."

Of course, Audrey wants to hear that she is doing great, that everyone appreciates her efforts. Naturally, they do because no one else wants to oversee picking out books.

"What if we follow Reese's Book Club? Or Oprah's or even Jenna's," Scarlet suggests.

"That's so unoriginal," Amber says.

"But they already put in the work," Dahlia adds.

Audrey's wheels are spinning, no longer completely irritated by the mutiny that just occurred. "Let's agree to look at some other alternative methods of choosing. I will send something out in an email."

They all nod in agreement before Abby makes a suggestion: "I think we should read *The Bridges of Madison County* next."

Abby has clearly given this some thought.

Audrey says, "But haven't we all read that book?" Abby scowls at her. Audrey pivots, acting quickly to appease Abby by putting it to a vote.

"All in favor of *The Bridges of Madison County*, raise your hand."

Everyone raises their hand except for Amber, who asks, "Isn't that a movie?"

Abby rolls her eyes. "Based on a book. A really beautiful book."

At least one person in the group has not read the book, leaving Audrey marginally satisfied that it will suffice for the next book club pick. Audrey seamlessly leads into the book on tap for the evening's discussion.

"Okay, so is Eleanor Oliphant completely fine?"

"No!" Missy yells. "Eleanor is not completely fine. She's a fucked-up mess. Likely alcoholic. Her mother. I mean, she tried. But, really—" She pauses and looks around the room. The other book club attendees are quiet. Stunned by Missy's angered statement. Margo's mouth is agape.

"For the record, my mom died not too long ago." More silence, this time of the puzzled variety. "Most of you just assumed she died a long time ago. In theory, she did. Kind of like Eleanor's, right? Maybe I'm mixing that up. But my mom died. And she was a mess. I hate that I'm happy she's finally gone, that the weight of her existence is lifted."

She means every word. What she can't say out loud is that her mother hasn't gone anywhere – not really. Since her death, she's been everywhere. Missy even scans the room, half-expecting to find her lurking in the corner.

A door slams in the hall. Missy flinches. *Yup. I knew it. You couldn't leave me alone now either.*

For a long moment no one speaks, the air thick with tension, until Audrey leans forward and says softly, "Missy, we had no idea. We're sorry."

Missy takes a deep breath. "Thanks. It's hard, you know? I've had some time to process, and I feel like she's been dead my whole life. And now that she's really dead, I feel like she's talking to me from the grave. Which is also bad because I start worrying I'm losing my shit just like she did." She stifles the urge to laugh at how much she's beginning to believe that.

The Divorced Women's Book Club has not seen this side of Missy. Since the book club started, Missy has been a pillar of composure, even if she likes to ruffle feathers. Most of these women have been in her outer circle. They knew her when she was with Cal. They did not know all the details unless Margo told them, which she assumed she did not, mostly because she didn't have many friends, which made her look bad, too. They knew of Travis. Even in her darkest moments after that, in public, Missy put on a brave face while struggling inside.

Missy excuses herself, shaking off Scarlet and Amber. Margo doesn't bother to check on her.

Missy walks outside, taking in the little bit of cold, which tells her that summer is ending and fall isn't far behind. It never gets really cold in Sullivan's Island. Cooler temperatures are a reprieve from hot and humid summers. The seasons here are part of why she loves her hometown so much. She inhales deeply and exhales slowly several times. As a cool breeze wafts up, she smells the salt air and is reminded of how far she has come to be there, to be unapologetically herself. She is living her best life and feels a genuine happiness rising inside of her.

It hasn't always been this way, she reminds herself. She'd given two decades of her life to raising her children. It was easy for her to get lost in motherhood. It has been eight years since she realized she'd gone missing. It has been eight years since she felt the wheels come off.

# Chapter 11

## *Milk Carton Missy*

Missy found herself missing on her forty-sixth birthday. She remembered it clearly. Macky was in her first year of college. Kaid was figuring out where he'd go the following year. Cal worked long hours, came home grumpy, and rarely spoke a word. She began to feel a void, as if a part of her had disappeared. She looked in the mirror and wondered who she was supposed to be when she was all that was left.

She had come to realize over the years that her worth and identity as a mom stemmed from her children's successes. Instead of being the former corporate go-getter version of herself, she put everything into giving them their opportunities. Her world had shifted to making sure they were properly nurtured. The sacrifices were so easily made, especially given how she had vowed never to be anything like her own mother. Motherhood was truly the most remarkable thing she had ever done, and she willfully let herself be consumed by them.

She and Cal were incredible at making it work. Despite his shortcomings as a husband, he loved and doted on his children.

She allowed herself to look past his narcissistic tendencies, chalking it up to working in a man's world. Contractors had to be bullies. They had to be tough. "They'll step all over you the second you're nice," Cal would say.

It was easy to ignore their relationship. He did not have the time or effort for her. He provided for her in the traditional sense, but he offered her nothing beyond that. If she asked him about it, he would say they were fine and that she was making things up. It became harder to imagine that their marriage could ever find a way back to them being equals, partners, friends, lovers. Sometimes, even to seeing each other as their fellow humans.

What bothered Missy above all else was the feeling that she had let herself get lost in the shuffle. She had lost her identity. So she began down a road that sought validation for herself, which manifested itself the year Kaid had gone off to college and peaked when she left Cal.

Shortly after Macky left for college, Missy found herself at a pet adoption event for one of the many charities she supported. Her job was to screen potential families to make sure they were a good fit. It took all of four dogs before Missy realized she needed to save one of them. And she did—a dog named Alfie.

Alfie had been found abandoned on the side of the freeway. No chip. No collar. She was no longer a puppy, as was evidenced by her perfect manners. She sat. She came. She peed and pooped outdoors. Alfie didn't need a manual.

When Missy first saw her, she thought Alfie was the mangiest mutt she had ever seen. She was a medley of colors: black, white, and gray all swirled together. Splattered. Blocked. Spotted. There was no speculating about what breeds she might have come from. There was no rhyme or rhythm to her. She was maybe fifty pounds. Alfie's most distinguishing feature, though, was the cowlick in the center of her head. It went straight up, just like Alfalfa's hair in *The Little Rascals*. The name fit. Alfie was as smitten by Missy as she was with her. It was love at first bark.

Alfie, she said, saved her in those first moments she realized she'd become lost. Or maybe Alfie simply delayed her further recognition that her utility as a mother—and in life—was nearing its end. She squelched the fear of a world that didn't revolve around her kids, leaving her with an empty marriage and a path forward that was blank.

On her forty-sixth birthday, Missy woke excited to celebrate herself. It was the one day she could count on that Cal would get her flowers, buy her some of her favorite Ferrero Rocher chocolates, and take her out to dinner. When she walked downstairs that morning, she found a note on the table. *Forgot to tell you last night that I have an early meeting with a new client and dinner after. I'll check in later. — Cal*

She looked around for flowers. For chocolate. For any sign that he had not forgotten it was her birthday. She should have reminded him like she usually did. Maybe it was a test. And he failed.

On her forty-sixth birthday, Macky was away at summer school, getting a head start on her freshman year in college. Sending her off had been harder than expected, even if it was only two hours up the road to the University of South Carolina.

On her forty-sixth birthday, Kaid threw a tantrum trying to figure out how he'd get into any college if his test scores weren't better.

"What's the point of even applying if I know I won't get in?" he screamed.

Missy simply replied, "That's why you have reach schools and safety schools."

He mockingly replied, "You don't even have to apply to get into community college, Mom. Duh. That's my safety school."

Kaid was a brilliant boy. He worked hard but sometimes got in his own way. He expected more of himself, even though he worked hard. His scores were well above average, as were his grades. On paper, he was smarter than Macky, and he knew that. He just had a flair for the dramatic in contrast to Macky's cool and calm composure. Missy thought it was funny how different they were: Same parents. Same upbringing. Totally different emotional IQs.

Missy struggled with the knowledge that he would be gone the following year, too, so when Macky texted her on the morning of her birthday and asked her to visit, Missy couldn't get to Columbia fast enough. With Cal's blatant disregard for her birthday, she now had the day free. Kaid promised to take her for her favorite ice cream when she returned. He could be a sweet boy when he wasn't panicking about life.

For her forty-sixth birthday, Macky gave her a gift card to get Botox. It was a sweet gesture. They had joked about the fine crow's feet Missy had and her elevens that were beginning to be more pronounced. "I hate being vain like that. It's a terrible example for you," Missy would tell Macky.

But somehow Macky knew she needed something; a reboot, a fresh start going into the back half of her forties. "I can tell you've been a little stressed lately. I thought this might help make you feel better. I don't know. But you're beautiful, Mom. Celebrate." Of course, Missy cried. And then promptly made an appointment to get Botox, paying a little extra for more as it seemed to make sense.

Later, Missy and Kaid had ice cream and laughed about how stressed out he was. He had finished studying for his final SAT test and felt good, just as Missy knew he would.

"So, what did Dad get you for your birthday?" he asked.

"I think he forgot it was my birthday. But that's okay. He's busy."

Kaid pulled out his phone, a furrowed brow marring his sweet face.

"Don't," Missy commanded, knowing that he was going to text his father.

He toyed with the phone for a moment before putting it away. "Sorry, Mom."

"I had a good day," she reassured him. "I bought myself a pretty dress to wear for the fireworks tomorrow."

Whether it was turning forty-six, watching her children grow up before her eyes, or that Cal had forgotten her, the stark realization that she felt lost hit her. Something was missing; the overwhelming sense of emptiness flooded her. She felt as if she might burst, a dam on the brink of breaking. The need for validation began to fill her.

Missy loved being a mom. She just hadn't anticipated that it would end—at least, end in its current state. When she said it out loud, it sounded stupid. Naive. Ignorant.

It pained her to recognize she didn't have anything in her life that was for or about her. She berated herself for having such a selfish thought. She knew she had the coolest job raising her kids. She was lucky they made it work on one income.

So she repressed the thoughts. She stayed quiet. Stuck her head in the sand. Ignorance could be bliss. But then reality comes and bites you in the ass. And it did.

Missy Kinkaid got lost. Without a map. Without GPS. With not even a compass to direct her.

* * *

Over the years, she helped Margo with her art, but she was no artist. They had written a children's book together, presented it to the kids for Christmas, and sold several copies in Margo's Etsy shop. Missy felt proud of that. Years of working in advertising had taught her she had a way with words. She would dabble with poetry on occasion and fashioned herself a Mrs. Seuss when it came to spontaneously creating rhyming bedtime stories for Macky and Kaid.

Cal did not share in the book's excitement. When she bounced the idea of doing more book collaborations with Margo, he thought it was a waste of time.

"It's not like you actually can make money at it, right?" he would say.

To which she would respond, "It takes time to build something like that."

He would scoff and repeat that it was just a waste of time. He was the one person she wanted to show interest, so she found herself discouraged instead.

It had felt like a personal affront that she wasn't interesting to him in that way. Or even capable of doing something for herself. It was as if she didn't exist beyond being the mother of his children. She let it bother her in those moments, wanting to scream that she was more than that, but eventually, busyness usurped her latent desire to write and the potential disinterest that came with it.

Cal and Missy celebrated their twentieth anniversary two months after her forty-sixth birthday, which Cal eventually did try to make up to her with a nice night out in her new dress and sloppy lovemaking when they returned home. He never did bring the flowers or chocolate.

Their anniversary was celebrated with a weekend in New York City. She had visited often for work and loved the buzz of the city, how it never stopped, the excited vibe emanating from it, but there was also a sense of anonymity in a place so full of people, where no one seemed to care that you even existed.

Cal reluctantly agreed, knowing he was still paying for forgetting her birthday. She had planned everything. The hotel. The play they'd see. Where they would eat. The sites they would visit. Cal did not share her enthusiasm. She felt like she was dragging a defiant dog on a leash everywhere they went. He wanted to piss on everything, and she had to clean up his shit. She could feel the emptiness growing inside her.

He did not speak to her on the plane, disappearing into his headphones and music. If she looked at him, it felt like she was looking at a blank wall. Missy recognized the empty feeling stemmed from their lack of conversation, insight into each other, and willingness to talk on a deeper level.

* * *

Kaid left for college the following year. Like his parents and sister, he, too, became a Gamecock. He abided by the same routine as Macky, but as an engineering major, his schedule demanded more of his time. He promised Cal he would pledge Phi Kappa Sigma. He tried his best not to get in, but legacy bore more weight. Missy thought it was the proudest Cal had ever been. "Just don't become a man whore," she told Kaid. He turned bright red.

Emptiness became a constant in moments when she slowed down enough to recognize the void. She was busy at first. Walking Alfie. Volunteering. Ideating books. It wasn't a sudden feeling that overcame her; instead, it was a gnawing, throbbing, pulsing feeling, like her heart needed restarting but was already tachycardic.

Missy found herself feeling increasingly stuck. She wanted to be seen. She *needed* to be seen. She had given so much of herself and asked for little in return. She had a full life as a mom, but who was she supposed to be in the face of this empty nest?

Missy's existential crisis hit pause when the rest of the world did. The pandemic struck, and the world came to a halt. It was a surreal time. Having both kids back in the house was a perfect distraction. She and Cal knew hard conversations about their marriage needed to be had, but the early days of COVID-19 were not the time to have them.

"We need to figure us out, Cal," she had told him before the pandemic. She didn't think she would blindside him with this, but he reacted that way all the same.

"What about us? We're good."

She was stunned. "We aren't good. You don't talk to me. You're not interested in me. It's always the same thing. The kids are gone, and it's like you don't even see me."

"That's so stupid. Of course I see you." Gaslighting. That was so Cal.

And, just like that, Kobe Bryant died in a helicopter crash. Australia burned. And the world locked down. Saving—or ending —a marriage was the least of anyone's worries.

# Chapter 12

## *Legacy and Lingerie*

Missy was in full mom mode until the pandemic gradually loosened its grip, and the world, once frozen in fear, began to stir, slowly at first, before racing forward. She shut off her emotions during that time, but as the world started to function again, so did the thoughts she'd forcefully suppressed. COVID had only delayed the inevitable. Missy and Cal had become increasingly estranged even as they sheltered in place in their home, feeling as if they were constantly walking on eggshells. The masks they were forced to wear became a haunting metaphor for their fractured marriage. Once removed, the truth was impossible to hide.

As things began to return to a new sort of normal, Missy was approached by her friend Tabitha. Tabitha had been going through her own sort of reincarnation. She took photos during the pandemic of Sullivan's Island and how life looked different during that time. She was working on a new project: the women of Sullivan's Island, and she wanted Missy to be a part of it.

"You're a legacy in this town, Missy. We all grew up admiring you and wishing to be you," Tabitha said as she pitched Missy on the idea. Missy was flattered but felt she was presenting a false front. She was miserable in her marriage, didn't know how to escape it cleanly, but needed something to make her feel again, like she was worth seeing. If she thought too much about it, it made her feel shallow and vain. She had been selfless for far too long, a voice inside her head insisted. It was time to remind the world who Melissa Jean Kinkaid Sutton was.

When she told Cal that she had been asked to be part of the project, he showed little interest. "You don't do anything. But I suppose it'll be good for business, too. Make sure you plug the company, hon." The hurt from his discounting her stung much deeper this time than it had when he aired his opinion about the children's books. It was clear to Missy that this was the beginning of her downfall and a clear sign that her marriage was on shaky ground.

Missy found unexpected joy in doing the photo shoot. She looked in the mirror and began to see a part of her old self emerge. She had her hair and makeup professionally done and bought new outfits and shoes. She chose things that she would not normally wear but said, as she and Macky waited in the checkout line at Nordstrom, "I can still rock this."

Tabitha gave her a safe space to express herself. It was a small studio with various props, including a couch, a desk, and a chair. There were coffee mugs, books, sheer drapes. Fans gently stirred the air and natural light filtered softly into the room. From the first moment she walked out in the green dress, Missy found herself empowered. Her inhibitions melted away. Tabitha directed her. "Jut your chin like this," she would say, pointing her jaw out slightly. "Be tall, stretch your neck just slightly.

"Ooh, I love those dreamy eyes. They are so expressive when you look at the camera. Tell the world you own it, Missy." She knew the words to cajole the looks from Missy.

It felt awkward at times sitting in a forced pose. Touching the side of her head with two fingers, crossing her legs and arms. Leaning in. Moving back. Big laugh. Coy smile.

"Beautiful. Do you know how hard it is to get people to do the not-smile smile?"

Missy laughed at that, but when she saw the photos, she knew exactly what Tabitha meant.

At one point, she put on a floor-length gown. It was tight around the middle, showing the rolls that she had. She felt self-conscious. Her hips were accentuated. She felt like Jessica Rabbit, just without the tiny waist.

"Are you sure I should wear this dress?" she asked Tabitha.

"It's the cover," Tabitha insisted. "I'm telling you. It's absolutely stunning. Just the right amount of cleavage. Perfect fit. Your eyes and that hair! Seriously, so amazing."

Missy loved Tabitha's enthusiasm. Missy had put on a few extra pounds during the pandemic. She told herself she should run to get in shape, but Missy knew better. She hated to sweat. She liked a good walk so long as she could continue a conversation and not get winded. Exercise was not her favorite. She surmised a few extra pounds were less torturous than the prospect of daily exercise.

Missy grabbed her belly and pulled on the fat. "This, though," she said to Tabitha.

"That is what makes you real, Missy. That is why you are such an influential woman. No one looks at you and thinks you are anything less than perfect." The words weighed heavy on Missy. What would Sullivan's Island think if she left Cal? Would they still believe she was "all that"? Missy did not know what overcame her. Maybe a fleeting thought that her marriage could be salvaged. "Would you do me a favor?"

"Anything," Tabitha eagerly agreed.

"One sexy lingerie shot? Maybe just this lacy bra and the

underwear?" She pulled up the bra under her dress to show it to Tabitha.

"Oh my God, yes! Of course." Tabitha sprang into action to set up the couch.

"It's not for the magazine, of course. I was thinking I could surprise Cal with it."

"Love it," she said, singing the words.

So Missy posed, contorting her body as Tabitha directed. Squeezing her boobs. Tucking in her tummy. Trying to be sexy. Inside, she was dying, wondering why she was doing this. Maybe it was really just for herself. She wondered if Cal would be upset with her. It had been a long time since she had felt sexy at all, let alone with him.

As the shoot neared its end, she began to feel her confidence rise. She'd concluded that she had long ago started to lose confidence in herself as a woman. Or perhaps she had forgotten she was a woman at all. It was easy to do, raising a family and living with a man who took you for granted and could see little about you. If he could see you at all.

She embraced the moment, seeing it as a pivotal opportunity in her journey. She didn't know what that looked like, but she recognized that it needed to be forward from here and all for her. Missy felt truly beautiful for those few hours in front of the camera. And the previews of the photos Tabitha showed her on the camera's viewfinder were stunning. She was on top of the world.

"Cal is going to be so hot for you when he sees you in these photos," Tabitha said. Missy's tummy turned at that, though she hoped her friend was right.

Missy came home eager to share her experience, but Cal did not even compliment her. His reaction to the preliminary photos she eagerly shared was a basic, "They're good." She felt deflated.

"I did a special one just for you." He did not seem interested, but she showed him anyway. She smiled, slightly embarrassed but also excited to be sharing it.

It was a stunning photo. Missy's pale skin made her look ethereal. Her eyes were dramatic and focused on the camera. Her long, red hair loosely flowed around the black, lacy bra she wore. Her hand rested lightly over her belly, not to hide it, but to encourage the viewer to use their imagination. Even Missy had admitted to herself that she looked sexy.

"Seriously?" Cal asked. Missy's smile faded as she heard him gear up. "Why would you do this?"

"Because the opportunity presented itself. Because I thought you might like something like this."

"Jesus Christ, Missy. You aren't in your twenties anymore. Keep your clothes on."

Missy was stunned.

"What does it take for you to see me anymore, Cal?" she blurted out, holding back tears.

"What does that mean? I see you. You don't have to play Barbie and get all dressed up to get my attention. Or take it all off."

"Clearly, because even that didn't work." She grabbed her keys and stormed out of the house. She drove to Margo, hoping she might have an empathetic ear. But even Margo did not take pity on her.

"Why are you trying so hard to get attention?" Margo asked. "Did you ever think how this might make Cal feel?"

Missy wanted to scream. She wanted to tell Margo that despite what she thought, Cal ignored her. Her husband of over twenty years treated her like an inanimate object, devoid of feeling, there to be tossed around, played with, and then put away.

How could she defend Cal? How could Margo even begin to understand what she was going through? Margo had been divorced for over fifteen years. She didn't raise a family. For the last decade, Margo had only ever thought of herself and been bitter about anyone in a marriage, who had children, or who was remotely happy.

"You should be glad I'm miserable, Margo," she snapped. "Isn't that what you've always hoped for? That I should be as miserable and unhappy as you?"

Margo said nothing as Missy stormed back out the door, and Missy felt even more alone in that moment. She had gone from a high, feeling a superficial sense of joy in having done something scary like a photo shoot. It was empowering, yes. She felt beautiful, yes. But despite appearances, she had been scared shitless.

In that moment, storming away from her cousin's door, she was overcome by a sense of resolve. "Fuck you all," she blurted out. "Fuck you for underestimating me. Fuck you for not seeing me. Fuck. Fuck. Fuck."

Missy was no stranger to sharing her life on social media. Mostly, she posted photos of her kids or her with her kids, usually with herself tucked away neatly behind Macky and Kaid. Rare photos with Cal made them look happy. Missy knew precisely what she was feeling in every one of them: See my pain with this man.

What Missy did not post were photos of just her. So when she left Margo's in a fit of rage, she sat in her car and posted the images Tabitha had shared with her. It was an uncharacteristic moment. "So this happened today. Excited to be a woman of Sullivan's Island." She hesitated before posting, deciding to add: "More to come. Thanks @tabithamoorephotos #womenofsullivansisland." She did not post the boudoir shot. She would save that photo as a reminder that Cal was beyond appreciating her, that he wanted to oppress her, that he was not worth it anymore.

Missy was not prepared for the onslaught of comments supporting her, telling her how amazing she looked. Some of the comments by male friends felt mildly inappropriate, but she knew what they meant. Above all, Missy would admit to herself that the validation felt good. Meanwhile, Cal did not say word one.

Missy embraced her role as a woman of Sullivan's Island. It fed her ego, filling that need for affirmation and making her feel seen as a woman. She told herself she could inspire others by putting herself out there and doing things that are scary, unconventional, and unexpected for a woman of her age. Long the person to hide behind others in photos, she was suddenly at the forefront. It was uncomfortable, but the response was incredible.

As much as she was feeling a new sense of self, she was still dying inside, trying to convince herself she could be happy pretending with Cal. But the voice of reason became louder with each passing day.

Missy tried talking to a therapist. She asked Cal if he would go to couples therapy with her. He reluctantly went once, annoyed by the touchy-feely parts of it. "I don't know. This is too foo-foo for me. I think we're good." In that moment, Missy knew there was no way back. Cal reverted to silence and avoidance, though he somehow thought that sex wasn't off the table. Missy would simply say, "I have a headache." In twenty-some years of marriage, she had never had a headache. Every two weeks, when he would try to initiate sex, she always had a headache. Eventually, he stopped trying, which meant she could stop pretending.

Missy was silently making plans to leave Cal. She was feeling confident. She had been suffocating and needed to find herself again, independent of Cal. She did not hold him accountable for her losing herself. She knew she was equally complicit, but only she could reclaim herself. They had both become lost in their marriage, and their tension and strain were insurmountable.

Missy tried to talk to her dad about it. She knew Margo wouldn't be of help. But Dex got COVID and was never able to recover fully. It saddened Missy to watch her once-vibrant father losing himself. He had been her rock. Her hero. Her true love. She decided to ask him, if only to share.

"What do I do, Daddy?"

He squeezed her hand. "You be you, sweet girl. You don't need me to tell you that." She smiled at him. "I never much cared for him anyhow," he added, his laugh turning to a cough. "You have a home to come back to."

Missy knew that. She just needed to hear the words that she had somewhere to go. Somewhere she could land safely and softly if things got out of control. She knew Cal was growing more bitter with each passing day, but he remained silent, opting for avoidance over confrontation. It had been a long time since Missy felt she was in control of her situation.

Missy had decided to ask Cal for a divorce once the kids returned to school after spring break. That would give them time to figure out the logistics without pulling Macky and Kaid into the middle of it. They could be adults about that. They both loved their children.

Missy could see a light at the end of the tunnel. She could see a way forward. When she came out of the tunnel, she would get to choose her path. There would be a direction. Unless, of course, the tunnel ended at a cliff, and it was a sheer drop down.

# Chapter 13

## *A Middle Finger Moment*

Missy found herself second-guessing the decision to get divorced. Was she just discontent because the kids were both off to college? Did she need to do other things instead? Maybe she should start reading more.

Instead, she booked a weekend getaway for them to the Shackleford Banks in North Carolina. It was an easy five-hour drive up the coast, and it had always been a favorite family spot when the kids were growing up. They were all fascinated by the wild horses that roamed the beaches freely, as if humans weren't even a factor.

The Thursday before they were supposed to leave, Missy reminded Cal. He informed her that he thought it would be the following weekend and that he had made plans with his buddies to try a new golf course.

"Can't you just switch the weekends?" he asked. She wanted to ask him the same. But she did not.

"It was a special for this weekend," she lied. In a fit of inspiration, she declared, "I'll just go by myself."

In an unusual gesture of affection, he leaned in and kissed her on the cheek. "That's my girl."

Cal left the room. As he did, Missy held her middle finger up high and waved it at his back. This would be her fuck-you moment.

She thought about asking Margo to join her. She knew her cousin would likely say yes. But she didn't want to have to explain that Cal chose golf over her. Margo already thought Cal was perfect. Margo was sweet to Cal. Almost flirty, Missy thought. He enjoyed the attention. "You don't find it odd how Margo flirts with you?" Missy once asked him.

"That's not flirting. She's a lonely woman. She has nothing on you, hot stuff," he would say. Sometimes he would follow it up by gently patting her butt, which still made Missy feel like a piece of meat. Cal pitied Margo, and she ate it up. Missy didn't have the heart to tell her otherwise, but she also wasn't open to a weekend of Cal conversation.

So Missy began her solo adventure driving north along the coast. It was fall. The leaves were changing color. The days were shorter. The nights started to have a cold nip to the air. She felt free and alive.

She arrived at the small boutique hotel. Built in the 1800s, it had Southern charm mixed with all the modern amenities. She could catch a sliver of the water from her bedroom window. She figured she would be spending most of her time outside anyway, walking, exploring, watching the feral horses as they frolicked along the sands and in the waters. She had brought a bathing suit but knew she would not be brave enough to go in the water at this time of year.

Missy unpacked, looked over the travel materials left in the room, and then decided to visit the bar in the large commercial hotel next door. She appreciated the amenities at the larger establishments but didn't like how busy and congested they always felt. A drink would be good. Or she could hit the liquor store and buy a bottle. She realized how quickly she had left home: She had forgotten to pack the good wine.

By her own admission, Missy looked a mess, and she kind of liked it. In her haste to escape home, she'd barely brushed her hair, wasn't even sure she'd brushed her teeth. Just in case, she squeezed a dab of travel toothpaste onto her finger, rubbed it around, then spit. It felt oddly freeing not to care.

She liked that she didn't have to worry about running into someone. If she ran around in sweats, no one would whisper that she was depressed or had put on too many pounds. She tried not to care, but a tiny little voice inside her kind of did. She hated to admit it, but years of petty criticisms from her mother left an imprint on her that would occasionally resurface. You can only be so strong sometimes, she'd allow herself.

As Missy ventured to the bar in an old pair of jeans with a University of South Carolina sweatshirt and her favorite pair of Cariuma leather sneakers, she caught a glimpse of her reflection. She stopped. She looked. She fussed with her hair, deciding it would feel better to pull it up into a bun, but she didn't have a hair tie. She always had a hair tie. She ran her fingers through her long tresses and reconsidered. She knew she had great hair. Tonight, by default, she would own it. She smiled at her reflection and headed toward the bar.

The place was virtually empty. She looked at her watch. No wonder. It was, after all, barely four o'clock. At home, she would have felt like a lush hitting the bar so early. And who was she kidding? At home, she would not be hitting a bar. She'd meet friends for a nice drink and dinner. She was dignified. She didn't drink alone at a bar. She almost talked herself out of it, but then a man at the bar smiled at her. And she decided to stay.

She wanted liquid courage to guide her toward him. He was younger. Maybe in his late thirties. He didn't have a ring. She felt for hers. It was still there. She wanted to pull it off, but she didn't.

She sat one seat removed from him, looked over at him, and smiled. He returned the smile, then effortlessly moved to fill the space between them. She could feel his breath. "Hi. I'm Spencer," he said as he put out his hand. "Buy you a drink?"

She took his hand. "Missy. Gin and tonic would be lovely."

"Top shelf okay?"

"Does anyone say no to that?"

He laughed. "Honestly, you're the first person I've ever asked." *Oh, he was so smooth,* she thought. *This is how the world has evolved over the years I have been married and raising a family.*

The bartender served their drinks, and Spencer clinked Missy's glass. "To new friends."

"To new friends," Missy said.

"What brings you to Shackleford Banks?" He mimed putting a hand to his forehead. "Don't say the horses. Please don't say the horses."

Her smile lit up. "The horses," she said and began to laugh, which made him laugh. Their conversation went from one topic to the next. They laughed constantly, and as they went from one drink to two, Spencer began to gently reach for her during conversation. She liked his touch. It wasn't aggressive; it felt genuine.

Spencer had been in town for a sales convention and decided to stay on through the weekend. "Make a mini holiday of it," he said. He was from Myrtle Beach. He knew Sullivan's Island as most people did. It was a small town with a considerable reputation. He had never been, which made Missy feel oddly relieved.

By the time he asked her if she'd like another drink, she was already feeling a little tipsy. One more drink would have put her over the edge. She got up and thanked him for the drinks and wonderful conversation. He stood up and whispered in her ear, "I think you're beautiful. Can I walk you back?"

She felt his warm breath as he spoke, felt her hair move as he whispered, tickling her slightly. She reached down and grabbed his hand and led him out of the bar.

They walked in relative silence to her room, taking quick glances at each other, giggling quietly between themselves.

They stopped at her door. "How old are you?" she finally asked.

"How old do you think?" he asked as he leaned in to kiss her neck.

She moaned softly.

"Doesn't matter," she confessed. "I'm still married, though."

He paused. "That explains the ring," he teased.

"I don't usually do this kind of thing," she said.

"I don't either," he told her.

She gave him a look of disbelief.

"Seriously," he explained. "My ex broke up with me a year ago. I decided to stop feeling sorry for myself and put myself out there." He ran his finger along the collar of her sweatshirt. "And then you walked in wearing this super sexy baggy-ass sweatshirt, and I thought, 'Okay.'" She would have laughed except he pressed hard against her, his lips finding hers, his tongue moving slowly inside her mouth. She had forgotten how lovely a good French kiss could be. His was especially delicious.

Missy and Spencer spent the next thirty-six hours together. Mostly, they spent the time in bed, exploring each other's bodies, reminding themselves what it felt like to feel pleasure at the hands of someone else. They came out to eat. They took evening strolls. They bought nice bottles of wine. They showered. When she went to put on clothes, feeling just the slightest bit self-conscious, he said her body was perfect and she should never hide it. He liked watching her move across the room naked. He liked how her red hair hung just past her nipples.

She found herself surprised by her attraction to Spencer. He had a boyish appearance. His hair must have once been blond;

now it is a mixture of brown hues. His eyes were a light brown, and with the right light, green drips appeared, as if they were part of a Janet Sobel painting. His skin was almost as pale as hers. "I don't get out much. It's the curse of working," he said.

He was built like a runner but admitted he only played squash on occasion, to which she replied, "Only East Coast Ivy League types play squash." He was silent. She looked at him as if to ask which one, to which he replied, "Princeton. I'm that transparent, huh?"

"Some things you just can't escape. If you had said tennis, I wouldn't have presumed."

"Fair enough."

Sunday checkout arrived. Missy had lived in an alternate reality for a weekend. Spencer was a gift. He made her forget she had another life. That she had a husband she needed to leave.

He asked for her number when they left and if he could see her again.

She thought about him the entire drive home. And he thought about her. She never did get his age, but it didn't matter. He was a distraction.

Missy and Spencer would meet twice more. The meetings were more for fulfilling sexual desires than delving into knowing each other better. Missy knew it would go nowhere, and Spencer recognized that dealing with a woman about to go through a divorce would not be healthy for him either. She suggested they should just be friends.

He laughed at the idea. "We can be text buddies," he joked.

"I don't know. I've never done this before," she said, frazzled.

He pulled her into a hug. "You are the most fun I have ever had with a woman. Truly. I will not lie that I will think of you often, might even visualize you when..."

Missy cut him off. "Stop. And ewww."

"Ewww?" He kissed her hard one last time. "You will never be ewww to me."

And she knew he would never be ewww to her either. It was the right thing, she realized. It was time to end things with Cal. To move on. To live her own life. A life that did not involve secretly meeting a lover.

* * *

Missy would remember that brief affair with Spencer fondly. He reminded her she was a desirable woman. He saw that she was smart. What had he said? Oh, yes, that she was "wicked smart." She liked that. It wasn't hot sex. It was good sex. She liked that he was real. That he made her feel. She knew any affair she had would likely do that. At least, she assumed it would.

Spencer had texted a few times over the years. He asked how she was doing, and she'd ask him. He married a woman he met at a bar. That made Missy laugh. He said she asked for a gin and tonic. That made her laugh, too. Missy told him he had come into her life at just the right time. He replied, "Ditto."

She had seen Spencer's face clearly that day in the cereal aisle. He had been the buzzy bee on the Honey Nut Cheerios box. He had seemed so basic and unassuming, except he was coated in sweet honey goodness.

# Chapter 14

## *Deliverance and Betrayal*

Missy could not pretend with Cal anymore, but asking him for a divorce would not be easy. He would avoid her. Make excuses not to talk. He must have sensed it. He was leaving early for work. Coming home late. Deflecting. He either sensed it or he was having an affair. *That would make it easier, wouldn't it?* she thought. Missy knew there was no good time to ask for a divorce, so she chose her moment and acted. She finally cornered Cal early one morning as he filled his coffee mug.

"You're up early," he said.

"You've been avoiding me," she countered.

"No. Just swamped," he said, irritated.

She took a deep breath, telling herself just do it.

"I'm done, Cal. I want a divorce."

He looked long and hard at her.

Finally, he snapped, "Saw that coming. Okay. Done. If that's what you want. Certainly explains your selfish behavior lately."

Missy wanted to scream at him. *Selfish? What the fuck?* How was she ever selfish in their marriage? Because she wanted some validation, because she wanted him to see her, because she wanted to feel like she was more than just arm candy?

All she could say was, "Yes. That's me. Selfish. But thanks for the divorce."

Cal slammed the door on his way out and did not return home that evening. Missy could not have been more grateful. She had been liberated. She had done the hardest thing she had ever done in her life. She had found her voice and used it.

As she slept alone in their bed that night, a peace came over her. There was no regret, only relief. But there was also a sense of foreboding: What would happen next?

When she woke, it felt like it was all a dream. Did she and Cal really agree to a divorce? Did she imagine it? Cal's side of the bed was exactly as he had left it, empty, and there was no part of her that regretted asking.

She called Macky to let her know. Her daughter was disappointed but not surprised. Kaid was surprisingly more emotional, wondering what would happen to their house, his surfboards, his collection of random objects he'd saved for no real reason over the years. Missy promised that nothing was happening overnight. "We're getting divorced, honey. We aren't there yet. Everything doesn't suddenly disappear," she reassured him.

It would be many months before the divorce was finalized. She didn't look forward to it. She had seen friends and acquaintances go through divorces, some messy, some easy. She crossed her fingers Cal would be civil, but she had hurt him. If he found out about her affair with Spencer, she wasn't sure how he'd react, so she hoped he wouldn't.

Missy told Dex later that day when she went to visit him. She swore she saw a smile begin to grow on his face. She peered down at him. "You aren't disappointed, Dad?"

"Are you kidding?" he blurted out. "That man was so self-centered. Didn't treat you right," he said in a gravelly voice. She hated seeing her dad become increasingly weak. He had a care-taker most days now, helping him manage the activities of his daily life. He didn't want Missy to see him suffer, he always put on a brave face for her, but she saw it. The man who stood above all others in her eyes was diminishing quickly.

"I don't think anyone will ever treat me like you do," she said, her own voice growing husky. "I've been lucky to have you my whole life."

"I'm proud of you. You did good in life, my girl. You'll be stronger and better without that man. And those kids are trea-sures." He closed his eyes.

Would she have married Cal if her dad hadn't approved all those years ago? But Cal asked Dex if he could marry her. At least, he said he did. She never questioned it.

She gently stroked his arm. "Daddy?" she said softly.

"I'm just resting my eyes." He opened them slowly and looked toward her.

"Did Cal ever ask you for your blessing to marry me?" She had been young. In love. Cal was forging a path forward. They had dreams.

He harrumphed, then took a deep breath. "Never did."

Missy felt a wave of sadness building. "Would you have said yes if he did?"

Dex looked at his daughter. "I saw how happy you were. With no crystal ball to guide me, I would have said, 'Love her with all your heart.'" He laughed. "And then I would have told him, 'I'll kill you if you don't.'" He started to cough, but he was amused nonetheless.

Even if Cal had lied to her about getting her dad's blessing, at least she knew that he would have said yes had he asked. It was a small consolation.

"A crystal ball would have been nice, though, right?" she said.

"No, sweetheart. Life is supposed to challenge us. So many

things we wish were different, but the parts to get there were sometimes the greatest moments in our lives."

With that one powerful statement, she knew her father wouldn't have changed anything. She would find strength and solace in those words and use them to guide her life forward. "Thanks, Daddy. I love you. Now get some rest."

* * *

The only other person Missy felt needed to know about the divorce was Margo. She could only imagine Margo feigning disappointment that her marriage had failed. While Margo had been making the most of her life after her own divorce, she was still bitter. Missy had made an effort over the years to keep conversations about Cal and the kids to a minimum. She tried to be respectful and kind toward Margo. She was her cousin after all and had always been there for her. At least on the surface.

She had texted Margo that she needed to talk to her, asking if she could come over. Margo did not reply until Missy had already pulled into her neighborhood. She was stunned to see Cal driving away as she turned onto Margo's street. A sinking feeling filled the pit of her stomach. Why was he there?

She knocked on Margo's door. She didn't answer. She knocked again and then pushed on the door handle. As she pushed open the door, Margo came out: bathrobe loosely closed, towel drying her hair. She looked stunned to see Missy.

"What are you doing here?"

"I texted you that I needed to talk. It's important." Missy saw the look on Margo's face. "I saw Cal leave. Did he tell you?"

Margo set the towel down, walked to the kitchen, and poured them both a cup of coffee. "I don't know what you're talking about," she said as she handed Missy a cup.

"Margo, what the fuck? Did he tell you?"

116

Margo took a deep breath. "I'm not sure what you want me to say. He said you asked him to leave, that you wanted a divorce."

Missy was flustered. "I asked him for a divorce because his narcissism became intolerable. I did not ask him to leave."

"Well, maybe not in those words."

"I'm sorry. Were you there? No. And you're going to choose to believe Cal over me? Me? Your cousin. The person who's been by your side our entire lives."

"He just seemed so broken. He said he needed me to help him understand."

Missy wanted to throw up. Or wring Margo's neck. She wasn't sure which would be better. Probably not attempted murder. Missy looked around Margo's home. It was obvious no one had slept on the couch.

"Did he stay here last night? He never came home."

Margo became uneasy. "He swore you found someone else and that's why you wanted a divorce. He thinks you're having an affair."

Cal had never said those words to her. She realized if he did, then it would be an admission he hadn't been good enough for Missy. A small victory. But out of context, she reeled herself back in.

"What if I did? It's not your business. And it wouldn't be his to share with you."

"So you did have an affair?"

"What? That's not the point. It doesn't matter... to you. Or to Cal. Or to anyone but me."

"Cal was right."

Missy hated Margo in that moment. Hated her for defending Cal. Hated her for assuming she had had an affair. Then she realized she had one more thing to hate her for.

"You slept with him, didn't you?"

Margo did not reply.

"You fucking bitch. You slept with my husband. I didn't think you could go this low, Margo. I didn't think you were capable of hurting me like that." Missy stared long and hard at her cousin. She wanted to scream. She balled her fists up, upper body stiffening, then turned and marched out of Margo's home.

She could hear Margo calling after her: "But Cal needed me. I couldn't let him down."

That was the story Margo would tell people. Whenever anyone asked why they never saw Missy together with Margo anymore, Margo would simply say, "It's not my story to tell... But she had an affair. Poor Cal. I tried my best to help him when he needed consoling."

For her part, Missy tried to remain neutral, hating Margo inside and treating her with as much respect as she could muster outside. She sometimes wondered if she disliked Margo more than Cal. He was just a stupid man being led by his dick and ego. Margo was just a stupid woman being led by an inferiority complex and a misguided desire to have something she wasn't supposed to, something that once belonged to Missy.

# Chapter 15

## *Coming of Middle Age*

Margo and Missy avoided each other for nearly two years. It wasn't until Missy turned fifty that she spoke with Margo again.

Missy's divorce from Cal had been predictable but not too messy. Her dad had died. Her kids were living on their own. She was figuring her life out. And she felt oddly sorry for Margo. She knew Cal had only used her; he had no intention of ever being more to Margo than a one-night stand. He never needed her again. Missy knew Margo would be embarrassed by that part.

Missy never shared that part of the story. She bit her tongue during the divorce proceedings. She wanted to lash out at Cal, see him squirm as she divulged what she had seen, what she knew, but she did not. She just wanted it to be over. And Cal, to his credit, whether he knew about it or not, never confronted Missy about Spencer. It was as if they each knew they had something to hold over the other, but the cumulative effect wiped out any benefit. It was marital mutually assured destruction, and there had been enough hurt throughout their marriage.

She couldn't imagine Margo ever telling anyone. Missy had

been her best friend. She wasn't quite sure who else she would have confided in, but maybe she'd made more friends without Missy. Perhaps Missy was the reason she didn't have more friends to begin with.

It was hard not to think of Margo during those lonely two years. It would have been nice to talk things through with her. After all, she had been there since the beginning. Missy longed for her cousin's shoulder to cry on when Dex died. Dex did not want a funeral. It was too soon after the pandemic lockdown ended. He didn't want others to get sick if someone unknowingly had COVID and shared it with attendees. He didn't want the weight of his death weighing on him.

"But Dad, does it matter if you're dead? You won't know." It was one of his final lucid moments before the final days he spent, drifting in and out of consciousness.

"It's my final wish, Melissa." He called her that in the end. "And I want to be with Charlotte. Spread our ashes together. I loved her so."

Missy wished she could understand that level of commitment. She wished above all else to have known her mother as a loving human, not a toxic, mentally unstable ward at a psychiatric hospital. Missy tried to imagine what her mother would have been like. She wanted desperately to believe she could have loved her had she not been ill. But she knew she was loved. Dex had loved her for both her parents. And if Margo's mother, Adeline, had been any indication of what a Goodwin mother was like, then Missy thought herself lucky to have been saved that same punishment.

Dex's was a peaceful death. Missy could hear him take his last breath, the brief exhale after it. And then silence. She had been holding his hand. She could feel his hold loosen, like he was letting go. She sat there, just watching him, waiting to see if she could witness his soul rising above him to the heavens. She had never seen someone die before, and she hoped she never would again.

Dex wished to be cremated and had already taken care of the details the first time he learned he had COVID. He thought it a certain death. It was not. It wasn't even the second time he got it. "Damn, what's the big deal if an old man like me can survive it?" he asked, half joking.

"You're a healthy old man, Dad. You're one of the lucky ones." Missy had known that to be true. But COVID had done its damage, and long COVID eventually prevailed.

Missy kept him in an urn on a high shelf in the living room. She knew he was there, watching, waiting to be reunited with Charlotte. She did not need visitors to be reminded that her dead father was in the room. If they asked about the urn, she willingly shared.

Two weeks after his death, she was notified by the cemetery that Dex's space was available for viewing. "Space?" Missy was perplexed.

"Yes. He has a space on the columbarium wall. And, of course, your mother's name is also included."

"She's not dead yet."

"I understand. It has her birth year. We'll add the rest later."

"So what do I do at this columbine wall?"

"Columbarium. There's a niche for the urn to go. For both of them."

"He said he wants his ashes spread."

"I'm just informing you that it's an option," the man said in a tone that did not waver. He was clearly used to this conversation. "The wall is in the middle of the cemetery. His is located in space 490A."

"That sounds like an apartment. How will I find it?"

"It will have their names on it. And if you stop by the office, we can show you a map of exactly where it's located."

Missy thanked him. She wasn't entirely sure what to do with that information. Her dad was in her living room. It felt weird to go to a wall and look at his name and her not-yet-dead mother's name. Not to mention the fact that they were on a wall with a bunch of other already dead people. Missy didn't like death. It was inevitable, she knew. She had watched her father die a peaceful death, and she has watched her mother live a painful existence. She wondered how much her mother really felt, how aware she was of her nonexistence, alive in human form but dead on the inside. God, she thought, death makes you think morbid thoughts —one that she quickly realized was redundant.

She wished for Margo then. Margo knew what it was like to lose a father. Even if Vance had been a drunk, Margo found a way to love parts of his memory. She kept photos of him. Margo was less resentful of Vance than of Adeline, who had lived long enough to make Margo see her for the woman she was—one she vowed never to be. Missy would argue that she only sort of succeeded at that. Margo was not whimsical like Adeline. She did not have boyfriends like Adeline. She did not have a child she resented like Adeline. She was bitter, though, much like Adeline. But no, Missy thought, Margo was too afraid to become her mother. She had shared her relief with Missy when Adeline died.

"Is that horrible?"

"I think you had a complicated relationship with her. But at least you had one," Missy said.

"Maybe now I can move forward in peace," Margo said, then never spoke of her mother again.

Missy didn't reach out when Dex died, and Margo didn't either. She was mentioned in the obituary, though. Dex had taken care of that, too. It was strange to think of all the details Dex had taken care of toward the end of his life. Missy's father had always been a planner. The obituary was short and sweet—father to Melissa Jean, husband to Charlotte. He didn't want a big fuss, just like he didn't want a funeral.

Missy would check her emails daily. Look for a voicemail from

Margo. A text. Some sign that she knew Missy was in pain. Margo was probably also in pain. Dex had been like a father to her throughout her childhood.

There were cards that came for a month after he died and flowers from well-wishers. Her father's house—now hers—had never felt more vibrant. The irony of death, she thought. Yet there was nothing from Margo. Missy had hoped his death might bring them back together. They were both now without parents, the only other family either of them had. But Missy knew this wasn't true. She had her children. It was Margo who had nothing.

* * *

Despite her grief over her father's death, Missy was determined to throw herself a fiftieth birthday party. She called it her coming-of-middle-age party. "Fifty and Fabulous" was her other idea, but it felt a little self-adulatory. It was an opportunity to celebrate with friends in a world that no longer wore masks, feared touch, or cringed at a sneeze or a cough. Even though she knew there would always be those people, in all likelihood, they existed before the pandemic and had thrived during it.

Inside, she was celebrating being single and being okay with being alone. She was confident in her skin. She was finding her way on her own. The years since the divorce had been liberating. Yes, losing her dad had been difficult, but she knew he would approve of this celebration. She was convinced he would have been proud of her independence, for choosing herself, and for celebrating the woman she was. Once during the party, she lifted her champagne flute toward the urn neatly tucked away and said, "Cheers, Daddy."

Missy did not know if Margo would show. She had sent her an invitation in the mail like all the others. Missy still liked the old-fashioned way of sending invitations. It felt more formal, as if it

123

were truly for a special occasion, not just another e-vite sent like an invitation to a business meeting. Margo did not RSVP. On the day of the party, Missy went through the RSVPs one last time, checking the mail to see if she had missed anything. She rolled her eyes, wanting to be disappointed but recognizing it was false hope. She said to herself, "At least I know I made the effort." She tucked the small envelope with Margo's name on it into the kitchen drawer. At first she wasn't sure why she didn't throw it away, and then she realized that she still had hope. Hope her cousin would get her shit together and come to the party, see it for the olive branch it was meant to be.

The doorbell rang ten minutes before anyone was expected. The caterers were all accounted for. The bartenders were in place. She expected no less than a hundred people to show throughout the night. Missy was excited, but she wasn't ready.

She hurriedly applied her lipstick, topping it off with a shimmering gloss. She smacked her lips together, poofed her hair just a little, threw on her new slingback two-inch heels, and headed for the door. She stopped briefly in front of the mirror. The black cocktail dress landed just above her knees. The halter top made her shoulders look strong, like those of a swimmer. She thought maybe she should start swimming. Or at least learn how to swim correctly. She wore the silver watch her father had given her for her twenty-first birthday. It was still her favorite piece of jewelry. She felt good in this body. And not just for fifty.

As she flung the door open, the smile she wore quickly dissipated. It was Margo. Missy stared at her cousin. A stranger, she thought. She had changed. How was it possible that Margo could look sadder, unhappier? How had she aged so much in those two years? Maybe she had COVID. Maybe she was sick. *God, what if she has cancer?* she suddenly thought.

"I didn't RSVP." That was Margo's opening line. Not even prefaced with an "I'm sorry." She wondered if Margo had ever apologized over the years. Were those words even in her vocabulary?

Missy didn't know what to say. She'd practiced this moment so many times over the past two years, but she simply said, "I'm sure you won't be the only one," and opened the door for her to come in.

Margo walked oddly past her and surveyed the empty space. "Oh, I'm early."

Again, no sorry.

Missy was reminded of the note she had tucked away. "I have something for you," she said. Margo looked surprised as she followed Missy to the kitchen. A man in a white uniform shirt with pressed black pants offered Margo a glass of champagne. She took one. The server then offered Missy one. She grabbed two.

Missy pulled the note out of the drawer and handed it to Margo without a word. She wasn't sure she could say the words she wanted without taking too many tangents or having it come out wrong.

Margo opened the note and read silently:

*Margo, I love you. You are my blood. I cannot forgive you. But I miss having you in my life. I want to find a way forward. — Missy*

Margo had barely finished reading before she was throwing her arms around Missy and bursting into tears. She did not apologize for what she had done because she really wasn't sorry. But she loved her cousin. And she missed having her in her life.

That night, Missy Kinkaid's friends celebrated her coming-of-middle-age party. They danced to eighties music. They didn't know how to move when Macky hijacked the Spotify account to play EDM, but they tried anyway. Missy felt like the belle of the ball. She would glance at Margo, hoping she would find joy in being there, being a part of her life again. She saw Margo shed a tear once, and she realized it was when she saw Dex's urn on his shelf.

Margo had missed much of the past two years, but tonight would be the start of many new things. A new decade. New freedoms. New adventures.

Maybe even love, Missy thought. She might finally be ready for that, too.

# Chapter 16

---

## *The Man of the Hour*

Missy and Margo found a way to move forward. They were blood after all. Cal left Sullivan's Island shortly after their divorce was finalized and their home was sold. Missy would occasionally ask the kids how he was doing. Kaid would shrug his shoulders while Macky would simply offer, "Dad is Dad."

*Whatever that meant*, Missy thought. They were loyal to their father, and that was enough for her.

Cal moved to North Charleston—far enough away not to bump into him and close enough for the kids to spend the occasional holiday with him, the ones they weren't spending with Missy. Missy decorated her home for every occasion; Cal did not. Missy made a big deal of spending time with them; Cal did not. Missy spoiled them with gifts; Cal gave them money.

Macky and Kaid debated the value of one over the other.

"Cash is just so practical," Kaid would argue.

"But Mom puts thought into our gifts," Macky would rebut.

"Does he ever ask about me?" Missy asked Macky once.

"No, but you know Dad. He's not a super-great communicator. Plus, he's stubborn."

"I hope he's happy. I hope he realizes he's better off on his own," Missy added.

Macky just shrugged. "He's happy when he sees me. That's all that I care about."

And she was right. Cal had always been a good father, and so far, he'd been good about paying her spousal support every month. He never texted, not even on her birthday. Missy took the high road and sent him texts complete with balloon and birthday cake emojis. He never replied, but that was to be expected.

* * *

Two months after she and Zander have started seeing each other, Missy asks Macky and Kaid to come home for a special dinner. She has someone she wants them to meet. Macky is elated by the news. Kaid wonders what's for dinner.

"Anything you want," Missy says.

To which he replies, "I'll get back to you on that."

As the older sibling, Macky always drives. They arrive early to take a walk on the beach. Kaid attempts to surf, but it's more of a paddle given the lack of waves. Missy knows he enjoys the solitude of water.

Missy makes them mini grilled cheese sandwiches as a snack. It's been a long time since she last did this. She finds joy in making them, hoping it doesn't ruin their appetite for dinner. She doesn't worry that they won't like Zander. She knows they will.

Missy opens the snack cupboard. As she moves the Triscuits out of the way and reaches for the bag of sea salt and vinegar chips, an image of a cereal box flashes before her. She sees it there: Grape-Nuts featuring Cal. She snickers at the idea of it. She hates Grape-Nuts. They're hard and unyielding. Cal saw himself that way—or at least acted that way. He was hard to chew, no matter how long he soaked in the metaphorical milk. He stubbornly avoided uncomfortable truths. The image fades, and she says to herself, "Of course he is." Divorce was the broken tooth from taking too big a bite.

Kaid gestures a spinning finger near his temple and rolls his eyes toward Macky. She giggles. Missy realizes they've witnessed her moment and mocks them back, "Yeah, yeah."

"So when do we get to meet the mystery man?" Macky asks.

"For dinner," she says.

Macky and Kaid look at their fake watches, then grab for their phones. She knows they want a more exact answer.

"Soon enough. Now eat." They inhale their mini grilled cheese sandwiches with a side of chips. Kaid drinks a beer while Missy and Macky enjoy a cider. Conversation is back to normal. They update her on their lives. They share.

"You're coming for Scarlet's wedding, right?" Missy asks them.

Kaid says it's the only weekend he has left before he takes his professional engineer exam. Memories of his meltdowns before tests flood back, so Missy understands. It's also his way of saying he has no desire to attend a wedding with a bunch of old people, with no hope of hook-ups among the guests.

"Emily will be there," Missy throws in. She knows Kaid once had a little crush on Emily, Scarlet's daughter.

"Over it. She's got a boyfriend. No point," he says.

Missy looks at Macky. "Did I know this?"

"Yes. You follow her on Instagram."

"Oh. That man is her boyfriend? That explains a lot."

"Scarlet doesn't say anything?" Macky asks.

"I think she's been a little preoccupied. I'm surprised, though. Mom and daughter both like those older men," Missy says.

"So old, Mom. Beau is ancient compared to Scarlet."

"A decade. That's not ancient."

"In ten years, he'll be decrepit and she's still going to be hot."

"She'll be ten years older too."

Kaid chimes in, "Yeah. But she'll still be hot."

Missy looks at him, confused. "You think Scarlet's hot? She's old—to use your words."

"Doesn't mean she can't be hot."

Missy shakes her head at both of them. "So Macky will be there. Kaid will not. Got it." They both give her a thumbs-up for finally understanding.

Later that day, Zander meets her children. She has warned them to be kind, not to judge.

Zander arrives punctually at five o'clock. If he's nervous, he doesn't show it. It still makes him smile to ring the doorbell at Missy's house. That door is where he first saw her, where he first realized she was something extraordinary. Funny to have such a strong memory about a door.

Missy opens it for him with an impish grin. She comes outside, closing the door behind him, putting her finger to her lips, and quietly shushes him. He is confused. She leans in for a long kiss. "No PDA in front of the children," she says as she turns around and opens the door back up.

He shakes his head, grinning from ear to ear. *This woman,* he thinks to himself.

Zander has brought a coconut cake from his favorite bakery in downtown Charleston. Missy takes it from him and sets it on the counter. Macky is immediately impressed. "Oh my god, that's my favorite bakery!"

*Score one for Zander,* Missy thinks. So does Zander.

Missy can't wipe the joy from her face as she watches her new man interact with her children. Even though they're adults, they are still her special humans, the creatures she carried inside her. The aliens that screamed as they left her body. Or maybe that was her. Their births are a beautiful, distorted blur. There's nothing on earth that makes her happier than their presence, but there's a new feeling accompanying it. The man next to Macky and Kaid is making her very happy as well.

Kaid had requested steak and potatoes, saying, "I eat way too much fish in the city."

So Missy bought filet mignon, which Zander grills to perfection. They tease each other about the amount of butter used, how a dollop of sour cream is more like a ladle, how chives are an embellishment, not a grass field. They drink the expensive wine. Missy knows the kids don't treat themselves to the good stuff yet.

Zander does not miss a beat. He jokes with them. Gives it back when warranted. He and Missy touch each other under the table. He watches her in her element, with her children, and thinks to himself, *Just when I didn't think she could get any more beautiful, she does.*

It's not lost on Macky how much this man adores her mother, and vice versa. Even Kaid recognizes this, which says a lot for him.

Macky sends Missy a text from the car after leaving: *Love him, Mom. I haven't seen you smile like that in a long time.* This makes Missy happy. She knows they both once adored Travis, thought him the perfect man for their mom. He had made her laugh. Had made her smile. Until he broke her into a million little pieces.

# Chapter 17

## *The One You Don't See Coming*

Missy met Travis Butler by accident. She was simultaneously the strongest she'd ever been but potentially the most vulnerable, knowing her heart had room to love. She had been content in her new life as a divorcee. She accepted that having an affair and leaving Cal meant that she was strong enough to survive. She had moments when she struggled with her decisions, but in the end, she had chosen to be true to herself. She contended that living with a man who had lost interest in her—both physically and emotionally (had he ever really had that?)—was worse than forging a path forward alone. The affair with Spencer was short-lived. He was too young, and she was too mature. It was fun while it lasted, she reminded herself. He was the excuse she had needed to leave her marriage.

So when Travis Butler was seated next to Missy at a charity event for homeless animals, she did not expect her life to be turned upside down. They began chatting. She noticed his calm demeanor, the subtle way he said things, and his striking blue eyes. He asked her about her interest in the charity.

"Dogs have saved me my whole life," Missy said.

"Same," he said.

"You do not strike me as the kind of man who needs saving."

He laughed at that. Then he turned to her and said, "It took me a lot of work to get to the point where someone might not look at me as the puppy who needed rescuing."

"I won't pry, but that's a pretty heavy icebreaker," Missy said, trying her best not to read too much into what he had said.

"Ask away. I've learned to share my truths. I've found it helps me as much as it helps others."

She was obviously curious. Was he divorced? Widowed? Recently paroled from prison? Was he running away from somebody? She found it incredibly refreshing that a man was willing to be so open about his life. She saw it as a challenge to learn his truths.

"So no ring," she observed. "I'm going with divorced. You are a workaholic who puts saving the world"—she motions around at the animal crates—"or dogs, as would be the case, first. Maybe in finance."

He exhaled, then smiled at her. "Perceptive."

"I nailed it?"

"No. Parts, maybe." Missy waited for him to continue. "Divorced." He paused, then held up two fingers. "Twice. Workaholic? Love my work. So probably. But I'm retiring, so that becomes less of an issue. I'll probably just save more dogs," he said and gave her another smile.

"Okay. First, congrats on the retirement. I don't think I know anyone in finance who loves their work. They're just workaholics. So, what do you do?"

"I'm a surgeon."

"Hmmm. Didn't see that one coming. You really don't fit the whole doctor look."

He gave a hearty laugh. It was unique, and she found herself drawn to the sound of it. "There's a look?" he said, putting up both hands and shrugging. "Who knew?"

She liked his sense of humor. He didn't take himself too seriously. He excused himself to get a drink, asking if he could bring her anything. She was surprised to see how small he actually was when he stood. She had expected a larger man based on the size of his laugh, but he exuded a confidence she found rare in a man. It was not arrogance. He was comfortable in his own skin. She sensed a man who had experienced heartache and loss in love yet was resilient.

He returned with two drinks, then handed her one. "I'm Travis Butler, by the way."

"Missy Kinkaid," she said as she took the drink from him.

They raised their glasses, saying, "Cheers," simultaneously, then laughing at their timing.

They spent the rest of the afternoon talking to each other, oblivious of the event going on around them. Margo would point out that she had been there that day, that she had seen their chemistry. "You two were in your own little world," she would tease Missy.

Travis had been a stark departure from the other men Missy had known. Conversation with him was fluid, not forced. They breezed from one subject to the next, pausing long enough to catch the glint in the other's eyes. She would admit that she did not initially find herself attracted to him. He wasn't her usual type. He was small in stature and a dozen years older than she was. He was soft spoken until he laughed; then he was the center of the world. He was modest about his profession and equally interested in what she did.

Missy struggled with that part of her story. She was proud of her kids. She felt lucky to have stayed home with them. When she and Cal finally divorced, she felt she could be whatever she wanted to be. She just wasn't sure what that was anymore. Her skills in advertising had become obsolete. She hadn't stayed up on trends. The internet had barely been a thing when she was working.

"I'm not really anything anymore," she answered, somewhat embarrassed. "The last twenty-five years were spent raising my family. Then I got divorced." She looked at Travis, wondering what he was thinking. "I know, not very exciting."

"Are you kidding? Working is way easier than raising a family. I admire that you did that," he said.

She shrugged. "Now I just do volunteer stuff. Sit on a couple of local boards. It's not a lot, but I'm busy that way," she offered.

He watched her face grow sad. "What? You okay?" he asked.

"No one really prepares you for when your kids leave, if taking care of them is all you've done. Caregiving became my identity, so when that was gone, I definitely felt lost." She marveled at the ease with which she could share her deepest sadness. She was in her fifties and didn't know anymore what she was supposed to be doing. This, in its own way, was freeing.

"It sounds like you're doing things that give you value," Travis observed. "That's important, right?"

"I feel like society looks down on that a little, but then I try to tell myself it was my career. It was twenty-some years of mom stuff. I'm allowed to do me now. So I try to be good with that and not beat myself up too much. I volunteer, sit on boards to validate my perceived lack of ambition."

Missy had struggled over the years, reconciling her role as mother with the internal expectations she had of herself. She was a product of her upbringing. Her father adored and encouraged her; the vitriol of her mother made her determined to succeed. When the kids came and Cal's business was doing well, it was a relatively easy decision to leave advertising to be a stay-at-home mom.

Secretly, she worried she would get bored or find herself intellectually under-stimulated. There were moments, yes, but she found a way to be engaged, to be relevant, front and center in her kids' world. It wasn't until Macky went to college that she found herself a little concerned about the next phase of her life. Kaid was a more challenging child, and she found herself putting out his fires most of his last year at home. When he finally left for university late that summer, she breathed a sigh of relief, silently high-fiving herself.

And then there was the silence. She'd done it. The kids were gone. The hard part was done. She sat at her kitchen table, stared numbly into the distance, and began to sob. What was she supposed to do now? She and Cal hadn't talked about that. He usually brushed any concerns she had about her well-being off. "You're a strong woman, Missy. You'll figure it out."

What if she didn't? she wondered. "Reinvent yourself. You always have," she would tell herself. Into what, though? She didn't have any real hobbies. She dabbled in writing but didn't know if she was any good at it. She could take up pickleball because everyone else was playing. She wrote it down on the blank notepad in front of her.

It occurred to her that she had done that job, the job of mom, for over twenty years. There were no pay raises or performance evaluations. There were the occasional thanks that caught her off guard. Cal took her for granted: expected a clean home, cooked meals, and biweekly sex. She realized the prize should have been herself. She should be allowed to finally take care of herself. If she wanted to read a book and not feel guilty, she should. If she wanted to exercise or sneak away for a pedicure, she should. There were no holidays. No paid time off. No vacation days as a mom. She and Cal never took trips together without the kids. She was actually relieved about that as the years went by. She felt selfish in that recognition. She had gotten lost over the years; it was time to reclaim herself, redefine who she was, and live her best life.

"Fuck society," Travis said matter-of-factly, bringing her back to reality.

She startled, then nodded. "That's what I tell myself. Also, that's easy for a man of your stature to say, Dr. Butler."

"I'm twice divorced. I'm pretty sure my dedication to my job played a role in that. I could tell myself otherwise, but I know better. And my kids would probably side with their mother, my first wife, and agree."

Before the charity event ended, Travis had asked for Missy's number and if she might like to continue their conversation over a bottle of wine. She had never met a man with whom she could so easily communicate, so she said yes.

Four months later, Travis asked Missy to move in with him. He lived just outside Charleston in a small waterfront home with impeccable views of the Atlantic Ocean. It was fast, she knew, but there was a chemistry between them that was undeniable. Travis had shown Missy that he was a man capable of both physical and emotional intimacy. Sex with him was fun. At this age, she thought, we know ourselves enough. She felt she'd met her intellectual match, someone who challenged her beliefs, shared his views with her, and made her feel like she was the most beautiful woman in the world by his gentle touch, sweet kisses, and kind words.

While Travis was nearly a dozen years older, she did not see him that way. He was handsome in an old school movie star way, a modern-day Paul Newman, she thought. Even though he wasn't a large man, he might have weighed ten pounds more than she—at her thinnest—but being naked with him felt natural. He was confident in his body, and he revered hers. She couldn't help but love and adore all of him.

In the beginning, sex happened often and everywhere. They had sex on the dining room table because neither of them had before. "We're having sex on the dining room table," he announced as he moved inside her, trying not to lose his balance. She laughed.

They had sex in the courtyard because that was a first, too. They made love under the stars on the front deck, laughing and giggling.

"What if the neighbors hear?" she whispered too late.

"They'll appreciate that old people still have sex," he said.

"Or they'll never have sex again," she shot back. More laughter.

They'd realized their prior sex lives had been safe, devoid of steamy, exciting fun. They were sexually compatible and invested in each other emotionally, which made their physical intimacy reach a level neither of them had ever experienced.

It was the emotional intimacy that Missy found especially appealing. Travis was a man who knew himself. "I've done the work after years of therapy," he would tell her. She knew that Travis was damaged, too. They shared that. But what two people with three marriages between them wouldn't be? A career in medicine. An early first marriage. Two children. A meteoric career. Divorce. A young nurse. Scandal. Moving. An unhappy marriage. A second divorce. He owned his place in both divorces, recognizing they were not born of one single act but of a cumulation of cause and effect with irreversible damage.

Missy recognized that Travis had a difficult time allowing himself to be loved despite his broken, glued-back-together pieces, but she pushed through. He allowed himself to be vulnerable, and she did the same. She was lost in him.

Missy knew she wore rose-colored glasses around him. Even if she tried to take them off, she only saw a beautiful, giving soul who reminded her she was worth seeing. She thought Dr. Travis J. Butler would have had more women hitting on him. She thought he would love it when she told him how handsome he was, but that just made him uncomfortable. He disliked compliments, saying it was not something he had been used to receiving, certainly not from either of his wives. Missy loved to shower him with compliments and adoration. She felt herself drawn to him like a magnet, not always sure she could explain the pull toward him, just that it was stronger than she knew how to explain.

"Hot for doctor. Come on. You haven't heard that one before?" She couldn't tell if he was kidding or sincere. How could a man who did what he did and looked like he looked never hear that before?

"I've been called a nerd. A geek. Weird. Those fit. Hot? No."

"Your wives never said you were hot?"

"Nope. Neither of them was very adept at giving direct compliments."

She playfully placed his arms around her, and he pulled her in. "Well, Dr. Butler, I am hot for doctor. And I think you're handsome, and your laugh is my favorite sound."

He kissed her. That was his thank-you, his way of deflecting. It was sad, she thought, that he could not see how beautiful she thought he was.

They traveled and explored together. They visited vineyards on both coasts, shipping bottles home and then doing blind comparisons to see if they could differentiate the coastal flavors. They joined way too many wine clubs but managed to keep ordering more. It was a shared pleasure. Travis upgraded his wine refrigerator to accommodate their expanding palates.

They enjoyed evening walks on the beach with their respective rescue dogs, Comet and Alfie. Both came with their names at adoption, and they somehow matched the mixed breeds of nondescript origins they were. Alfie had no problem bonding with Comet when they moved in together. The dogs shared their bed. Comet was especially keen on morning kisses, even if his breath was in dire need of refreshing. Alfie would stand over them, daring them to get up, then bounding away as soon as Missy or Travis flinched. It was a shared joy to wake up next to each other, slightly stiff from being squeezed between dogs but simultaneously relishing that they had been wrapped up in each other all night anyway.

Although it took Missy a while to find her footing in Travis's home, she felt she belonged there with him. He cleared out space in the closet for her. She had her own work area. He allowed her to bring her University of South Carolina coffee mugs even though he would have preferred the University of North Carolina ones he had. They giggled in the mornings with their rival coffee mugs in hand.

Missy loved listening to Travis talk about his career in medicine. He had experienced forty years of change in the field, innovating, improving, researching. His perspective on healthcare, on humans, and on the financial and emotional toll of the industry was eye-opening to her. If poor health didn't affect you personally, it wasn't always top of mind. She began to see the world a little differently through his eyes. Macky even said her mother seemed softer since she was with Travis.

"Softer? What does that mean?" Missy asked her.

"You're maybe not so quick to judge or assume something," Macky said with slight trepidation.

"Me? Judgy?"

Macky rolled her eyes. "I'm just saying, sometimes you can be a little bullheaded. It's a good thing, Mom. I mean, I always loved you, but I think you could scare people sometimes, too."

Missy wanted to defend herself, but she could see herself in her daughter's comments. "I suppose it's why I was always chosen to lead things, huh? Bull in a china shop? Get it done?"

Macky shrugged.

"Okay, so I'll take softer. I think of it as having an open mind and being willing to hear differing perspectives and having the courage to admit that I wasn't always right," Missy said matter-of-factly.

"I like Travis, Mom," Macky repeated. "I think he's good for you." And she left it at that.

# Chapter 18

## *And Then the Wheels Fall Off*

It was exactly a year and a half into their bliss when the wheels fell off.

A week before Christmas, Missy was up early, wrapping gifts and writing Christmas cards, cursing herself for maintaining the tradition, even though it seemed passé. She was two cards shy and began searching the basket of cards Travis kept in the office. It was a basket she had been in many times over their relationship. She had never noticed the plastic bag at the bottom of the stack, full of cards differing from his usual stack. "Keeping the good ones from me, huh?" she said under her breath.

She opened the bag and pulled out the top card. It had writing in it. She saw only a few words: "your messy hair" and "enjoy your weekend with the boys." She did not recognize the name until she remembered his nickname for her: Ollie.

Missy quickly closed the card. Still curious, though, she opened the second card only to see it was written in, too. She did not read another word; She did not look farther. She felt sick to her stomach at the sight of the pile. She had intruded on his privacy, even though she knew the man had a lifetime of trust issues.

It bothered her all day. She didn't care that he had saved them. She'd kept things from her past, too. At dinner that night, Missy told him she had stumbled across the cards and that she had read a few words, didn't register who it was from at first. Then she mentioned Ollie, and his face went white.

Travis finished his dinner in silence, eyes fixed on the window as he drained the last of his wine. He rose, cleared only his plate, and moved slowly, as if carrying a weight. At the doorway, he turned.

"Why would you do that? Why wouldn't you see it as an invasion of privacy? Why not just stop?" His voice stayed calm—he was not a man who yelled, ever the stoic doctor.

"It was an accident."

"I'm just not understanding. And before I get really angry, I'm not going to speak." He left the room.

Missy sat stunned. She hadn't meant to find the letters, hadn't been searching for secrets. She never doubted her place in his life. After Cal's indifference and Travis's own trust issues from past marriages, honesty had seemed the only way forward. They had shared so much—histories, hurts, vulnerabilities—that openness felt essential. But she had not expected this.

Wasn't truth more important than burying some letter from years ago? They'd been living an idyllic life together, bound by the very confessions that once wounded them. Why now, of all times, did he recoil? They had never fought seriously before, always found their way back to steady ground. But this—this had struck something deeper. If she'd known, she would have locked it away, thrown out the key, and never spoken of it again.

"You know I have trust issues," Travis said when he finally broached it.

"Which is why I told you," Missy replied gently.

"I don't understand why you even needed to look." The hurt in his voice was unmistakable.

"I did not intend to find the letters. I would never intentionally hurt you. I was honest with you. That's what we do." Her desperation hung just as heavy in the air.

Missy felt the thud of her heart as it dropped into her stomach. She felt Travis start to slip away, then and there, in that moment. There wasn't an answer. She couldn't explain it. Maybe it was the same reason he took the stack of emails from his first wife, when she'd been having the affair, and burned them. Missy never asked if he read them. He had to have, at least enough to know what their content was, but she did not offer that in her defense.

As Missy recounted those months before she was asked to move out of Travis's home, the one they had shared, she recognized the emotional torture he had been putting her through while he unilaterally grappled with their relationship ending.

It took him three months to ask her to leave. Even then, he did not ask. She made it too easy for him, asking if he wanted her to leave. To which he simply replied, "Yes." He offered no explanation.

She wanted to fight, to tell him he was wrong. But in that moment of pain, her voice collapsed beneath the weight of her grief. The only sounds she managed were smothered by sorrow.

She checked in with him constantly over those months, desperate to know what she could do to make things better. "Tell me what I can do," she'd plead, but his answer never changed. "I don't know. I need to figure this out." The words sent her spinning.

On the rare occasion when the tension seemed to lessen, she would hope. "Are we okay?" she'd ask. His reply was always the same, always brutal - "I don't know." Each time it cut deeper, sharpening her anxiety instead of soothing it.

Once, he even said the words she did not think possible, "I stopped loving you." Then, as if that weren't enough, he added, "I'm not sure we can ever get back to where we were."

"It's a growth opportunity," she pleaded. "Going back just

means the parts that were new and exciting. This should make us better, not break us."

But she couldn't give him the distance he craved. The more he needed space, the more she moved toward him. He stopped holding her hand. He no longer kissed her good night. He didn't touch her as he walked by, gently reminding her he loved her. He started picking at little things, such as how she moved her mouth when someone else talked or how he preferred the toilet lid to be down. He stopped asking her questions. He lost all interest in her.

The last time they had sex, he closed his eyes. When they finished, she sensed that she would never feel him inside her again. The way his eyes loved her when they had sex had been the most beautiful part. The way he smiled the entire time was magical. Watching him with his eyes closed made her feel cheap for wanting a man who no longer loved her.

Her autopilot said she should fight for him. Prove him wrong. You can't just stop loving someone. *He was just trying to hurt you with his words. You're good at that. He's doing it, too.* But he wasn't. The harder Missy fought to prove her love, value, and worth to him, the more Travis pulled away. Until he had the opportunity and the courage to say "yes" when Missy asked if she should leave. He said "yes" again when she asked if he was sure. And then he said there would not be a second chance. He'd already made up his mind.

Missy knew she was being immature. Her heart hurt. She couldn't understand the pain as she attempted to process why he would let her go when she loved him so much. She wondered if she was just a challenge to him, a way to prove he was still capable of being loved and lovable. And what had flipped in her head to make her worry? She tried to tell herself he was too old anyway. He had a hard time with her energy, and he was not always sure he could sustain it as they aged. Yes, he was an older man. He was lucky she loved him. But she knew better. She didn't care that he was older. She had fallen in love with the man, all of him, even the things she thought quirky or odd.

She added up all the parts and pieces of their relationship. The beginning was beautiful. He had swept her off her feet, let her be her, let her forget the painful parts of the years with Cal and the brief affair she'd had with Spencer. She felt she glowed in his aura. His friends said they had never seen him happier. They were perfect despite their age difference or the lack of a perceptible difference between their heights and weights. She didn't care. Until she did.

Her mother's voice would sometimes haunt her in moments of doubt and insecurity. She had worked hard throughout her life to suppress that voice, but after finding the letter, confessing to a partial read, and Travis's reaction, she began to fall, making missteps, losing her balance and way. She panicked that she was too much, that he might no longer find her attractive. A tiny rational voice said he was lucky to have a younger woman who looked as good as she did, who worshipped his smaller size. In hindsight, she would reflect that she had always worn rose-colored glasses with him. She didn't care about those things when she was with him; he was perfect to her.

She replayed their relationship on an endless loop, focusing on the parts before the letter, the admission she regretted. Missy had been there for his retirement, smiling as his friends and colleagues congratulated him. She listened as he recounted his career and milestones. She learned from him. She asked questions. She doted on him.

And then he broke her. The man who made a living fixing people shattered her heart. It was a pain she had never had before, a gut-wrenching, uncontrollable emotional roller coaster that would change Missy in ways she did not know possible.

Had it been a perfect storm? Was the letter the lightning strike that shattered her perceived fairytale? It felt like a reverse fairy tale now: Her prince charming had turned into a frog.

* * *

Missy spent two days moving her things out of Travis's home. There were a few pictures of them together scattered throughout, but once those were gone, there would no longer be any evidence that Missy had ever been there. She looked around and wondered if he'd ever loved her enough to make the house theirs. She was especially hard on herself as she scrutinized their relationship. She hated herself for loving him so much. She hoped someday she would be able to unlove him.

Then there were the dogs, the unknowing victims of the relationship ending. Comet and Alfie were also breaking up. They were dogs, though. They'd be fine. Not like Missy. She held Travis on a pedestal, knowing he didn't deserve it. She told herself all those things. She tried desperately to believe them.

Missy was grateful for Alfie during that time, too. She faithfully lay by her side as Missy silently suffered. She nuzzled in tightly as Missy cried hysterically. Those moments even confused her. She hadn't cried once when she and Cal divorced. But she realized that she'd had years of mourning before their marriage ended. It was easier letting go of her marriage than it was to let go of Travis, which made her feel even more pathetic.

Margo was the first person she called after she moved out, and even that took Missy a week. While the cousins' relationship was back on solid ground, she hesitated to share that her happiness was no longer. She wasn't sure if Margo was bitter that Missy had found happiness after Cal or if she was genuinely happy for her cousin. It was hard to read Margo anymore. She was always there, though a little more reserved than she had been. Maybe she worried she'd misstep, say something wrong, and Margo knew she could not afford to lose Missy again. Even if she knew she would never quite fit in, that she'd always feel a little like an outsider, a little like the world was judging her, Missy was her only family.

Margo came to Missy's side as soon as she called. She was stunned to find her cousin a wreck. She had lost weight, looked almost too thin. "I'm not hungry," was all Missy would say. She'd pick at food but would never finish her plate. Even chocolate had lost its appeal, and wine was a reminder of nights spent with Travis. Months later, when she began to see the light again, she would rediscover her love of wine, vowing not to let Travis take that from her.

Margo stayed with Missy for several days. They talked. Well, mostly Missy talked. They both cried. They never spoke of Cal. Or of Russell. Margo listened. She felt Missy's pain, though inside, she silently found joy that her cousin was hurting. She hated herself for that. Life hadn't been fair to Margo. That's the story she told herself. Watching Missy suffer felt like a small vindication for her sad, lonely life.

Sometimes Missy would see Margo smirking as she sobbed, thinking to herself, "You bitch. And you're right. I deserved this."

Missy did not know how the months passed after she left Travis's house and returned to her childhood home. Maybe deep down, she had known they weren't going to be forever, but no one had ever broken up with Missy before. They say the first heartache after divorce is worse than the divorce itself. She had given all of herself to him. For the first time in her life, she had allowed herself to be completely uninhibited. She wondered if her mental break was Charlotte haunting her, telling her she was no different than she was. Had Missy been faking it her whole life? Had she kept her insecurities so well under wraps that it wasn't until they went unchecked that they were allowed to escape? Travis went unchecked. The monsters, the doubts, the voices in her head seeped through the fissures until they exploded. Just like her mother's doubts had.

"The self-reflection is exhausting. I'm imperfect. I get it. I have flaws. I have triggers. I always thought I knew all that. But I wasn't prepared for this," she explained to her therapist, Melanie, as she begged for medication. "I need the voices to stop. I need my head to quiet down."

Melanie was a good therapist, who was available by Zoom, so Missy could wallow in the cozy, homebound comfort of her own depression when they spoke. Even if she were twenty years younger than Missy, Missy felt understood by her. She would begin and end her call, "I'm here to help you heal, Missy," and then Missy would mostly talk, cry, and apologize for how out of control her emotions were during their conversations. Melanie provided kind words, offered moments for reflective pauses, and shared some valuable insights.

Her therapist agreed that medication would be good. "You don't feel suicidal today, do you?"

"I have really dark moments. I question my purpose. What's the point? To die like my dad? Be locked away like my mom? I feel like that's where I'm headed right now. So dying would just be so much easier." Missy feels so dramatic as she says that, but she knows she has Macky and Kaid. They may not need her like they used to, but they did.

Macky has told her as much. "Mom, if you died, I'd be lost. So don't get all dark on me. Please. I love you."

"I love you, too. I'm hurting."

Macky understood in the ways a twenty-something could understand. She had not known heartache like this, and Missy hoped she never would.

After she hung up with her therapist, questioning her own life, its purpose, she called her doctor, who immediately prescribed her an antidepressant. "Relief won't be immediate, but it should help."

She was no longer sure if it was the Zoloft, her therapist, Alfie, or Margo who saved her during this time. She imagined it was Zoloft first, Alfie second, Margo third, and Melanie last. *God,* she thought, *it took a fucking village to get me through.*

# Chapter 19

## *Burn, Baby, Burn*

Scarlet knocks on Missy's door before turning the knob to let herself in. It's an enormous home, yet the likelihood that Missy is anywhere but in the kitchen is slim as both women have eagerly awaited their scheduled coffee and walk to catch up.

"Hello?" she calls out as she enters the home, gently closing the door behind her. She hears Missy call out in her singsong voice, "Just finishing in the loo. Coffee's ready to go."

Scarlet finds two coffee mugs neatly placed by the finished pot of coffee. The fancy creamer container stands empty next to the bottle of Coffee-Mate French Vanilla. She imagines Missy impulsively grabbing the small carafe, thinking she needs to keep up her Southern etiquette, and then realizing that it's just Scarlet after all and she won't give a shit.

Scarlet hears the toilet flush as she pours both cups of coffee, grabbing them in one hand and the creamer in the other. She sets them down on the table and notices a picture of Missy and a man she doesn't recognize. She knows enough to determine it isn't Cal.

Those photos were neatly stored away with the albums of her children. The man in the photo is too young to be her father. Her curiosity is piqued.

She holds up the photo as Missy walks into the room. "He's handsome," Scarlet says. Missy smiles, taken aback that she has left the image out. She takes it from Scarlet, then walks it to a drawer, placing it far in the back, then slams the drawer shut.

"A secret lover?" Scarlet chides.

"A broken heart," Missy replies. "Mine."

Missy sits at the table across from Scarlet. She takes a sip of her coffee.

"You know how they say the first heartbreak after divorce is the worst?" She looks at Scarlet, knowing she won't understand. She's been lucky to find Beau—and keep him—after her divorce. Scarlet shakes her head, but Missy sees she's triggered a thought within Scarlet. She quickly adds, "God, I would never wish it upon anyone. And I hope you and Beau are solid enough."

Scarlet thinks so. They have weathered some trying times in their relationship, and Abby continues to look for ways to interject. Plus, there's always that little bit of awkward space when Ben visits. But she and Beau have worked through all that. He asked her to marry him. They were living together. It was fast, but it felt right. Whatever they might get thrown next, she hoped they could work through it. She knew she could hurt with her words at times. That was her defense mechanism. She would always apologize, and he would admit that he might have set her off, intentionally or otherwise. They always ended it with a kiss, acknowledging that not all days will be good days, and the challenging ones were the ones that would make them better, even if they hurt in that moment. There was always a whispered "I love you" as a reminder that they truly did.

Scarlet focuses on Missy. She sees the pain in her friend's words. "When was this, Missy?"

Missy wants to shrug it off. Instead, she feels tears begin to well up in her eyes. She grabs a tissue from the table and dabs at her face. If she speaks, her voice will be a muffled, phlegmy quiver caught in her throat. Scarlet says nothing, anticipating that Missy is finding the words.

"Before I knew you," she says. "Man, had I known you, I might have handled it better. You met me just as I came out on the other side." Her voice loses its hitch, becoming fluid, but it's filled with melancholy.

She stops to take a sip of her coffee, reflect, regroup. That makes sense to Scarlet. Missy was her rock and guiding light, the humor and common-sense voice that helped her navigate the unexpected chaos that came with being part of a divorced women's book club in a small town that wasn't always as kind and welcoming to strangers as the smiles on their faces suggested.

"That was Travis," Missy continues. "He was the first man I let myself love after Cal. It's been a couple of years. We were together for a year and a half, and then we weren't. Pretty much just like that." The pain on Missy's face is still evident.

"I'm so sorry. You've been such a rock for me here. I just assumed..." Scarlet stops herself, realizing that sounds horrible. "I'm sorry you have had to hide the pain, especially from me."

Missy swallows hard. "It's more that I'm embarrassed and caught off guard that I still had that reaction to him. I was doing so well. Then today, Macky asked me to find something for her, and I found the picture at the bottom of the stack. I should have torn it up. I managed to delete them all from my phone over time." She opens the drawer, takes out the photo once more. She looks long and hard at the picture before setting it down between them. She wants to trace Travis's lips and the outline of his ears, remembering what it felt like to run her fingers through his salt-and-pepper hair.

She feels a familiar wave of anxiety. It's an awful feeling, one she has worked so hard to overcome. She silently counts as she breathes in a pattern: 1-2-3-4 inhale. Hold 1-2. Exhale 1-2-3-4.

"I'm trying so hard to be okay," she says after this first series of breaths. "I feel weak again. Not like the strong woman who came out the other side. I can tell you this. You didn't see me after. I tried so hard to hide the pain. I couldn't tell Margo everything. I wondered if I was going crazy like my mom, but I wouldn't let the demons win. Thank God for Zoloft," she says, giving a slight little laugh.

"I had never loved like that, Scar. It was crazy. It was beautiful—"

"Then it wasn't, obviously," Scarlet finishes her thought.

Missy laughs bitterly. "I thought I was so fucking strong. But even a strong woman can be blind when she gives all of herself to love."

From the other side of the kitchen table, she grabs an open letter. "I forgot about this. He always said he'd send me a letter explaining why. He never gave me a reason when we ended. It was abrupt. I waited for it to come so I could have some closure.

"I wished for months that he would give us a second chance, see that we were better together than apart. People would ask me why I would ever want to go back to a man like that. At the root of it all, I let him love me in all my hot madness"—she tries to laugh —"but he extinguished my flame with a fucking fire extinguisher."

She begins to laugh, but the laugh becomes a sob. The tears fall freely from her eyes. Missy knows she can't speak, taking in deep breaths every time she opens her mouth to say something. She clears her throat, making a path toward articulation.

She blows her nose, giggling at the trumpetlike sound it makes. Her body feels like an off-key symphony playing broken notes. "Pathetic, right?"

Scarlet shakes her head and hands Missy the box of tissues.

"Thanks. God, it's been two years since he broke my heart. I was doing so well until that letter. I should have burned it then."

"Or you can look at it as a reminder that he hurt you. You were wounded. But you have healed and moved forward."

She takes a deep breath. "This is going to sound terrible, but my whole relationship life, I had never been dumped. I was always the dumper."

"*Building Back After Divorce?*" Scarlet asks, citing the book that helped her to better understand her own divorce.

"Something like that. So many fucking self-help books. I was swimming in them. Trying to understand what happened. Spiraling. Blaming myself. I was like that freshman cheerleader who doesn't get it when the senior quarterback breaks up with her, groveling, begging, humiliating herself. All so he'll change his mind. We know he never does. Who the fuck ever does?" she wonders out loud.

"The novels with happily ever afters. The ones we all want to live," Scarlet says, knowing that she is living that version of divorce and love later in life. "They say the rebound heartbreak is harder than the divorce."

Missy knew that. And Travis had been her rebound. Had she been his, too? She knew his story inside and out, she thought. She believed she understood how he had become the man he was, the brilliant surgeon. She knew his two divorces were complicated. In those moments, she only felt love, not like either of them was a rebound. Hindsight offered that reality.

By the time his letter had arrived, she felt like she could breathe again. Her life was in less of a fog. She had accepted her version of what happened and stopped blaming herself for their relationship ending. She tucked the letter far back in the stationery drawer beneath the one picture she did not burn because she looked too good in it and because someday she might like a reminder of a younger time.

She knew he was a damaged man, broken after two failed marriages. He allowed himself to love her until he was reminded that pain was real. While she believed Travis knew the man he was, she didn't think he was capable of letting someone love him completely. His job was to fix people, to put them back together again, but he was guarded; his heart needed protecting. From her.

Over the course of months, she had done her best to process, admitting it was two steps forward, one step back. Somedays, it was all three steps back. She read books on divorce and relationships. She tried radical acceptance. There were the nagging parts, residual reminders, the ones she tried to rationalize as to why this was better for her.

She reminded herself how hard it was for Travis to say the words *I love you*. When he did, it was like they were gifts one should appreciate receiving. Scarlet, on the other hand, wanted to scream from the rooftops how much she loved this man. Sometimes she did. Often, it was met with silence or a kiss.

"How messed up is that?" she says after she mentions this to Scarlet.

"Hurtful. Not okay. Not if you both loved each other," Scarlet says.

"I'd tell myself his actions proved it. But then those stopped when..." She pauses as if she has found the stack of cards all over again.

"I know he loved me. All of me. But I was too much. The glitter was gone, and I no longer sparkled. He couldn't trust me. I'd triggered unimaginable pain and sad memories. The brilliant surgeon couldn't forgive. Then we lost things in translation. I pulled when he pushed. I had never known love like that. I was allowed to be unapologetically me. I thought this was it. This was what love was supposed to look like. A man who looked at you when you made love and you felt special. Not like you wanted to hide your belly roll. But the kind of look that made you smile back and think how lucky you were to have this man inside you. You knew it wasn't just physically, but inside your head, too. How do you just let that go?"

She knew he was like a drug, an addiction.

"When he broke up with me, I spiraled. My drug had been taken away. My memory played the good parts on repeat, not the shitty ones. Those I would beat myself up about later."

Missy knew her answer. She hadn't let it go. She'd died inside, felt herself break into a million little pieces, ones she had worked so hard to make whole after Cal. One man did not deserve the amount of pain she was experiencing, but she couldn't shake him. She knows she has to let him go. She reminds herself of the purgatory she felt in those months before he told her it was over, that she needed to leave. No explanation. Who doesn't go down a rabbit hole of self-capitulation in those moments?

Heartache is like grieving, they say. Mourning a loss, taking the steps to grieve. "God, Scarlet, if you knew what I did? I begged. I pleaded. I blamed myself. I said I would change. He fucking said he stopped loving me. Why would I want him?"

"Because you loved him," Scarlet says. "And gave all of yourself to him."

"I told him the truth. I read a little part of a letter. He couldn't forgive me. I would have given anything to take that moment back."

"First, not to make light of this, but I'm impressed you only read part of it. I don't know many women who wouldn't have read the whole thing, all of them. They just never would have said anything. You were brave. You risked it. But you can beat yourself up about it, or you can recognize that something else would have set him off anyway. He wasn't capable of loving, let alone someone strong like you."

Scarlet is right, and over time, Missy has recognized that too. It's taken therapy. Not years, but a few months. It took some anti-depressants because she knew she needed something to ease her pain and allow her to heal. It had taken Margo, her shoulder to cry on.

"I woke up six months later," she concludes. "I swear I was a zombie for that long. And then I decided I needed to take control of my life. He didn't deserve to hold me hostage any longer. I lit a fire and threw everything about him in it. Then I danced on the ashes, said a curse, wishing he'd be alone forever. I hated him. I moved on. A week later, that letter came. Finally. The fucker took six months to finally write it. I didn't open it. Until today."

Missy could have gone her entire life without opening that letter, without feeling the pain sear across her body as she recognized his handwriting. Her fingers had trembled slightly when she opened it earlier. She reaches for it now on the table, holding it up toward Scarlet.

"I believed that at this age there wasn't anything we couldn't tell each other and not get through it. I believed it would have made us stronger, not broken us."

"It was obviously a deeper issue for him," Scarlet offers.

"We'd be living our happily ever after like you and Beau," Missy laments.

Scarlet feels the weight of Missy's pain, shaking her head in a resigned admission. "That wasn't always easy either. And it went fast with us. You don't think we've had hiccups?"

"Okay, hiccups, but..."

"Beau questioned us once." Missy looks stunned at Scarlet's assertion, but her best friend nods. "Yep. I didn't say anything. I was embarrassed and confused. The harder I fought for him, the more he pulled away. I was spinning in a cycle of overthinking and self-doubt. Just like you."

"But you obviously got through it. You're still together."

"Because we both recognized we weren't perfect, that there would always be some part of us that could rear its ugly head at any moment, but that was nothing compared to the love we share. The sense of relief I felt in that conversation was enormous."

"God, Scarlet, imagine if I hadn't told him."

The words make Scarlet ache inside. She hates seeing her friend in such pain. In Scarlet's eyes, Missy is the epitome of strength and courage. She embodies that confident, fifty-something woman who does not want or need to be defined by a man. And while she knows Missy admires her relationship with Beau, she does not envy it. She knows Missy is moving forward. She sees how just speaking of Zander makes her light up.

Missy experienced unimaginable pain in her heartbreak with Travis, but in the end, it made her stronger. Made her better. She knew that. Every book, every podcast, every person with an opinion told her time would heal, that she'd be better, stronger than before. She hates to admit they were right, but they were.

She keeps her optimism about Zander at bay. She recognizes it is new, and all new things feel magical. She knows she will move cautiously with Zander. Missy feels whole again. She is wiser. Less eager. Less hopeful. More metered. Controlled. Confident. She is better.

"Why did you open the letter today?" Scarlet asks.

"Because it's like the fucking stars aligned, sending me to that drawer. First, Macky's text. As I'm texting her back, a text from Travis comes through. Then I see his picture. It's a fucking train wreck. Oh, and my cursing him apparently worked. He's sick." She reaches for her phone and shows it to Scarlet. "He has cancer. Said he'd like to see me. So after two years, I finally dared to open his letter."

Scarlet studies the message, wondering why someone who

knowingly hurt another human, told them he stopped loving them, would want to see them. He had asked Missy to leave his life and his home. He had told her she was too much, that he didn't think he could sustain her energy.

"Who says they don't think they can sustain your energy?" Missy says, as though reading Scarlet's mind. "Geez, I was keeping him from getting old. I probably would have kept him from getting sick, too. That's on him," she says, trying to be lighthearted.

"Are you upset by the letter, the fact that he wants to see you, or because he's sick?" Scarlet asks.

"Yes," she replies. "Yes to all of it. I feel like the wound that healed, that made me stronger and better, was ripped open again a little." She takes the letter and walks to the kitchen sink. She opens a narrow drawer next to the stovetop and pulls out one of the multicolored lighters from within. She holds the letter out, clicks the lighter, and watches as the flame climbs up the paper, engulfing each word. Small parts of her want to wail in pain, but she stands strong, knowing she is better now despite all she has endured. She releases it before it singes her finger. She turns on the faucet, allowing water to extinguish the remaining flames. She grabs a paper towel and wipes up the burnt and soggy letter, tossing the remnants in the trash.

"No dance?" Scarlet says with a wry grin.

"He belongs in the trash." She walks over to the kitchen table and sits back down; a tear moves slowly down her cheek. "I loved him unlike anyone else. He wasn't the kind of man I thought I would ever love, but I think that's why I loved him even more. And I allowed myself to give all of myself to him. All the parts I protected before. He was so easy to love." She wipes at the tear. "He said he had loved me once, but he couldn't forgive me for reading the letter, even if it was just parts of it. For him, it hurt on a level that made him protect himself. Our relationship was barely two years old, so he thought it was better for both of us if it ended.

He could guard his heart, and I could go on with my life. He stopped loving me because he was afraid of what might happen. His heart had been broken twice before. It was time for him to take it back before it could be broken again. No discussions. Of course, he said I deserved to be loved by a man who could tell me every day that he loved me. That I deserved more than he could give. That he was too broken. And alone was his decision."

Scarlet hands her a tissue. "Was that what you thought or expected?"

"I told myself so many things those first few months. I blamed myself for loving him too much, for not giving him space, for failing to recognize that I was a little overwhelming." She points to herself—"Me? Really?"—and lets out a muffled laugh.

"The man gave out 'I love yous' like they were gifts, thinking it made them more special. I wanted the world to know how much I loved him and how lucky I felt to be sharing my life with him. Five years of therapy taught him to love himself first, and if that became threatened, I told myself, he would have to end it."

It was hard to imagine Missy as anything less than a strong, resilient woman. She knew she was fortunate to have had her own home to return to, but it was big and empty. Her father was gone, and she recognized he was the only man who truly loved her. She tried to feel his presence in the house, to imagine his warm hug as he reminded her she was worth so much more.

"I came here, to my sad childhood home. I opened the windows, let in the air, rolled up on the couch, and cried. Margo tried to console me. The kids were great on the phone. I felt like a horrible role model. Neither of them had ever experienced heartbreak—breakups, yes, but what I had, and on the scale I had, no. I wasn't sure what my purpose was supposed to be anymore. I hate even admitting to that. I knew I was better than him. That I deserved more than him. But I so completely loved all of him. And now that fucker's dying and wants to see me."

Scarlet studies her friend, seeing the depths of sadness this man's memory still brings her. "If you decide to go, I'll go with you for support."

Missy smiles at her friend, wishing she had met her years earlier.

"I don't think I can. I did not wish for him to be happy. Horrible, I know, but it's just who I am." Missy's honesty borders on brutality at times, but it's an enduring quality those who know her best appreciate.

"I would have done the same thing," Scarlet admits. "I mean, look at you. If a man couldn't have been happy with you, then he's a fool."

Missy knows, though, that what people see on the outside is not always who she feels she is on the inside. As her relationship with Travis began to slip away, she spiraled, her mind spinning, panicking, overcompensating out of fear he was pulling away. He no longer kissed her neck in the mornings as she sat on the sofa reading her email. When she told him how much she loved those things, he reacted as if it were an indictment of neglect on his part. She was stunned by those words, wondering when giving someone a compliment had turned into an assault on their character.

In the months of loneliness, adjusting to a new normal, repulsed and frightened by the prospect of opening her heart to another man, she reminded herself of Travis's passive-aggressive demeanor those last months when she felt her heart beating out of her chest, wondering when he might say she repulsed him after what she had done. He stopped holding her hand, just like his ex-wife had done. She realized that all the things that hurt him in his breakup with his second wife were on full display in their relationship.

Missy had been whole when she met Travis. She was an independent woman, exuding confidence after her divorce, living alone as a divorcee. She hadn't been looking for love, but it had found her. It was beautiful. Those are the parts she always wants to remember, but she ultimately let Travis destroy her. She gave him too much power that way.

There will be no visit, she decides. She picks up her phone and types: *I'm sorry you're sick. You broke me. I healed. And you've been dead to me since.* She shows the phone to Scarlet.

"That's a little harsh, no?" Scarlet says as she reads the message.

"The dead part?" Missy asks, chuckling. She deletes the last sentence and replaces it with *I can't.* Scarlet nods her approval, and Missy hits send.

If it were only that easy, Missy thinks as a wave of pain makes its way up through her body. She wants to wail in agony. She wants to scream that he can still evoke those emotions in her. And she wants to run to his side and hold him until he takes his last breath. She looks at Scarlet. "I would have taken him back a hundred times if he had asked. He was such an asshole to me. Treated me so poorly. Psychologically, he was probably borderline abusive with his avoidant and dismissive ways in those last months, but what he gave me always outweighed those things."

"It's good he never asked you back, Missy. Really. Would you have ever believed he changed his mind and forgave you?"

Missy would reflect on the time she had spent with Travis for the rest of her life. He had given so eagerly at first but then recoiled like a snake after it attacks. She damned his two prior wives, mainly the second, for damaging him.

She finally remembers the cereal box on which she saw his face. "Toucan Sam," she says out loud. Scarlet looks at her, confused. "Travis was the box of Froot Loops. He was full of color and flavor. I loved all of him. But my nose didn't know even though it should have."

Missy proceeds to tell Scarlet about her breakdown in the cereal aisle. About Malcomb. About the ghosts of men past. Her father. Cal. Travis. Spencer. Random men she couldn't remember or recognize but was sure they meant something to her once.

"I'm not sure I understand the symbolism of it all, but I keep coming back to that day." She pauses for a moment as a light bulb goes off in her head. "I think I was like the prize at the bottom of the cereal box for Travis. I was the shiny, sparkling toy waiting to be discovered and unwrapped. But the hunt is always way more fun than when you finally open the prize and realize it's just a comic or a flimsy toy. I was shiny until I wasn't. Until I triggered an old pain. And with that, my own insecurities were triggered."

Her phone pings, bringing her back to reality. It is a reply from Travis, simply stating: *Understood.* With a heart emoji. She wants to send him a black broken heart, but she doesn't. God, she hates him. She really, truly hates him for sucking up so much of the good in her life.

She flashes her phone to Scarlet, who sympathetically smiles. "If I go, I'd take pity on him. And I don't want to do that."

Missy breaks into a sudden giggle. "I will give him this. Even though he didn't have a huge penis," she deflects. "Such a weird word, right?"

"'Dick' isn't much better," Scarlet says.

"Actually, I called it 'friend,'" Missy coyly replies.

"Most women say that about their vibrator."

They both snicker.

"But it fit me perfectly. He was the first man I had vaginal orgasms with. I always found that ironic, given how much importance men put on that part of their anatomy. Sex was fun. Until it wasn't. Fucker."

Scarlet adds, "Amen and hallelujah," for dramatic effect.

Missy stands up from her chair, places the picture she keeps—"Because I look amazing"—back at the bottom of the pile, slams closed the drawer, and announces, "We're going for our walk now.

You know the story of Travis. You know my pain. And you know I came out the other side better and stronger than before."

Scarlet mostly believes it; Missy slightly less.

Charlotte watches in silence. She wants to give Missy a sign, tell her she's there. Instead, she nods in silent approval, a single tear drop slipping to the floor. Later, Missy notices the faint iridescent ring it left behind, shimmering like a halo.

# Chapter 20

## *Dating Apps, Unhinged*

The Divorced Women's Book Club has become a monthly event. While the divorcees were initially enthusiastic about meeting twice a month, the reality was they couldn't keep up with the required reading. They took a vote, and, much to Audrey's chagrin, they agreed that once a month was more realistic. Audrey lived for her books. The rest of them lived for the chance to bond over shared perceived injustices in their lives. Even then, they sometimes tired of the drama.

Scarlet's Harlots, on the other hand, has mandated weekly meetings with few exceptions. The four women enjoy the time catching up on their days. Some weeks are more intense than others, but when that's the case, they provide a sympathetic ear or offer a pass. They always enjoy each other's company, though.

While Missy feels compelled to invite Margo, Scarlet and Amber have slowly softened on her. Maybe she's capable of compassion and change after all, Missy wonders in moments of pity. She finds herself torn between loyalty and disdain, but they have been through too much for her to discard her cousin entirely.

"I might have met someone," Amber offers as she opens the second bottle of wine one week in late October and begins to pour.

"I thought you went off the apps," Scarlet says.

"It wasn't an app."

"How's that even possible?" Missy wonders. "Unless your mom dies and the hot attorney hand-delivers her voice from the grave, of course."

Amber has been on the apps for months, trying to connect. Her standards are high after what she's been through. While she didn't disclose the apps she was on, the women were convinced she had access to the more elite ones. Amber does not like to flaunt her prior priority status, but she works it when she needs to. She loves her newfound friends and their support, but she misses some parts of her previous life.

"Do tell," they say like a well-rehearsed choir.

"His name is Tyson. He's in hospitality."

"Like he's a waiter? Was he your server? Love at first martini?" Missy jokes.

"He sounds like a boxer," Scarlet says. Margo has no input.

"Haha. He's super cute. I think he's younger. I don't know. We met once for drinks. But there's something there." Amber does not tell her friends that she has plans to meet him later, nor does she mention that he owns a chain of upscale restaurants. "He made me laugh. And, by the way, he did bring me my drink. But it was a Cosmo." She laughs at herself. "I would love to never go on an app again."

"Imagine being our age on the apps," Margo chimes in. They all gawk at her, to which she replies, "What? I just look."

"God knows, I did the apps thing once. It was all I could do," Missy admits.

"When did you do that? You never told me," Margo says.

"Margo, seriously, you are just recently back in my relatively good graces. I'm sorry to say it that way, but I was not about to tell you that when I wasn't sure what you might do with the information."

Margo sits on that thought for a moment. Missy wonders how blind she can be to her own shortcomings sometimes. She has spent a lifetime taking everyone else's leftovers. How does she not see that? Or is it just who Margo is?

"No, you're right," Margo finally admits. "I haven't always been understanding about what you've gone through."

It's a light bulb moment for them both. Maybe there's a way for them to find each other again. Inside, they both ache for the sister they had lost, metaphorical or otherwise.

Amber chimes in. "I gotta know about the apps. Where? When? Good? Bad? Do tell, please."

Missy takes the bottle from Amber, finishes topping off the other glasses, and meanders to the sofa.

She begins with a simple, "Ugh. Not where I wanted to be. Not after Travis. But there I was..."

* * *

She hated the idea of it, but she knew she needed to do it. If Missy was ever going to find her fire again, she needed to see what the dating pool was like. She dreaded it. Disliked the idea that she had to make up some version of herself that might appeal to men. Men? What did that even mean? It was so broad and unappealing. She did not want to feel Travis on her shoulder, whispering in her ear or showing up peripherally, reminding her that she once knew what a man was. And that he had greatly disappointed her. She was resolved not to let his perceived presence hinder any part of her forward motion.

She was hindered enough. In those days, Missy felt like a lighter without liquid fuel. Her flint kept clicking when she flicked it, but it wouldn't catch. She needed to add fuel. She wanted to flick her BIC again.

Despite her mother's reminders that she was too chubby, wore too much makeup or not enough, that her hair was too wild and should be better coiffed, she was still able to look in the mirror at her fifty-something self and see a woman who had withstood the test of time. And boy, she had been tested. No man—not Cal, not Travis, no one—was going to be the reason she no longer looked amazing. Well, maybe the couple of times she afforded herself Botox gave her an added boost, but that wasn't anything drastic. And it helped with her headaches. She could believe anything she told herself if she wanted to.

Dating within a twenty-mile radius of Sullivan's Island felt risky. The chances of running into someone somewhere that might fuel gossip, speculation, or outright vitriol were not part of her plan. She would go to Charleston, stay with Macky for a couple of days, and explore the dating scene.

"I love it, Mom. I think that's awesome. Can I pick the guy?" Macky said with way too much enthusiasm.

"I'm not sure I'll have a lot of choices," Missy equivocated.

"Oh, please! I think you need to go younger. Like, way younger. You did that old man shit." Macky pretended to shiver. "Seriously, didn't get that one in the long run. But anyway, be a cougar."

"Okay, you are way too excited about this."

Macky chose not to acknowledge this but instead helped her mother put together a profile. She picked relatively recent photos, said smart things about her, and put her on three platforms. "If you're going in," she said as they hit "Publish" on Hinge, "you're going in."

Missy hated the idea. Men had always happened organically for her. Even after Cal, her brief, steamy affair with Spencer had been organic. And Travis was unexpected. It was easy when it just happened. But this felt contrived, forced, like she was pimping herself, unsure if anyone would want her. If she thought about it too hard, she knew she would have deleted the apps faster than Macky set them up.

The first four men to reach out to her were all in their late sixties or older. She wondered if Travis looked as old now as these men did. He couldn't have. Or were her glasses so rose-colored, she didn't see how old he really was? She swiped "no," "X," or whatever the app called for.

"They just want a caretaker at that age," Macky agreed.

"This is not helping my self-esteem," Missy confessed. "Why are the only men I appeal to old geezers?"

"So you know you have to be patient. It's a game. And I think men your age just want some young hottie by their side. They need Viagra to get it up, but the girl looks good."

Missy cut her eyes to her daughter. "You sound like you know about this way too well. Should I be concerned?"

Macky physically recoiled. "Eww, gross! That'd be like dating someone Dad's age. But I have friends who have done it. Mostly for kicks. It's kind of cruel. They get these old guys all worked up, and then they can't even perform. I know better."

"I don't think that's fair. Not all men in their fifties or sixties, even, are unable to get it up."

"Oh, they get it up. But then it's down just like that."

"Now, you're just scaring me. Who are you dating by the way?" Missy wondered.

"I did the apps *for-ever*, Mom. You know that. There were some super nice guys. And some super weird ones. I told myself I would need to date a bunch of frogs to find a prince. I'm still kissing frogs." She laughed at herself. "Actually, if I'm being totally honest, I am sort of, kind of, but not really sure yet dating a guy from work."

"Ooh, do tell," Missy said, distracting herself from her lack of interest on the three apps.

Macky blushed. "It's new. He works in accounting, but he's not like super nerdy. Or weird. Maybe a little quirky, but it's cute. He's an excellent kisser."

"Good kisser is good. Accounting means stable. Local man?" Missy wondered.

"No. Grew up in the Midwest. He's divorced. Has a teenager."

Missy's alarm flags went off. "How old is this man?"

Macky squirmed a little. "He's not that old. I am mature for my age. But he's forty-ish."

"Ish? Oy. I don't think I want to know more."

Macky was glad to end the conversation there. It was a new relationship for her, and it was different than anything she had known before. It was fun. She knew that this new guy liked her young body, enthusiasm, and zest for life. She got that from her mom. Missy may not have known it, but she had always been a role model for Macky. She had persevered in trying times, which she had so many of. She wore a brave face, even when she was breaking apart.

Macky stared long and hard at her mom. "You know, I don't know if I've ever told you this, but you're kind of a superwoman to me."

"Nice pivot," Missy snarked.

"Seriously! You have been through some shit, Mom, and every time, you seem to come out stronger. More beautiful."

"I'm getting old, but thank you."

"Are you kidding? You are a fucking bombshell. Men are just stupid." Before Missy could answer, Macky grabbed her phone from the table. She opened Bumble. "It's time for you to pick a few. We're not waiting for them. Bumble gives you the power. Well, at least to like them. It says you have over fifty likes so far."

Missy grabbed her phone. "But I can't see them. They're blurred out."

"Of course, they want you to pay. But don't. Let's just see what happens."

Together, mother and daughter sat side by side on Macky's apartment couch, perusing the men who would earn a "check" from Missy. *Why were there so many single, divorced, or widowed men out there?* she wondered to herself. They couldn't all be failures at relationships. But who was she to talk?

She especially loved the men who had specific physical requirements. "Not too short. Not too tall. Petite. Curvy fine. Fit." She especially loved it when men with big bellies wanted fit women.

"In what world does a man think a fit woman will like a beer belly?" Missy wondered out loud.

"In the one where there is CEO or MD next to his name. They're afforded a lot of slack."

"Not in my world. No way. You want me to be a certain way, then I expect it back," Missy said proudly. Not that Missy would have said she was fit. She wore her curves just right. Her little bit of middle fit perfectly inside high-waisted pants. She knew how to choose clothes that highlighted her assets and downplayed her flaws. She was confident in her body.

On the rare occasion she doubted she might still be a sexually attractive woman, she would allow herself to remember how Travis had loved her and how Spencer had devoured her. Cal, on the other hand, was routine. They had been together so long, knew how to please the other, and she was no longer sure if they even truly saw each other in the last years of their marriage. Sometimes she attributed that to their busy lives with kids, but other times she pinned it to Cal's narcissistic tendencies to put himself first. In later years, she would fake orgasms and then sneak off to the bathroom to satisfy herself. It just wasn't worth it to ask him for anything better.

Missy put down her phone. She had hit "like" five times on a range of men. "That's enough for now. Where's your wine stash?"

Macky hopped up from the couch, dashed to her pantry, and pulled out her mom's favorite Chardonnay. "I splurged and bought your favorite."

Missy smiled in deep adoration. Her kids had turned out all right despite the turmoil of the past few years. She had kept herself together, raising them even when she felt herself slipping away. Watching Macky now and knowing that Kaid was also succeeding after his tumultuous teen years allowed her to afford herself some grace.

Ambition had become her least favorite word in those early post-divorce years. It had defined her before. It was easy to do when a paycheck, promotions, prestige, and power were attached to it. It became clouded when it meant you stayed home with your kids. She had learned to accept that she was still ambitious, continuing to volunteer and sit on local boards, but she also recognized that it wasn't anyone's business how she chose to live her life and define herself.

It was in those moments that she was most grateful for her friendship with Scarlet. She hated the cliché that people come into your life for a reason, but Scarlet was a kindred spirit, a sister in life. She understood what it meant to be the one to leave a marriage first, to be the one to choose herself after years of giving to everyone else. Scarlet had come to South Carolina to find herself. She knew that was scary. Like Missy, she had struggled with the same "ambition" demons.

"The mom part didn't suck," Scarlet would say. "The part when they move out does. And you're left wondering what you're supposed to do now, especially if you did something in the pre-Internet days."

They would both laugh at the reality of that statement.

"The internet barely existed when I quit working. Shit, I think we even still had dial-up internet back then. The only reference young kids have to that anymore is from *The Proposal*," Missy said.

"Seriously, my kids used to look at us and ask if that was a thing!" Scarlet said.

Scarlet understood her. She was equally grateful that Macky and Emily had become fast friends. Emily rarely stayed with Scarlet when she visited. Macky was much more entertaining, and Charleston was a much more exciting city than Sullivan's Island.

Macky poured two glasses.

Missy laughed as Macky rejoined her on the couch. "You know, you're not supposed to fill the glass to the brim."

"I know. But it kind of defeats the purpose if you're going to fill it up again anyway. Besides, it's just us."

"I guess that makes a weird kind of sense." Missy raised her glass. "Cheers."

"Cheers," Macky said as they clinked their glasses.

Two hours later, they had caught up on life, and Missy had forgotten all about the dating apps.

* * *

"Hey, Mom, guess what?"

"What?" Missy said as she came back from the bathroom. "Whoo, I really had to pee."

"Me, too. But take a look at these two guys who liked you on Bumble. They are totally age appropriate. By that, I mean young and hot. Be a cougar." Macky handed her the phone with a smile and scurried off to the bathroom.

Missy felt her tummy tie in knots as she peeked down at the phone in her hand. Was she really ready for this? A cougar sounded so predatory. She wasn't a predator. She simply knew that she had enjoyed the company of men, and she'd been alone long enough after Travis. She knew she wasn't going to open her heart to love again any time fast, but that didn't mean she couldn't test the waters, even if that sounded tedious and scary. Her new mantra, though, was to do things that scared her. Wasn't that what women her age were supposed to be doing? Life was short. And, she thought, if she died doing something that scared her, at least she had lived a good life.

"Okay, here goes," she said under her breath as she clicked on the profile of Brian, a forty-year-old software engineer. "Oh, you're cute." She clicked the "like" button and found out it was her move. "What do I do now?" she asked as Macky came back into the room.

"Ask him if he'd like to meet for coffee tomorrow. Tell him you're only here for the weekend."

"That seems kind of aggressive, doesn't it?" Missy wondered.

"It's kind of the point."

Missy felt uneasy, but she found herself typing exactly those words. Fifteen minutes later, she had a coffee date with Brian just around the corner from Macky's house.

Macky practically danced in her seat. "Seriously, Mom, I'm not sure anyone in the history of apps has scored a date faster than you just did. It must be that cougar energy!"

Missy growled. It was a frightened, dying kind of growl, but she did her best to own it.

"What about the other one?" Macky asked.

Missy clicked on Jesse, who was in his early thirties. He was most definitely hot, but he was Macky hot, not Missy hot. Macky agreed and let her skip past him. Missy felt relieved, though a tiny part of her felt good knowing a much younger man liked what he saw enough to like her photo. She didn't allow the voices in her head to say he was either a psychopathic lunatic with murderous tendencies or a horny former frat boy thinking she was a MILF. Oh, how she hated that one.

"It's a compliment, Mom. Seriously, a MILF means you are hot!"

Missy picked up her wineglass and cleared her throat. "I'll take the compliment and leave it at that."

# Chapter 21

## *What If He's a Serial Killer?*

Macky helped Missy get ready for her date. She handed her a razor with a grin. "Trim up the lady parts. Just in case." She plucked a few rogue chin and nose hairs, then brushed out Missy's hair – an unexpected role reversal that warmed Missy to her core.

Macky pulled an outfit together: flowing pants and slightly fitted white T-shirt. Missy looked in the mirror and felt suddenly juvenile. "I don't know about this," she confessed.

Macky twirled her mother, sizing her up. "I mean, Mom, if I were your mother, I wouldn't let you go out looking like that. You are hot."

Missy laughed, the nerves loosening their hold. She let herself believe it.

Missy tried not to overthink her impending encounter with Brian. She didn't want to second-guess herself or him. In the back of her mind, she heard her mother's voice saying, *He's going to stand you up.* But he did not. In fact, he was the one waiting for Missy's arrival. He smiled as she walked into the coffee shop. She felt relieved, knowing that the awkward moment of figuring out if the picture matched the person had been bypassed.

He gave her a small hug and said, "You look exactly like your profile." He seemed pleasantly surprised.

"I sure hope so," she said.

If he expected her to look like anything else, she wondered why he would have bothered to like the older woman in the photos. She was fifteen years his senior. He had to anticipate she would not look like she was forty, but there was something in the way he looked at her that made her recognize his interest was genuine.

For his part, Brian exceeded his pictures. She had expected him to look less normal and more nerdy. It was a safe assumption, she thought, and it made the prospect of him seem less overwhelming. Had he been a pretty boy, she would have had more questions. She liked his hazel eyes and the way they changed color depending on the way he moved or how the light hit them. His hair was simply brown, a little grown out, and flowed nicely when he ran his hands through it. And he was tall. She liked that. Skinny, gangly. That part of the nerdy engineer he delivered on, but his air was confident. He owned who he was, and that made him appealing to her. She couldn't remember many fortyish men over the years who had pulled confidence off. They, like Cal, had been arrogant, thinking they had earned the right to look down their noses at others.

They ordered coffees, and Brian insisted he pay. She appreciated that. They sat at a table for two, removed from others. As they began to talk, she told him this was her first time doing the apps, that he was her first date. She wondered how someone as attractive, intelligent, and witty was not spoken for.

"Because women my age are boring," Brian said. "They want to get married. Have kids. They cater to me. I like a woman who's lived a little already. There's more excitement there."

She liked his candor.

"So it's all about the hunt?" she said, feeling a little flirty.

"It's way more fun than having scraps thrown at you," he said, building on her analogy. She found his wordplay sexy. "I've been married. I've been divorced. Thankfully, no kids were involved. I'm just looking to have a little fun right now."

That felt like an invitation. Macky had told her to go with the flow, say what felt right, be in the moment. "I like fun. It's been a while, though."

Brian and Missy finished their coffees. He asked her to go for a walk along the waterfront. They talked about themselves on a superficial level. It was easy to talk to Brian. He made her feel pretty, sexy. When they stopped in front of a charming townhome, he asked if she'd like to come in.

"This is yours?" she asked, craning her neck up at the colonial architecture.

"It is. I'd love to give you a tour," he said with a promiscuous smile.

She didn't know what overcame her. Missy was usually a woman totally in control. Was her vibe screaming, *I'm an easy lay?* Why did he assume she would walk inside with him? He made her laugh. Touched her gently when they walked. He had done everything right. She ignored the reality that Brian was younger than Macky's boyfriend. That was irrelevant. Missy was not going to have a relationship with this man. She was just testing the dating waters again, figuring out if she still knew how to after a marriage, affair, and heartbreak. This was her pass, her moment to be free, to go with it, to explore.

"If I walk in with you, you promise you won't kill me?" she said, half joking.

He laughed hard. "Why? Because I'm an engineer? Kind of the stereotype for killers, right?"

"You're too smooth for an engineer."

"I'll take that as a compliment." He opened the front door, and she walked in, immediately stunned by the beauty of his home. It was modern, with stark grays and whites and subtle reds mixed in with black. The walls were relatively bare, with the exception of a few small pieces of art, framed elegantly. She looked at them closely, recognizing the artist.

"Your home is impressive. Ex-wife?" she asked as she gently moved her hand across the small, framed art.

"You'd think, right? But, no. All me. Well, and the art is my mother's."

"Your mother is Eleanor Burns?"

"You know her?" he asked, hovering somewhere between surprise and appreciation.

She stared at the three pieces hung closely together. "My father loved her work. I have one of her pieces in my bedroom at home. She's exquisite."

"She's nuts, but that's beside the point."

Missy laughed at that.

"All mothers are nuts," she offered.

"I knew you'd get it." He walked behind her, pulling her hair up to expose her neck. He leaned in to kiss her. His skin felt smooth against her neck, his lips soft as they gently made contact with her skin. She turned around to face him, his lips brushing hers. She could feel his hand press against her neck as he kissed her slowly, then with more intention. She liked how he kissed her. She made every effort to stay present in the moment, not to let her mind wander back to the last time she'd been kissed. Or the last time she'd had sex.

"To new beginnings," she said under her breath.

"What was that?" he asked, briefly coming up for air as he made his way along her blouse line.

"Let's go to the bedroom," she said, taking herself by surprise.

"I prefer the couch," he said, pulling her hand and leading her to the cream-colored sofa.

The next three hours were a blur to Missy. She had set out for a coffee date and ended up sleeping with a much younger man. Her body reacted to his touch. She could hear herself quietly moaning, feeling the release of pent-up desire. Her body welcomed his hands as they moved across her bare flesh. She felt selfish taking it all in, not wanting it to stop, but then she realized she should reciprocate. As she reached for him, erect and waiting, she played with him, teased him, licked him, and then took all of him in. His reaction reminded her she had been good at this once, that she enjoyed giving a man pleasure.

He pulled her up to him, gently straddling her legs over him, then moving to be inside her. She moved her hips, and they moved together. He did not speak. She was relieved. She did not want to have to say something back, to come up with something sexual. She just wanted to be in this moment. She closed her eyes as she felt her body react as he moved his finger over her, rubbing just perfectly. And when she came, she was stunned at how quickly. He smiled, flipped her over, and allowed himself to come inside her.

They lay side by side on the couch. She liked that he didn't get up, didn't need to wipe himself off right away or hop in the shower. It was refreshing to be next to him.

"That was nice," she finally said.

"That was fast," he offered back. She was surprised by the answer. She wasn't sure if it meant he was disappointed or surprised at how amazing she was in bed. She almost laughed out loud at that thought.

"Fast, huh? I was quite content with that."

"I'm not complaining. I just don't have to be anywhere for a couple more hours, so I think we need to draw this out a little longer."

She laughed. She had not heard herself laugh that hard or loud in a long time. "I might be up for that."

He rolled on his side and began playing with her breasts. "I'll start here and see how long we can make this last."

Missy felt herself let out a small groan. She watched him as he devoured her. The last time she'd had sex with a man he'd closed his eyes, hurting her in the process. Brian had his eyes wide open, taking in every part of her. That, above all else, lit a fire in her. She hoped her vagina could handle all the stimulation.

Later that afternoon, she made her way back to Macky's. She felt only slightly slutty as she adjusted her T-shirt and attempted to finger-brush her hair before walking into her apartment. Missy smiled as she entered, and Macky squealed. "I was starting to worry," she said.

Missy knew she had her location on her phone, was capable of finding her within seconds if she really needed to.

"You didn't check my location?" Missy asked.

Macky, much like her mother, did not beat around the bush. "Of course I did," she giggled. "Well? Do dish."

"No. You're my daughter." There was only so much she could share with Macky. Neither of them needed details about their love and sex lives; it was enough to know they had them.

"Okay, but..." Macky persisted.

"Yes. We had sex. It was delightful. Everything is still in working order."

Macky wiped her hands together. "My work here is done," she proudly proclaimed.

"Let's go get dinner. I'm famished," Missy said.

"I bet you are."

"Okay, stop. Thank you. Momma's still got game. I want Italian. And wine. Lots of wine." They grabbed their purses and headed to Macky's favorite Italian dive two blocks from her apartment. It wasn't lost on Missy how lucky she was to have the relationship she did with her daughter. And for her part, Macky knew how important keeping your mother close was after watching Missy lose her mother, even when she was still alive.

The unexpected fun of Brian had left her feeling satisfied, a *How Stella Got Her Groove Back* moment. But she also recognized she did not like one-night stands anymore, or whatever the equivalent of what they had done was. It felt good to feel again. Her lady parts still fully functioned, responsive to a man's touch. She enjoyed that. But inside, she knew she much preferred relationships and the physical and emotional intimacies they provided. She had hope, though. The lighter had fluid again. There was a spark, and there was a flame. She was determined to keep it lit.

* * *

Later that night, long after she's told her friends about Brian, long after Scarlet's Harlots have left and she's tidied up, a cereal box flashes in front of her eyes. It's Cocoa Puffs, with Brian's face on it. "Cuckoo for Cocoa Puffs," she says under her breath, realizing his face had been among the many she'd seen the day she broke down in the cereal aisle. She had been a little crazy and reckless for doing what she did, her first time on the apps, but he was munchy, crunchy, chocolaty delicious at a time she needed it.

"Why cereal boxes, Mom? I don't get it. You hated cereal."

In those moments when she finds herself talking to her mom, she wonders if she is losing her mind just a little. She'd never talked to her mom before she died. Conversations in her care facility were one-sided monologues her mother used to revisit the past or chastise her in the present. She knew her mother couldn't differentiate between the two, but it still hurt Missy. It was challenging to be Charlotte's daughter mostly because Charlotte didn't want to be her mother.

Since her death, though, it feels like she is everywhere,

inserting herself when Missy least expects it. In these moments, Missy allows herself to mourn her mother, the parts she wishes she'd known, the ones she wishes she could forget. She sometimes sheds a tear wishing she had her mother's arms to wrap around her as she navigated these painful last few years of her life.

Above all, she wishes Charlotte could have known her children. "They are pretty amazing humans, Mom. Macky and Kaid are my light. I think you would have loved them, too," she says under her breath. Her mother could never love her, so why does she think she could love her children? She immediately answers the question: "Because I fucking killed it as a mom in spite of you." Then she wipes her tears, composes herself, and moves forward in life, pretending that talking to her dead mother is absolutely normal.

Down the hall, a light flickers on and off. Missy dismisses it as just another thing she needs to fix. Still, in the back of her mind, she wonders if Charlotte is trying to say something.

# Chapter 22

## *The Ick*

Missy was open to the idea of dating after her tryst with Brian, but she wanted it to happen organically. She knew this to be a double-edged sword in a small town. It narrowed her options. But Missy was okay with that; she was okay with continuing alone. She had mastered it once she recovered from the heartbreak of Travis. She still cursed his name on occasion for allowing herself to give up so much of her life to wallow in self-pity.

Several months after Brian, she would find herself in perfect company, as Audrey invited her to join the Divorced Women's Book Club. There were four of them on the list: Margo, Dahlia, Audrey, and Missy.

"How is that even a club?" Missy remembers asking Margo.

Audrey insisted they meet at the library. "It just makes it so much more official."

The four women sat awkwardly in a circle, spaced way too far apart from each other. The room had torn posters on the walls and chairs that dated back to when they were all still in high school.

"God, is it scary this place hasn't changed since I made out with Carl in here?" Dahlia asked, half kidding.

"You made out with Carl, too?" Missy sassed.

"Didn't everybody?"

Neither Margo nor Audrey responded. Missy briefly wondered why Margo didn't want those leftovers. She remembered Carl was a good kisser.

They decided on the rules of their book club. They would be ambitious, attempting to read two books a month. They decided on books about strong women. It didn't matter if it was romance, historical fiction, or some new genre they were discovering as they perused Amazon's top 100 lists. "I never realized there were so many categories of books," Audrey said. The women agreed to let Audrey run with it. It had been, after all, her idea, and she was clearly the most enthusiastic about the concept.

"Of course, we don't want to get too big, but let's see if we can find a few others to join our group," Audrey said as she embraced her first call to action as the newly anointed group leader.

"There's Abby," Margo said. "She had a nasty divorce and might like to have other women around for support." Missy was not fond of Abby, but that was because she preferred her ex-husband, Beau. Missy did not veto it but would sometimes regret the bitter pill that Abby was. She had even, for a tiny moment, considered asking Beau for a drink to piss Abby off, but Missy knew she would probably do that anyway.

As they left their inaugural book club meeting, Dahlia mentioned that her brother Harris was coming to town.

Missy looked up from her phone. "Harris? How is Harry?"

"You always did have a little crush on him, didn't you?" she chided.

Missy put her thumb and pointer fingers together. "Just a tiny one. He was so frickin' cute, thinking he was the goth king of the high school."

"Oh my god, I forgot about his dark phase. He'd borrow my eyeliner, and when he couldn't do it, he'd ask me to help him. Don't tell him I told you that." Dahlia giggled.

"I think your secret's safe. It's been, like, thirty-five years. Jesus, we're fucking old."

"Speak for yourself," Dahlia said.

She proceeded to set Missy and Harris up on a date. It was the first of three Missy would go on before pledging to only let the universe bring her men organically.

* * *

"Harry. Oh my. You look good." She beamed as she walked toward him in the bar.

He awkwardly embraced and then corrected her, "It's Harris."

She crinkled her nose, as if to say, *You're shitting me right now.*

But he was not. The early correction was indicative of the evening. Harris had once been fun. He had been edgy in the best ways, challenging the system, defying his teachers. He once even mooned a bus with very impressionable elementary school children inside. He was promptly suspended for three days and had to read to them once a week for the remainder of the school year. No one knew who would be more embarrassed by the situation. Harris played it cool. Because Harris was cool. But he went by Harry then. And Harry was way cooler than Harris.

It seemed Harris had outgrown his rebel stage. Now he wore fitted slacks, button-down polo shirts, and loafers without socks. He no longer required hair gel as he had none. The boy with spiked hair had become a bald man. He looked good bald, Missy thought. He did turn out handsome, but the stick up his ass was not the least bit attractive.

She wasn't impressed that he had earned his Ph.D. in astrophysics. Or that he worked on various secret government projects.

Or that he had the inside scoop on Area 51. She didn't believe in flying saucers, UFOs, or extraterrestrials. "ET was cute. But he wasn't real either," she said.

He didn't appreciate her humor, and she didn't understand his lack thereof.

She finished her glass of wine, wishing she had ordered something a little stronger. She put down her glass. "Well, Harry—" she said.

"Harris," he corrected her again.

"Well, Harris," she said, long and drawn out. "This was fun. But I liked you better in high school." She gave him an insincere kiss on the cheek, and he watched her walk out, completely befuddled by what had just happened.

She would later tell the Harlots that she now understood what Macky meant when she used the word "ick." "He gave me the ick. So cringey, a total turnoff," she explained. She told them she would not allow herself to waste one more second with a man who was not the least bit interesting to her. She would tell Dahlia that they didn't have anything in common.

But Harris/Harry beat her to the punch. He told his sister Missy was not really his type. "Too full of herself. And that energy? It's so overwhelming."

Dahlia sided with Missy. "He's become a total prick." She apologized for setting them up. "Don't lose your energy, Missy. It's what makes you special."

Missy found she liked Dahlia in that moment and wondered why they weren't better friends in high school.

In between dates, Macky had convinced Missy to check in on the apps. "Scroll on occasion," she would say. "You never know what might happen. You have subscriptions. Might as well use it."

"Why do I have subscriptions?" Missy asked, having no recollection of paying for them.

"Because you told me to. Remember? You handed me your

credit card and said, 'Sign me up'? So I did. On three apps: Bumble, Hinge, and Silver Singles. To be safe."

"Silver Singles? I will not look at that one. Sounds old. And don't you dare say that I'm old."

Macky zipped her lips closed and smiled, so Missy reluctantly agreed to keep the apps a little longer. She occasionally browsed, but she saw nothing of interest. She refused to look at Silver Singles.

She barely considered Harris/Harry a date, and she no longer considered Brian a date. She simply referred to him as "the app experiment." He was like a feral unleashing that couldn't be defined. He had reminded her of the hidden treasures inside her body, but she learned she could be choosy. No man was worth sacrificing your principles, once you remembered what those were. You take those things for granted in a marriage. And when you're mindlessly in love.

Her second date was a man named Sheldon. Missy's sorority sister, Amanda, had texted saying she had a friend from California who was visiting Sullivan's Island for a few days. "Would you be willing to meet him?" she texted. "He's single."

Missy knew she was being set up.

"We can discuss at the gala," she texted back. Missy's involvement with her Delta Delta Delta sorority was limited to the annual gala. She had gone more frequently when Macky was in college. Now the two of them attended the Tri Delta gala together. It had become a yearly event they looked forward to, but Missy did not go the year Travis broke up with her. She barely recalls receiving an invitation and vaguely remembers the conversation with Macky.

The following year, Missy and Macky attended in matching dresses. "Let's make a statement, Mom," Macky had said. "Let's let the world know you're back, hotter than ever. No man can take that from you." So for the first time since Macky was seven years old, they wore matching outfits: floor-length, floral, one-shoulder gowns in bright shades of pink and red.

Macky does not have her mother's fiery red hair. Her hair is strawberry blonde, and her eyes are a shade of hazel. She stands at the same height as Missy, but her skin is a soft olive that absorbs sun like a sponge, much like Margo's. Their smiles, however, are identical. When they entered the gala, all heads turned.

It was the first time Missy felt alive again. And she knows her sorority sisters felt a pull to help her find a new man. Most of them genuinely wished for her happiness, for which she was grateful. Even at their age, women could be petty. She had learned to wade through her genuine "sisters" and those who weren't. Missy hated anything petty. She'd dealt with Margo her whole life, but while Margo was family, her "sisters" were one degree removed.

Amanda squealed when she saw Missy. "Oh my God, she lives! And look at how goddamn gorgeous you are. Seriously, stunning. Just isn't fair how you haven't aged."

This was the fake part of the gala Missy hated. Amanda hadn't aged either, but how could she retort with that when it was clear Amanda had paid a significant amount of money to have her face altered to look like Meg Ryan, distortions and all?

Missy leaned in to hug her, the insincere hug of someone who doesn't want their makeup smudged. "You look great," she said, lying.

"I've been thinking about you. I told you about my friend, right?" Missy had hoped she'd forgotten her earlier text. "Well, my friend has a friend. He'll be near you for a few days. And I think you should meet him."

"Have you met him?" Missy asked.

"I've seen his picture. He's adorable," she said in her perfect South Carolina drawl. Then she begged, which was very unbecoming of her. "Pleeeease."

Missy agreed, and Amanda jumped up and down like a small child.

Sheldon seemed like a charming man when they spoke on the phone. He was staying nearby for the golf tournament his company was sponsoring. "It's the Rudolph Open. To be clear, it is *my* company," he made a point of saying.

"Got it. Let me guess, you specialize in reindeer," she attempted to make a joke. The phone was silent. "Kidding," she threw in at the last minute.

He gave a delayed laugh, then ignored her comment altogether. "Financial services."

"Got it."

They made plans to meet for dinner at The Obstinate Daughter on Middle Street. "They're known for their seafood," she said as she made the recommendation. "Plus, the name reminds me of my daughter, though my son is my obstinate one, but it's good nonetheless," she found herself rambling. "You do eat seafood, don't you?"

"I'm particular, but I am sure it will be fine."

Missy was ambivalent about meeting Sheldon. He sounded arrogant and lacked any sort of personality on the phone. She assumed his looks were what got him dates. And when he entered the room, she realized that was the case. He was a handsome man, dark hair with graying temples. His eyes were an even darker shade of brown, large and intense. His brows were thick yet perfectly combed. Missy wondered if she remembered to brush hers. She thought she did, but gently finger-combed them just in case. Sheldon was a solid inch shorter than she was, though, and that was before her two-inch heels. And he had a slight build. She suddenly felt like his mother, which she found strange because he was sixty.

They sat at the bar while waiting for their table. "We had a huge party earlier, so we're a little behind. Feel free to get a drink at the bar while you wait," the hostess said without looking up from the iPad in front of her. She handed Sheldon the table buzzer. "It'll flash and vibrate—"

"Got it," he snapped as he took it from her.

Missy learned that Sheldon enjoyed talking about himself. He told her how he started his company and made his first million before he turned thirty. "I made the Thirty Under Thirty list when I was twenty-nine," he said.

*He's been telling people this for three decades*, she thought.

He shared that he was divorced, had twin daughters and a son. Missy thought they finally had something they could talk about.

"Do you see them often?" she asked.

"Never. We're estranged."

"Oh, I'm sorry."

"It's all my ex's fault," he said without prompting. "She poisoned them against me."

"Your ex-wife did that?" She couldn't imagine ever saying anything so horrible about Cal that her kids would hate him. Thankfully, he never said anything terrible about her either. Or, she realized, maybe he had, but they were smart enough to reach their own conclusions.

"No. My ex-girlfriend. We were together for five years." He stopped, motioned to the bartender to bring two drinks. "What are you drinking?" he finally asked.

"Red. Pinot."

"Pinot and a scotch," he barked to the bartender.

She mouthed, "Please," embarrassed by Sheldon's lack of manners.

He continued as if he had never stopped talking. "Five years. Turns out she's a fucking alcoholic. Like closet drinking. I'm finding empty bottles around the house."

"You lived together?" she asked.

"Yeah. Then I say I can't do it anymore and ask her to leave. But I said it nicely."

Travis had said it nicely to her. It didn't make it hurt any less. It would have been easier to hate him if he'd been a dick. Sheldon seemed like a dick. Missy couldn't imagine he would be nice, but she also couldn't imagine that his girlfriend was very smart. Why not just throw the empty bottles out? Was leaving them behind a desperate cry for help? Missy didn't know any alcoholics intimately enough to make an accurate assessment.

Missy grabbed her wineglass and contemplated guzzling it. "I'm sure that was hard for both of you."

He took a big sip of the scotch the bartender served and agreed. "Then she tells my kids it's my fault. That I was mean to her. So now they won't talk to me."

There was so much wrong with his story, Missy thought, but she did not pursue it.

She wanted to change subjects, but he added one more tidbit, "So I'm suing her for defamation of character." Giant red flag thrown; Sheldon was swimming in a sea of red flags.

Missy changed the topic. "How do you know Amanda?"

"Amanda? Who's that?"

"My friend who set us up."

"Oh, Amanda." He took another bigger sip of his scotch and motioned for another. She wondered who the alcoholic really was in that relationship. "I don't. Not really. I dated one of her friends, Daphne. And Daphne said to look up Amanda. So I did. But she's married. Or engaged. Or something."

"So you just find people to go out with wherever you go?" she asked, curious about his methodology.

"Look. I'm a busy guy. I travel a lot for my job. Next week, I'll be in New York. Then it's Paris for a week. Rome for another. It gets lonely. So I like to date wherever I go."

"So you're a serial dater?" she said, joking.

"No. I don't know. If I find the right woman, and there have been a few I liked. Like Jaz in DC. Oh man. Jaz and I had a thing. But it didn't work."

"Does this telling women you're dating a lot of other women thing work for you?" Missy was genuinely curious.

"I'm honest. That's all I got."

He finished his first drink and started on the second. Missy decided to down the remaining wine, thankful in that moment that it wasn't a full pour. She put her glass down and, for the second time in as many dates, gave her date a piece of her mind. "Sheldon, this was eye-opening, but I must confess that this was a huge mistake."

As she got up, she made a point to tower over him as he awkwardly stood. She put out her hand to shake his. He took it and gave her the weakest handshake she had ever experienced, male or female. "But what about the fish?" he asked as she walked away.

"You should get the swordfish," she said. "It's amazing."

She exited the restaurant proud of herself for not enduring his company any longer than was necessary. She wondered how someone like him ever got more than one date. She texted the Harlots: *Even ickier*.

Sheldon had surprised her. She didn't know why any woman would be amenable to being with a man who had a girl in every city. Where was the moral compass on that? Not to mention the potential for STDs? That was something, she realized, she needed to consider moving forward. And, dear god, his endless self-talk. Had he even asked her any questions? He liked himself probably more than his money. More than anything, she couldn't get past the very asymmetrical nose he had. It just made everything about him seem off.

"Seriously, the nose knows," she said later when she saw Scarlet and Amber. "I'm not sure I can handle one more date.

Maybe I'm just meant to finish this part of my life alone." If she were, she would be okay with it. Divorce had been freedom. Travis had been the most beautiful love she'd ever experienced, trumped only by the devastating heartbreak she experienced when he told her to leave. She didn't want loneliness and heartache in a relationship. Alone with herself, she was guaranteed little disappointment and complete control.

"You haven't been out there long enough," Scarlet reminded her.

"You are my role model, my spiritual advisor, my hope," Amber said, half joking, half hoping the dating landscape wasn't as abysmal as Missy found it.

"You're young, Amber. You've got the gift of youth. And beauty," Missy said.

"Maybe youth. If you consider your forties youth."

"We do," Missy and Scarlet said in synchronicity.

"But aside from that, you are beautiful. And funny. And smart. And men must just get stupider as they get older." Her takeaway was likely not wrong. "Which is why I am going on a weekend getaway with Tyson."

"So from a Cosmo to a weekend away? That was quick work," Missy said.

"Not really. We FaceTime every night. Sometimes we..." She was flustered.

"You do *not*. Have you even fucked?" Missy asked directly.

"Once," she admitted. "He's divine." She told them that he was rich, ten years her junior, had no baggage, and was secretly in love with her when she was on *The Bachelor*.

"I'm having fun. Like, really enjoying this process. I'm not in front of cameras. There's no paparazzi following me. He's not famous even if he's well connected. I don't think he's my forever, but if men keep getting stupider as we get older, then I might as well take advantage of this now." The logic made sense.

"Now who's the cougar?" Missy said. Amber and Scarlet look at her, perplexed. "Brian," she reminded them. And they nodded in remembrance.

* * *

Missy sent Amanda a note saying that Sheldon was a disaster and provided a list of bullet points of all the reasons she should never set him up with one of her friends again.

"Unless you really hate that person. You don't hate me, do you?" she asked, half joking.

Amanda replied quickly, promising her she adored her and saying that she had no idea he was such a "smarmy ass."

It was several weeks after Sheldon that Missy went on her third and final date before allowing herself to acquiesce to the universe. It took her that long to feel the ick factor of Sheldon cleansed from her psyche.

Lance had seemed promising. He was a radio personality in Charleston, and she had first met him at a fundraiser when she was still married to Cal. He had one of those smooth, velvety voices, speaking in a melodic, almost hypnotic tone. It was very nice to listen to. She doesn't remember what he talked about, but she does remember he was smitten with her. After a few too many drinks, he suggested they meet to discuss opportunities for him to help with local Sullivan's Island charities. She had declined the offer then.

Margo, however, had recently run into Lance at a coffee shop. They struck up a conversation, and he asked about Missy. She imagined the question went over about as well as a lead balloon. "I gave him your number," she said matter-of-factly.

"Why would you do that?"

"Because he asked if you were still married. I said no. Then he asked if you were seeing anyone. I said no."

"Margo, ugh. I hate this. I hate dating. I hate random strangers."

"But he's not a stranger. You know him. You'll have lots to talk about," she said enthusiastically.

"You like to see me suffer, don't you?" Margo wasn't sure whether her cousin was joking or serious. Missy didn't know either.

Lance texted. Then called. He sounded nice enough on the phone. He asked thoughtful questions, didn't seem arrogant, and was able to hold a conversation. Missy thought this at least sounds more promising.

Lance and Missy agreed to meet for lunch. "And maybe a walk after," he said. It sounded like a lot of time, but she was practiced at escaping these awkward dates.

Lance was as big as she remembered him. He was tall, at almost six and a half feet. His build was thick. She couldn't tell if he was fat or fit in his jeans and button-down shirt. He attempted to look hip, with funky bracelets collected in third-world countries and a gold chain. Missy does not like jewelry on men. There was something off-putting about it, she thought, like he was trying too hard to be cool. He had tattoos on both his forearms. She didn't remember that. But, then again, they met at a formal charity event.

"I imagine the tattoos have stories," she said, feigning interest.

"Yes, they do. They're very personal reminders for me." He offered nothing more.

"Why put something on display for everyone to see if you aren't prepared to answer the question?" she asked.

"I do answer. I say it's personal." He was vague for a man whose job it was to talk for a living. "They tell a story. And they look amazing, right?"

Missy wondered how to answer this. She was not a fan of tattoos. She'd seen too many that faded over time or had become distorted because gravity was Mother Nature's idea of a cruel joke;

a happy face became a sagging, sad face; big boobs hung as distorted blobs.

"I'm not a fan." She didn't mean to offend him, but he seemed a little hurt by her response. At this point, Missy felt herself done with the date. But it had only been fifteen minutes. They had just ordered food. She gave herself a mental pep talk.

As the conversation settled, she realized they had many things in common. They both had children of the same age living and working in Charleston. They were both divorced. When she asked how long Lance had been divorced, she wasn't prepared for his reply. "The first time was for fifteen years. The second time was for twelve. And the third time was for five years." She was speechless.

"Three divorces? Wow."

"I'm a sucker for love. I just made some bad choices. But I've done the work. Lots of therapy over the last few years. I know myself now. Know how to be better as a person."

She knew she shouldn't judge. She didn't know the details, the whys, the reasons for his divorces. She knew Travis had been married twice, and those relationships had shaped him in ways she didn't think were for the better. If anything, she always thought they made him bitter and close-minded to the future. He certainly never would have considered a third marriage. At least not to her. She, meanwhile, would have married him in a heartbeat. Disaster —and divorce—averted there, she reminded herself, if not reluctantly.

She and Lance got through lunch. She smiled and laughed when she was supposed to. He touched her leg when she spoke of having her heart broken and proceeding with caution, something she hoped he would hear. But Lance kept talking. He was excited by her, but she couldn't figure out why. She hadn't been bubbly or enthusiastic. "I love your charisma," he said. What was he seeing in her?

They finished lunch, and he asked her to go for a walk. "I love exercise. It just makes me feel alive!" he exclaimed.

"We're just walking," she reminded him.

"But isn't it glorious? The ocean. The air. The sunshine."

"Yes, it's very lovely." She did agree. Ocean, air, and sunshine were some of the many reasons she loved living on her little island, hidden from the rest of the world.

"I hit the gym for two to three hours every morning. Rarely miss a day," he announced.

She couldn't tell. Lance did not appear to be a man who regularly went to the gym. Where were his muscles? she wondered. She looked at his arms, checked his biceps, and wanted to squeeze them to see if there was something muscly there; she only held back when she realized he might take it as a sign of interest. His ass didn't look particularly solid either as they walked out of the restaurant. She felt herself objectifying him, then laughed under her breath, loving the idea that women can do it too.

His looks did not scream gym rat, but how would she know? She hated the gym. Walking, yes, at a pace where talking was not labored. Scarlet tried to get her in the water to swim, but she had no desire to get her head wet, her eyes foggy, or her skin salty. Scarlet always replied, "Cap, goggles, shower," to which Missy said, "I'll just stick with the shower."

Missy felt relieved as they approached his car, parked off to the side by the restaurant. It was a fancy sports car. "Oh, it's nothing," he offered even though she said nothing. What was it about men and their vehicles?

"Today was so much fun," he said. "You check every box for me, Missy. But I knew you would." Missy wondered what it meant to check every box. She didn't know there had been a checklist.

She smiled. Lance did little to check any boxes, whatever those were, for her. He did make her wonder, though, if she should have some mental checklist moving forward. Three disastrous encounters with men in the last few weeks, men who came with highly rated pedigrees, with high anticipation that they'd meet the standards of Missy Kinkaid. How could anyone know what those standards were if she hadn't formally expressed them?

"Lance, you were lovely," she lied, "but I'm still really struggling with my last relationship ending, and I just can't, in good faith, lead you on to think we could be anything more at this time. It just wouldn't be fair."

He smiled, hiding his disappointment. "I understand," he said. He leaned in to hug her goodbye. He squeezed extra tight, and when he pulled away, he said, "I could get used to that." She wanted to cringe. It sounded so horribly, awfully cringeworthy.

"God, is that what men have come to these days?" she bitched to Scarlet and Amber later. "And then, I'm driving home, wondering what that smell is. He had on so much cologne, it was stuck to my clothes, and I swear it permeated my skin. Like, seriously, who thinks that much cologne is good?" She wiggled her nose.

"Maybe because he's on the radio, he overcompensates," Amber said. "There were women like that on *The Bachelor*. I wondered how any man would find a woman so full of perfume attractive. I'd be wondering what they were covering up."

They laughed at this.

"Yes, my preferred fragrance is Secret body powder," Scarlet said.

"Exactly," Amber offered.

Missy smelled her armpits. "I should probably consider that in the future." They all laughed.

Missy let out an exasperated, exaggerated exhale. "Dating is exhausting at this age. So I am officially done. I am done being set up. I am done scanning the apps. Done. Done. Done. I assume die a lonely spinster." She paused for dramatic effect. "Me and Margo. Spinster cousins. That'll be so fun and jolly."

Amber and Scarlet recognized that this would not be the case. There was too much love, fun, laughter, friendship, and sex left in Missy to wither off and die.

"Good riddance. I am unhinged," she announced as she deleted the final app from her phone.

"Good one," Amber says. "I love when I get the pun."

Missy went to bed that night relieved. She did not have to or need to check any of the apps to see if someone liked her, checked a box, sent a rose, or left a message. That was gone. Life would happen on its terms. When it was supposed to.

She double-checked her nightshirt and sniffed her skin to make sure no part of her smelled like Lance's overwhelming stench. She did not dream of tattoos, cologne, or checked boxes. It's likely, her brain cells had been poisoned by his overbearing parfumerie.

* * *

It is Halloween night. Missy and Zander skip handing out candy in favor of a quiet romantic dinner in downtown Charleston. They dress up, of course - he as Woody from *Toy Story* and she as Jessie. Walking into the restaurant, they simultaneously blurt out, "There's a snake in my boot!" They begin laughing hysterically. They are the only ones laughing, which only makes them laugh harder.

They are seated next to a plainclothes man and his significantly younger date, who seems bored by the evening. The man's eyes landed on Missy, "Well, all be. If it isn't the righteous Missy Kinkaid."

Zander looks over to her.

"Zander, this is Charleston's one and only man of the airwaves. Lance...shoot, what's your last name again?" It is meant to sting, and it clearly does. Lance said nothing else the rest of the evening.

Later, Zander and Missy make love in character. Of course, he can't resist saying, "There's a snake in my pants."

"So cheesy," she teases, following it up with, "Trick or Treat?"

"Treat," he murmurs. She gives him a devilish grin and proceeds to lick him slow like a lollipop. He nearly loses control before she pulls back, then climbs on top, riding him with Jessie's fire.

Afterward, as they lay together, he asks, "What if I picked trick?" And she shows him.

Zander quickly falls asleep. She likes the feel of her cheek on his chest, feeling as his chest moves in slow rhythm.

As she closes her eyes to fall asleep, a surreal vision flickers: a box of Rice Krispies cereal dances across her mind's stage. Snap! Crackle! And Pop! She couldn't quite make out their faces, but she knew it was Harris/Harry, Sheldon, and Lance dancing on those boxes. "Good one, Mom," she whispered into the dark.

# Chapter 23

## *You Get One Life*

In the months between deleting the apps and her mother's death, Missy found renewed purpose. She bought three Moleskine notebooks in black, pink, and blue. She planned to save the blue one for Margo's next birthday. It had been a long time since she had gifted her something meaningful. The blue Moleskine has blank pages so Margo could draw sketches for her paintings. The other two were lined even though Missy prided herself on her ability to write straight without them. It felt more ordered.

Missy also bought her favorite pen in blue and black. At home, she put the black and blue notebooks in the top drawer of her desk. She had cleared the top, made space for her writing, for creating, for ideating. It spoke to her now, encouraging her to be bold in her choices, to do the things that brought her joy.

She set the pens next to the notebook. She gently opened it and pressed along the binding. The paper felt so soft and silky as she ran her fingers across it. She considered a formal title page as if she were an author writing her debut novel, but she decided a blank template was more forgiving. She began to write a list.

Across the top of page one, she wrote *The Rest of Missy Kinkaid's Life*, then underlined it. A to-do list, of sorts. She bulleted each line, her way of not being tied to an ordinal system of accomplishment. On the first line, she wrote: *Margo*. Next came: *Love*. After that: *Visit Mom*. Then: *Be Me. Always be me. Write another children's book. Try swimming (with my head in the water)*. She remembered one of her favorite sayings and wrote it in all caps at the bottom of page one: LOVE YOUR FUCKING LIFE. TAKE PICTURES OF EVERYTHING. TELL PEOPLE YOU LOVE THEM ("Yes, Travis, because that's what normal people do," she said to no one but herself). TALK TO RANDOM STRANGERS. DO THINGS THAT SCARE YOU. FUCK IT, BECAUSE YOU GET ONE LIFE. LIVE IT. She knew it was not exactly verbatim, but it was the gist. It was her mantra. Beautiful words she wanted to live by. She found a pink highlighter and drew a pretty, scalloped bubble around them.

The Harlots kicked off that summer with a medley of rosé wines. "I think they're underrated," Amber opined. "And it feels like summer. And it's pink. I love pink. I feel hopeful again." After they had finished three bottles, they were all fans. Their thick heads the next morning did have them second-guessing their enthusiasm, though.

Deleting the apps had been liberating. Not going on dates freeing. Focusing on herself felt selfish. But Missy loved it. "I love being alone. I love not worrying about what someone else is thinking. Or what someone else needs. I get it."

Margo rolled her eyes at this. She had never loved being alone. But it was an accepted fact of life for her.

"You really haven't checked the apps this entire time?" Amber asked.

Missy confessed she doesn't miss the complications, the innuendo, the misguided good intentions of others. Dating was simply exhausting.

"If there is a God and he sees it upon himself to intervene, then let it be divine intervention that inserts a man in my life," she proclaimed.

This was the South, but Missy knew she was in the company of women who questioned if there was a God, wondered why he got all the credit, how he could sometimes be so cruel. They were spiritual in their own ways, she supposed, but no one toted a Bible or quoted scripture. In that regard, she felt lucky.

* * *

She recalled going to church when she was younger, when Charlotte was still around. Charlotte was always so uptight when they did go, constantly correcting Missy. *Stand tall. Look straight ahead. Put your head down when you pray. Don't fidget.* Church with Charlotte was a lot of direction. It did not give Missy a sense of belonging, community, or understanding.

But once Charlotte was gone, Dex never took her to church again. Maybe that was his way of showing doubt that a higher power existed. Or maybe he was ashamed. But Missy never thought to ask him about church or why they suddenly stopped going. Instead, she and Margo would meet on Sunday mornings for playdates while Dex read his morning paper, occasionally peering over the top to watch them play. In those moments, Missy would stop and smile at him. And he would smile back. She loved those memories.

Years later Missy would pose the question to Margo. "Why didn't you have to go to church when we were kids?"

"Daddy was always too drunk," she said, "and Adeline was too embarrassed. And you stopped going. Momma said if the Kinkaids didn't owe God anything, then we didn't either."

Missy remembered thinking at least they'd all end up in hell together.

* * *

"Amen, sister. And if someone wants to pray for me, they can do that, too," Amber said enthusiastically.

Margo reminded them, "God does not insert himself in dating affairs." She took a sip of wine. "I know. Because I have tried very hard to get his help." They laughed.

*When was the last time Margo said something intentionally funny, not funny because it was stupid?* Missy wondered.

Missy was fully aware that the most important men in her life did not come from an app. They were men whose paths she crossed at exactly the right moment. Cal. Travis. Spencer. Maybe it was God who put them there, then left her to her own devices to figure them out.

* * *

She believes it is divine intervention, after all, that brought Zander into her life. God took Charlotte home to him and sent Zander to deliver Charlotte's last words to her daughter, like an angel delivering glad tidings. She wants to believe it is Charlotte's doing, that she couldn't show Missy love in life but was delivering a gift in death. She knows it's silly to think that, but she also wants to believe just a little tiny bit in miracles from heaven. She wonders if she should start going to church again but quickly dismisses the idea. *I am spiritual in my own way*, she reminds herself.

Zander has quickly found space in her once-reluctant heart. She did not expect him. Did not intend to do more than sign papers when he showed up. But she believes this is how love is supposed to happen.

"When you least expect it, dance in your kitchen, answer the door barefoot, and meet a handsome stranger ringing your doorbell. Does it get more organic than that?"

# Chapter 24

## Say "Yes" to the Dress

Missy and Scarlet meet for a day trip to Charleston to find Scarlet a dress. The wedding is three weeks away, yet she remains remarkably calm.

"It's not my first one. I feel silly having a wedding. I would have been fine with a ceremony. My kids. My close friends. Beau's kids. No Abby. That would have been so nice," Scarlet admits.

"So, why are you doing this?" Missy asks.

"Believe it or not, Beau wanted it. He said his wedding to Abby was too much, a spectacle in fuchsia. They were young. And she was a bit of a bridezilla." She quickly qualifies that with, "According to Beau."

Missy insists on driving them to Charleston, which thrills Scarlet. Despite her California upbringing, she has not adjusted to driving in the big city.

They arrive at the bridal boutique, a small store on a side street downtown. Scarlet is nearly run over by a horse-and-carriage tour as they go by. "I will never get used to that. Except at Disneyland."

"It's the South, darlin'. We love us some fairy princess magic."

"Fairy princess? Thought it was a throwback to the colonial days," Scarlet says.

"You have your version. I have mine. Daddy always said a prince should someday whisk away a princess like me in a horse-drawn carriage," Missy says this with an aristocratic tone, making light of herself.

"How'd that work out for you?" Scarlet chides.

Missy gives her the finger as they enter the boutique.

Priscilla, a woman schooled in the finest etiquette of wedding retail, greets them with an overly exuberant but clearly fake smile. She holds her hands at her waist as she looks Missy and Scarlet up and down. Once she decides they are suitable to serve, she addresses them. "Ladies, welcome to Sherman's Bridal Boutique. You must be here for the mother of the bride attire," she says presumptuously.

Missy ups her Southern drawl to the most appropriately condescending level. "Oh, darling. You are sorely mistaken. My friend here is the bride, and she requires the finest matronly bridal attire."

Before Priscilla answers, Scarlet looks at Missy. She speaks in her worst Valley girl voice. "Oh my God. Matron's bridal attire? What the fuck? I'm, like, *so* not a matron." She has barely finished when she and Missy begin laughing hysterically. Priscilla stands somewhere between mortified and petrified.

They stop laughing. "Seriously," Scarlet says. "I am the bride. Second wedding. Nothing too fancy. Maybe something more silk, less lace. And it must be able to hold my boobs up." She motions to her chest. "They tend to have a mind of their own these days. Plus gravity. So something that says they aren't grandma boobs yet."

Priscilla doesn't know what to do with this. She simply says, "Of course. I'll bring some options out. Please feel free to have a seat or look around." She walks off quickly.

"Okay. I wish dress shopping had been that much fun my first time," Scarlet says. "My mom made it so hard with her endless nagging. 'I am, after all, paying for the dress,' she would say."

"At least you had a mom to shop with," Missy replies. Scarlet looks apologetically at her. "I had Margo instead. That was awesome," she says sarcastically.

They sit on the sofas in front of the giant mirrors. Priscilla's associate, Samantha, brings a tray with champagne. They each take a glass, clinking them together before taking a sip.

"I came in here once when Travis and I were together. I know he didn't want to marry. But a girl could still dream. I never told him," Missy confesses.

"Did you find a dress?"

"Two. And they were so pretty. One for the wedding. One for the reception. I even tried them on. I knew it would never happen, but I loved him enough to." She takes a sip and points to a hideous dress with puffy sleeves and a collared neck. "I think it was that one."

Scarlet knows she's kidding but senses there's more there.

"You okay?" she asks.

"I dreamed about Travis last night," she admits. "I dreamed he came back to me, but it was so strange. He had this giant felt eraser, and he started erasing me. I was disappearing. He was laughing as he did it, finding joy in every stroke of the eraser. And I could see myself in a mirror. I swear it was this metaphor for how I had lost sight of myself in the end. And when all that was left of me was my heart, he put down the eraser. My heart turned to paper. He walked up to it and tore it in half. He was shaking his head and repeating, 'Too much,' like I loved him too much, so he had to make it go away. I woke up panicked. It felt so real."

"That's awful. But it's not too much when it goes both ways. And I know you said it did in the beginning. He didn't come with a manual that says, 'If you love me too much, too hard, I will put on the brakes and invoke the lemon law,'" Scarlet says in her best New York mechanic voice, which makes Missy laugh.

"That would have been good to have. Like a warranty." Missy laughs as she blurts out, "Men should come with warrantees. Or maybe relationships should. At least we'd go in thinking that something might go wrong even if it's running well. Fucking brakes." She shakes off the past. "Loving too much is okay, I know, if you feel that love in return. Then it's not too much; it's just right."

"Exactly," Scarlet says. "Don't you dare close your mind to it. You're smarter. You learned. You healed. You're owning it."

And she was right.

Priscilla returns with seven dresses. "Like Snow White," Missy muses. Priscilla is not amused yet attempts humor, "Will you be one of the dwarfs?"

To which Missy replies, "Every one of them."

Scarlet immediately discounts three of the dresses for being too sexy or too frumpy. She tries on the other four. "It's a late fall ceremony. I don't think strappy is good."

Priscilla assures her that there are no rules on straps for weddings, so she tries on one. Then she tries strapless, followed by an off-the-shoulder gown. Scarlet doesn't mind any of them but loves none of them.

Missy is also not convinced they've found the one until Scarlet tries on the final dress. She walks out of the room after Priscilla helps her with the back buttons. She stands on the bridal circle in front of the three mirrors placed to see every angle. Neither Missy nor Scarlet says anything. Scarlet begins to smile. As does Missy.

They stare at Scarlet in the dress. It's a beautiful yet simple crepe-draped U-neck column dress in ivory. It is open in the back, revealing Scarlet's strong swimmer shoulders and nicely defined back. A long row of buttons descends the short train.

"It has a boned bodice to hold my boobs," Scarlet says finally.

Missy wants to cry. "I have never seen boobs held better." But really, she wants to cry because she has never seen anything look more beautiful on someone than it does on Scarlet in that moment, and she feels a sense of relief that she didn't marry Travis after all. Maybe that's what the dream was supposed to tell her: Not that she loved him too much, but that she was worth more than what he could give in return.

"Yeah?" Scarlet asks.

"Say yes to the fucking dress, Scarlet." And like that, Missy is back.

They purchase the dress off the rack. Priscilla promises the alterations will be ready the week before the wedding.

"Isn't that cutting it close?" Scarlet asks. "What if it needs more?"

"I do this for a living. Trust me." Priscilla has proven herself, so they do.

They leave the bridal boutique, which fills with Priscilla's pomp and pride as soon as Missy and Scarlet close the door.

# Chapter 25

## *Pinky Promise*

"I'm bringing Zander to the wedding," Missy announces on the drive home from Charleston.

"I assumed," Scarlet says.

"Really? Do I talk about him that much?"

"No. You don't talk about him at all. But I think I get why." Scarlet studies her friend as rogue strands of her hair dance in the gentle breeze from the cracked window. She looks happy. Maybe even happier than Scarlet can remember.

Scarlet was the newcomer, an outsider let in to a group of divorced women. Then she was embraced by Missy as a kindred spirit in the world of anti-women scorned. Missy was a pistol. Unfiltered. Relentless. Fierce. As fiery as her red hair. But Scarlet saw a different Missy the day she read the letter from Travis. She saw a woman who had been beaten down by love. She understood better why Missy was larger than life in its aftermath. She had learned to overcome, to conquer, to face fear, to feel pain. She knew her heart was deeply wounded, that she was guarded, tempered in her thoughts of loving again. She knew her story was more than Travis. And more than Cal. It was a lifetime of loving, giving love, then losing it.

"Why?" Missy wonders if she is that transparent.

Scarlet studies her friend. "When I first came here, I had no idea what I was doing. What I was getting into. I was newly divorced. I hadn't been on my own since my early twenties. I wanted to be brave. But I was scared. And then Ben. Oh my. I can't even believe that one anymore."

Missy suppresses a giggle. "If only you'd known me before that," she says.

"No shit. Imagine the lack of drama." They both laugh. "But seriously, there was drama. I didn't think women could be so mean and judgmental," Scarlet admits.

"Really? They don't do that in California?"

"No, they do, I suppose. But I'd never found myself in a situation like that. It just got so messy. But then you took me for Porn Star Martinis and my world changed." Scarlet holds back tears.

"God, you're a sentimental fool, aren't you?"

Scarlet reminds Missy how she defended her with the other women. How she stood tall with her when they learned the truth about Ben. And Beau. How Missy confessed to understanding Scarlet's position as the anti-woman scorned, that she, too, had made the decision to leave her marriage in less-than-auspicious circumstances.

"I guess I just kind of sensed you were my person," Missy says.

"Aww. I've never had a person," Scarlet says. "And as your person, I am going to tell you that I am so happy you found Zander. I know it's early"—she pauses for dramatic effect, then continues in a thespian voice—"but your fire glows outwardly like a tempered burn that radiates love."

They both giggle.

"You seem happy," Scarlet doubles down. "And content. It's

nice. So no, you don't talk about Zander much. But I see he makes you happy."

Missy wonders how she got so lucky to have a friend like Scarlet who really sees her.

"So far, he does. We're going slow. And I like it. I have absolutely no regrets about anything past or present," Missy says.

"It's why you're an inferno," Scarlet insists. "You are fire, girl."

"Damn straight." Missy believes this. She feels it inside her.

"So don't keep your heart closed because you're afraid."

Missy chances a look at her friend, just before they merge onto the highway, and she knows she is right. *Thank goodness*, she thinks. Because Zander has already found a way to penetrate the protective layer around her heart.

* * *

Things between Zander and Missy have been moving at a comfortable pace. There are moments when Missy wishes they saw each other more, and Zander tells her as much, but he still works in Charleston. His job is demanding, and Missy doesn't want to be that girl who begs her boyfriend to spend more time with her.

"What do we call each other?" he asks her over dinner one night.

She snickers. "I call you Zander. I could call you 'Z' if you'd like."

He rolls his eyes at her. "Haha. You're funny. Also, you can call me Z. Lucy called me that. So did my parents." She isn't sure if she should call him something his dead wife called him. She lets it percolate.

"Do you want to be my girlfriend?" he says like a middle school boy asking the popular girl to go out with him.

Missy crinkles her nose at him. "That sounds so creepy."

"Girlfriend? Or the way I asked?"

"Both, maybe. It just feels so juvenile to call each other boyfriend and girlfriend."

They continue to discuss the merits of titles in relationships. They aren't teenagers navigating romantic firsts. They are adults with experiences, disappointments, heartbreak, and joy on their résumés.

Their experiences included guarded hearts. Both of them feel equally afraid that, by allowing themselves to be truly open to love again, they might be swallowed up in grief and sadness. Missy had sworn she would move with gentle trepidation should that day come. Zander promised his dead wife he would not leap blindly, though he knew Lucy would have wanted him to love someone like he loved her.

Early in their marriage, they had promised each other that if anything happened to one of them, the other would live a life for two, imagining the other's presence, a voice, a shadow. Love that ends abruptly, without warning, means you live with a part of that person, forever finding a way to make space for new experiences and opportunities. That would include being with someone else, knowing that person would never replace them; they would just walk alongside the original pair. Zander only ever considered it might be he who died, conceding Lucy should move on without him. He never thought he would be the one to fill the void left by Lucy's death.

For her part, Missy never considered what it meant to fall in love with a widower. Zander seemed too young to have suffered such loss. She has promised herself a future with Zander will not be full of wondering how she compares with Lucy. She accepts he loved his wife deeply, just as Zander will learn that Missy has loved deeply and been broken by her own loves. Missy knows her greatest fault is the voice that says she is not enough. It's always in her mother's tone, so real, so clear, that she finds herself looking around the room for her withering stare.

Missy and Zander sit bundled on her front porch, the nip of early autumn in the air. It's pleasant to sit outside again. They sip a lovely Cab Franc gifted to her by Scarlet, from Scarlet's favorite winery in Napa.

"Have you been to a winery before?" she asks Zander.

"Can't say that I have. I really didn't become a wine drinker until it became part of the job, shmoozing with clients. I quickly became a fan after that, though. Lucy and I talked about taking a trip out west. For ten years. But it obviously never happened. You?"

"I have been to a few. But there are so many. I keep a list of the ones I want to visit."

"Then we should go. When's your birthday?" They are discussing labels, yet Missy realizes she doesn't even know his birthday, or he hers.

"July third," she says. "And we both know I'm older, so I'm not affirming the year. When is yours?"

"May seventh. We should go in June and celebrate our birthdays that no longer come with numbers or years." He winks at her, which makes her smile. She likes his subtle sense of humor and effortless banter.

She holds her glass toward the setting sun, appreciates how the light turns it into a dazzling ruby. She dislikes the shorter days and wishes, not for the first time, that long nights and early mornings were not reserved for summer.

"I would like that," she says. "Maybe by then we can figure out what to call each other."

"I'm sticking with Zander." He cracks himself up.

"My Zander," she mimics, but he likes the sound of that.

"My Missy," he says back. She thinks that has a nice ring to it. "Also, it's October. June is a long ways away."

"You don't think we'll make it to June?" she teases, pushing down the thrum of anxiety that comes up if she thinks about that question too deeply.

"I'm not keeping track of time. I'm horrible with dates." He looks at her. "If that's important to you, you'll have to send reminders. Otherwise, I will disappoint you."

Missy loves his honesty. "I like that kind of stuff. I can go all Hallmark at times." She pauses. "So should I send you text updates or just a Google calendar invite as reminders?"

He laughs, appreciating her ability to make light of his shortfall.

"Google invite. Definitely."

This is the best part of falling in love later in life: There are no rules. There are no conventions that imply following a certain order. You can do what you want, how you want. Skip steps. Create steps. Avoid steps. Take giant leaps or stutter steps. If only young love were that easy.

But they both know it isn't. Love is a loaded gun that sometimes shoots blanks, but it also comes with the potential to shoot a live bullet, sometimes disguised as betrayal of trust. Sometimes as death.

They understand that's what love later in life does. You learn to take those losses, heartbreaks, and build a foundation for the future. It doesn't mean that pockets of insecurity, comparisons, seeming weaknesses won't glare their ugly heads.

Missy does not want to question that she might be allowed love again, but she knows as strong, fierce, and resilient as she is, these attributes don't preclude her from recognizing she could slip.

She shares this fear with Zander. He promises her he is far from perfect and will have his own moments, too. He has been on his own for a decade. "God knows what hidden emotional beasts you might unleash," he says, half joking, half knowing it might be truth.

He puts up his pinky finger and says, "Pinky promise me we'll talk. If it seems like I'm dismissing you, tell me. And I'll tell you. We can talk about our pasts, the good parts, the painful ones. Let's not perseverate on those things, though. Let's focus on making our own relationship organically." He laughs. "Whatever that means. I paid for years of therapy. Might as well get my money's worth."

"I was hanging on 'perseverate.' That sounds serious." She puts up her pinky, and they lock them together.

"Repeat after me," he says. "I... say your name, and I'll say mine."

They do.

"Do solemnly swear that I will hear you," she says this. The pattern continues. "To speak kindly... to apologize profusely even if I have a good argument..." She rolls her eyes at this one. "Is that foreshadowing?"

"I see your fire. I do not want you to lose that. But I do imagine that sometimes it might just get in your way a tiny little bit." She opens her mouth to speak, but he continues. "I promise to use my voice even if silence is my preferred weapon."

That's an interesting promise, she thinks. She loves how open, honest, and forthcoming Zander is when they talk. She knows it's the newness of their relationship, that it's like discovery for trial.

"I'm not that kind of lawyer," he says when she points that out.

She hopes that she will never stop asking him questions, wanting to understand how he evolved into the person he did. She knows she will need patience sometimes, that there are even parts of her own story that will take time to share on a deeper level.

"Lastly, I swear to squelch the pesky voice in my head that makes me question. If it becomes too loud, I will not suppress it but will choose to share it with you so that we might find a way to support the other without minimizing or taking it for granted."

After she repeats everything, she looks at him and says, "Did you just make that up?"

He simply replies, "I've had a lot of time to think about what matters most."

"I hope you have that written down," Missy jokes. "I'm getting old. Losing parts of my short-term memory."

He gets up, walks to the kitchen for a paper pad. He feverishly writes on it, then returns. Missy has never noticed how he sticks his tongue out of his mouth just a little when he's concentrating. She finds it endearing. He hands her the paper titled *Pinky Promises*, and she sees it is nearly verbatim what they just said. She looks up and smiles at him.

"You know I'm going to frame this, right?"

To which he replies, "I expected as much."

* * *

It has become routine for Zander to arrive on Friday nights and leave in darkness on Monday mornings. Missy cherishes the three nights a week they are together. Imagining a future beyond a June trip to Napa isn't something either of them feel compelled to do... for now. While Missy's heart is decidedly less guarded, she finds herself reluctant to share some truths of her life in detail. Zander senses this when the conversations of the past head in the direction of Travis. She knows he deserves all of the truth, even the part where she has to admit to reading a letter not addressed to her.

They sit on her porch one Saturday evening after a wonderful dinner of homemade risotto, her favorite. Missy does not enjoy cooking. As it turns out, though, Zander is a bit of a gourmet and fancies himself an experimenter in the kitchen.

"I told myself I could eat out for the rest of my life or I could learn to cook," he once said. "I've had ten years of learning to cook. And learning to love it."

"I had twenty-some years of people with strong opinions and clashing taste buds," Missy says. "Once I was free, the idea of

219

cooking was not something I looked forward to. DoorDash, Grub-Hub, Uber Eats. Trader Joe's frozen meals. A single woman's best friend."

He laughs at this.

"You give such a sophisticated air, but are really..." He stops and stares.

"Words fail you?" she teases.

"Not," he pronounces. "You are so normal. So real. So beautiful."

"You know you don't need to flatter me. I'm going to sleep with you."

"And witty. You are very witty. And intelligent."

"Again, I will be sleeping with you."

Zander leans in, moving his hand along her jawline. Her smile begins to fade as he studies her. "You haven't been honest with me," he finally says.

She is stunned by the transition. "About what?" She knows he means Travis.

"Tell me what he did to hurt you so badly," he says. "You're remarkable. And I've been trying to imagine how someone let you go, especially when you loved him so much."

She knows she doesn't owe him this. It's her story. But she knows to move forward: She must share it. She rolls her eyes and stares away momentarily to formulate the words.

"Just so you know, I'm sharing this because it was a long time ago. At least, it feels like a long time ago. And he said I was remarkable, too, which scares me more than a little that I might let you down someday. Or that the way you see me might change as time goes on. That you might see something different once the glitter is gone."

Zander laughs gently as she says this. "I probably will see you differently. I think that's what happens in relationships. But I imagine that part of seeing you differently will be appreciating the parts I don't see now, that will emerge over time, that will become the parts of our story."

Missy feels a grin ripen on her face. "You really are a sweet romantic. Will you love me if I get huge hips and my boobs drag on the floor?"

He lets out a guttural laugh. "I will get a dolly and help transport those boobs. Although I don't think that's going to happen. And you're avoiding the topic."

Most men would have been sidetracked in thought by the visual Missy presented to misdirect them from the conversation they were having. She appreciates that he remains on task even if it pains her to share the story.

"Okay," she says, taking a deep breath. "Here goes. When we were living together, I found some old cards and opened the top one. I didn't read most of it, but I didn't put it away when I recognized it was written on." She watches for a reaction but doesn't get one. "It was from his ex-wife."

"First or second?" he asks. She loves that he pays attention.

"Second. I didn't read all of it. Just saw a few words and how it was signed. I wondered if I should say anything, but we were so open and honest. There was no intimate detail I didn't share with him. So I told him I found some letters and read a little bit of one. I tried to be funny, but that was a huge mistake. It triggered him. All his prior trust issues were thrust to the surface, and I was the reason why. I tried so hard to prove to him I loved him. That I didn't intend to hurt him. But he pulled away. He stopped touching me. He stopped having our deep conversations. The laughter stopped." Missy takes a deep breath. "I realized too late, after we were done, that I was making excuses for my actions instead of asking him how it made him feel. I went into full Cal defensive mode."

She looks at Zander to see if he looks at her differently.

"I get where that could hurt," he says, "but it seems more like a learning opportunity than an ending."

She shakes her head. "He couldn't get past it. But it was deeper and more complicated than that for him. We were good until we weren't, but I don't think it would have changed things in the end. If I am honest with myself, there were little signs leading up to it. I think we were different enough. I was a lot of energy. He was a more subdued cerebral man. But he became disinterested, and my heart broke on a level I didn't know was possible. So me letting you in, sharing that with you..."

He doesn't let her finish. "Thank you."

Missy feels a weight lifted as she leans into him and he kisses her head.

# Chapter 26

## *The Sleepover*

"So I was thinking we could spend next weekend at my place," Zander whispers, twirling the end of her Jesse braid between his fingers. It is the morning after Halloween, three months into their relationship.

Missy hasn't given much thought as to why they always stay at her place until he says those words. Until now. She meets his eyes.

He smiles, soft and reassuring. "Mostly, I want you to meet my dog."

This makes Missy smile. Alfie passed away a year after her breakup with Travis. She misses Alfie but cannot bring herself to get another dog. She was her rock in those last years with Cal, in the heartbreak of Travis, and a true companion when Margo disappointed her. Alfie had been strong for Missy, enduring endless tear soakings and hours of cuddling in silence. It was as if Alfie knew Missy needed her, and when she sensed Missy had found her way again, she let herself fall into eternal sleep. Missy's heart broke to find Alfie dead next to her in the bed. But she was old. It was time.

"Thank you, sweet Alfie," she had said. "I wouldn't have made it without you. I love you." She snuggled Alfie in death, shed tears, and took on the day as Alfie would have commanded.

"My dog sitter is gone," Zander was saying, "and it's probably time you see my humble abode. It is not anything like this."

Missy is beside herself. "Oh my God. I never once thought to tell you to bring the dog! I love dogs."

"I know," he says, "but I just wanted to focus on you, on us. Enzo can be a little demanding, and, I will guess, he might get jealous."

"I'll work my magic on him," Missy assures him.

Zander turns up one corner of his mouth. "I am completely confident of that."

Missy treasures the moment. She has shared her truths, and he has not passed judgment. They promise each other to always share, that if one of them approaches something the wrong way, they will talk about what the right way looks like. She appreciates having the conversation early in their relationship when they both wear rose-colored glasses, shiny wrappers, and glitter.

Missy finds herself excited as she packs for her weekend with Zander. She likes seeing his toothbrush next to hers. She smiles at the small pile of clothes he's left: boxer briefs, two collared shirts, a pair of shorts, and a pair of jeans. She makes a mental note to clear out a drawer for him. It's too soon for more, she decides, but a toothbrush and a drawer are appropriate.

She calls Scarlet on her way to Charleston. "Why am I nervous?" she asks.

Scarlet laughs. "Is it the dead wife thing? I'm sorry. I don't know how else to say that."

"Right? I don't know how else to explain it either. Dead means gone. Former or ex or past wife means she's lurking about some-where. You know, like all the women we have lurking about in book club." *Or like Charlotte*, Missy thinks. A shiver weaves down her spine. *God, what if Lucy has a ghost, too?* She squelches the thought.

Missy knows she's overthinking. She's making something out of nothing. She hates that she's good at that. As if on cue, Scarlet says, "You're overthinking. Let it go. Have fun. Fall in love."

"I think I've already fallen," Missy says.

"I know. Love you. Bye." Scarlet hangs up.

Missy drives the next few miles with a huge smile spread across her face. She reminds herself Zander has never given her a reason to believe she is being compared to Lucy. He shared their story. It was beautiful and tragic. She hates that she equates losing a wife to losing Travis, but she knows they have both experienced the pain of grief. They have both addressed their demons. Most importantly, both are open to reclaiming their happiness.

Missy pulls up to the front of Zander's townhouse. She marvels at its beauty, but she knew Charleston's French Quarter would demand it. Trees line the streets. Large mansions alternate with historic homes. She imagines how lucky Zander and Lucy were to have bought their townhouse when they did.

Zander opens the front door, and Enzo comes bounding out to greet her. He has a goofy run that is playful and determined. He jumps on her as if to give her a big hug. She is immediately in love.

"Enzo, down," Zander commands to no avail.

"You were holding out on me with him!" she says as Enzo kisses her face. "Ooh, and he's such a good kisser too."

"I know, right? Like, seriously, I don't know what I'm doing with you."

Enzo gets down, running back into the house. Missy wipes the slobber from her face, then walks over to Zander and begins licking him.

"Yeah, no. I don't think so," he teases, then pulls her in and kisses her tenderly.

"Oh, why, Mr. Hancock, I do believe your kisses are divine," she says in her best Southern accent. Enzo barks. They both laugh. Zander takes her hand and leads her inside.

Missy hasn't given much thought to what Zander's place would look like. She has entertained the fleeting wonder of whether it would be a shrine to Lucy or left exactly how it was when she died. She instead finds herself pleasantly surprised at the aesthetic. It is contemporary in varying shades of grays, blacks, and whites.

"White can be challenging with a dog," Zander says.

"White is just challenging. Dogs. Kids. Red wine. Guacamole."

"So you know white?"

"Intimately. Yet I keep making the mistake in one form or another." She wipes at a small smudge of dirt on the white shorts she's wearing. She smirks as she does, and he knows not to apologize.

He gives her a tour of the townhouse. It's simple, clean, organized, and minimalistic. She sees no pictures of Lucy as she walks through the hallways, looks in the spare bedroom set up with a pullout couch and TV.

"Do you get many guests?" Missy asks.

"Just family. And not often. My sister has a bigger place. She has kids, so my parents prefer that we all meet there. And it's halfway for them and me. Fine by me. Makes family get-togethers way less stressful when you aren't hosting."

"You close with your sister? I never had siblings. I only ever had Margo. You'll meet her someday. I'm never quite sure what to do with her." Missy laughs as she says this.

"We were closer when Lucy was alive. Before my sister had her triplets. I think she feels guilty or maybe bad for me. I don't know. She doesn't talk about it. Neither do my parents. It's been weird. But that's my family."

Missy knows about weird families. About not being able to talk about important subjects like dead people or crazy ones. When you had to imagine a world without them, it was all the same.

When they enter his office, she sees a picture of Lucy on their wedding day sitting on his desk. She looks stunning in her very ostentatious dress. She was tiny compared to the puffy sleeves and large ballgown, but her smile said it was the most beautiful day of her life. Zander sees Missy's eyes study the picture. He walks toward it and then hands it to her.

"This is Lucy. You would have liked each other." He says this so easily, without any awkward pauses, like it's the most natural thing in the world for her to meet his dead wife.

Missy holds the photo. "She was beautiful, Zander. I can't even begin to imagine the pain you have felt."

His breath hitches. "I wouldn't wish it on anyone. But I tell myself how lucky I was to have loved her for as long as I did. I never had to share her with anyone. She was mine until she wasn't. She is always with me. You need to know that."

Missy understands. "I get it. I would never expect anything else."

"But I have had a decade to process, to figure out how she fits with me moving forward. I think she led me to you."

That sounds strange to Missy. She looks at him, confused.

"Honestly. It's not customary for any of the attorneys to go to a client's home in person. We have people for that. But I remember the morning I went to your house. I had actually taken those documents and put them into an envelope for a courier to deliver. I dropped the letter from your mother and saw Lucy's photo on my desk. I swear—and I know this is weird—but I was overcome with this sense that I needed to do that in person. That what was in that letter was so important that I should deliver it. Not some random stranger."

"You were a random stranger."

He shoots her a look. "Don't ruin my story," he says with a grin. "I really think Lucy sent me to you. And then you were dancing in the kitchen, so free, so unencumbered even though your mother had died." Missy thinks if he only knew the real reason why, that Margo had once again gone too far. But in that moment, it didn't matter. She also believes Lucy sent him to her. These days, preternatural forces felt like a natural part of her existence.

"I think I would have liked her a lot. Except that dress," she says.

"If it helps she hated that dress," he offers with a smile. "Her mother picked it out."

"Then I like her even more."

They continue to the last room upstairs: his bedroom. It's a small primary bedroom. A queen-size bed sits between two long windows with sheer curtains covering them. She likes the lightness of the room. There are matching nightstands on each side of the bed. A charging mount sits on the right side.

"Do you prefer the right side of the bed?" she asks. He has never mentioned a preference before. She has slept on the right side when they're together. It felt so natural with him on the left. Her left hand fit nicely with his right as their fingers intertwined on occasion during the night. And it felt easy to rub her left foot with his right, to rest her right knee on his right leg when she slept on her side. His left arm draped nicely around her when they spooned.

He glances at the nightstand. "I sleep in the middle when I'm alone. But I'm a lefty and it's easier to reach to the right."

She is relieved to hear they have not been sleeping wrong, if there is such a thing. She wonders why she doesn't sleep in the middle when she's alone.

"Where does Enzo sleep?" she asks curiously.

"Wherever he wants. And he'll let you know it, too." He wraps his arms around her as they stand in front of the bed. "You're our first overnight, share-a-bed-with-us guest." He kisses her neck, gently moving her light, collared sweater toward her shoulder cap as he kisses the makeshift trail he's created along her collarbone. He pulls her sweater off. Then she pulls his off. Enzo barks.

"Don't move," Zander says, and he leads Enzo out the door and shuts it. There is a momentary whine, then silence.

"Where were we?" he says as he gently lays her on the bed.

They make love and spend the next two hours satisfying each other. They doze tangled together, her on the right, him on the left. They laugh. They talk. They wonder at the beauty of the other without saying the words. Zander looks out the window as the setting sun catches openings in the curtains, sending reminders of the day ending into the room.

She smiles an acknowledgement that it's time to get up. Time to feed the dog dinner. Time for them to eat dinner.

"I've worked up an appetite," he says. "I'll feed the dog. Then let's go grab a bite to eat. I have a favorite little Italian restaurant I want to take you to. I've reserved a seat in the front window. Watching the people go by is the best part."

She likes that he wants to share this part of his life with her. There is nothing about Zander she doesn't like, but she knows she felt like that about Travis once upon a time. She hates those reminders. She knows better now, though. She knows how to proceed, how to move forward, cautiously optimistic. The hardest part, Missy thinks, is the internal argument she has, the one where she is forced to recognize she is already in love with this man. If she allows herself to, she can see he is in love with her, too.

As Missy drives home after their weekend together, she finds she can't stop smiling. Her latent fears of feeling Lucy's presence are allayed. She imagines somewhere there are pictures and objects that are special to Zander. If she ever stumbles upon them, she promises herself to look past them, never to question them, never to perseverate over them as being more than what they are: memories. The consequences would be more than she could bear.

# Chapter 27

## *Special Delivery*

Missy arrives home from Zander's house at the same time the FedEx man pulls up. Anthony has been the only FedEx man Sullivan's Island has ever known. He no longer moves that quickly. He smiles even though his body aches. She asks when he plans to retire. He says when he dies. She hates that answer. He hands her a cardboard box, and she immediately knows what it is: her mother's ashes. It feels so impersonal having her delivered like this. She felt the same way with her dad.

She takes the box inside and leaves it by the door. She returns to the car for her bag. She thinks it feels lighter since she left a toothbrush, some underwear, a sweater, a pair of jeans, and a light jacket at Zander's townhouse. Zander laughed when she asked if she could leave a few things.

"Too much?" she asked.

"Nope. Nope. Not at all."

"I mean, this at least equals what you have at mine."

"Missy, you could move your whole closet in, and I'd be just fine with it." He watched her thinking, the wheels in her head spinning at high velocity. "But don't."

She looked at him, pouting. "I can just buy new stuff and leave it here. Then I don't have to move my closet."

He was speechless.

"I'm just kidding. Too soon. I know."

In his mind, he didn't think it felt too soon. Everything about Missy felt perfectly right in those moments.

Missy drops her bags by her front door. The best part of living alone is not having to pick up your crap or anyone else's until you want to. If you do at all. But Missy hates disorder just enough that she doesn't go to sleep at night until the dishes are done, the groceries are unpacked, the mail is sorted, and her bags are unpacked.

She takes the box to the dining room table. She imagines her mother sitting at her end of the table, the one with her back to the ocean. She places the box with Charlotte there. She sits in her old spot, the one far enough away from her mother's fork that if she misbehaved or put her elbows on the table it wouldn't stab her arm. "Manners. Manners. Manners." She doesn't remember her mother saying anything else at the table.

Missy has perfect table etiquette as a result. She knows the correct order and placement of the various pieces of silverware. She knows to eat with her left because you cut with your right. "What if you're left-handed?" she asked once.

"Don't be a silly girl. Rules are rules."

She was glad she was not left-handed.

She knows where the water glass goes and that there are differences between white and red wineglasses. "And of course, the port. Don't forget the port," she'd say. Charlotte would laugh when she said that. She never understood it. She looks at the box and asks her, "Why did you laugh at the port glass placement, Mom?"

The doorbell rings, startling her. She looks at the box again and shakes her head. She looks up to the skies, something she finds herself doing more frequently since Charlotte's death. "You need to stop."

She opens the door and is surprised to see Margo standing there.

"I'm sorry I didn't call," Margo says as Missy opens the door for her to come in. They are long past showing each other affection when they greet each other. "I had to tell someone. And, of course, you're the only one who *might* care." *Might* feels harsh as she says it.

They walk to the kitchen. Missy looks at the clock. It's early afternoon, too early for wine. The sun hasn't yet started its decent. Or is it the earth that hasn't yet spun away from the sun? Even if Missy doesn't like the shorter days, fall sunsets are her favorites. The colors are more dramatic, more enhanced. The sun's light seems to dance with the autumn leaves as they change from green to orange, brown, and red. Then they die and have to be raked. She is glad she has someone for that.

Margo sees the box on the table and looks at Missy questioningly.

"It's Charlotte," she explains.

"Oh. She looks different," Margo says, trying not to giggle.

Seriously, when did Margo develop a sense of humor?

But she can't seem to stop giggling. Missy starts to giggle, too. They giggle together for what feels like minutes before they find themselves trying to breathe, blowing out air, inhaling slowly several times before regaining their composure.

"Should you open her?" Margo finally asks.

Missy takes the box and gently moves her fingers along the edges, breaking the tape with her nail, and pulls the flaps open. It is an eerie feeling, unpacking your mother's ashes. Her urn is exactly like that of her father's, sitting high on the bookshelf. *Charlotte Goodwin Kinkaid* is engraved across the front in italics. The urn looks like a trophy: shiny, with ornamental handles, a pointed top, and a tapered base. Missy wants to hoist it up and take a victory lap. Not because her mother is dead, but because that is how the urn makes her feel. She hadn't felt that way when she got Dex's urn, but then she was just so overwhelmed by sadness. Her hero was dead. The sadness was, of course, tempered with the hope that divorcing Cal had given her. Too many emotions were co-occurring when he died, she thinks.

Missy places her mother's urn next to her father's. She looks at Margo and says, "Let's pick a time to take these to the cemetery. They have a spot."

Margo smiles in agreement.

Missy looks at the clock again. "You know, I think the reunification of Dex and Charlotte is worthy of a toast, don't you?"

She pops open a bottle of her favorite bubbles. They sit in the living room with a view of the Atlantic Ocean on one side and Dex and Charlotte's urns on the other. Missy feels observed and moves seats so that they are both now facing outward, toward the ocean, away from death. She hates this new awareness that her mother is everywhere, like a holy spirit. Or a genie in a lamp.

They sip their champagne.

"So you needed to talk?" Missy finally says.

"Oh shit, I almost forgot." Margo never cusses. She reaches for her phone and begins to read. Missy watches intently.

"'Dear Margaret...'" She looks up at Missy. "So this is an email I got today. An email. Not a phone call. Not a letter. A fucking email." Missy thinks this must be bad. Again, Margo does not cuss. Margo hands Missy her phone. "You read it."

"'Dear Margaret, On behalf of the family of Russell Jones, we regret to inform you that you have no interest in his estate.'" Missy looks up. "When did Russell die?"

"Keep reading."

She does. "'It was the request of Mr. Jones that all his belongings, including money, homes, automobiles, and business enterprises be left solely in the name of his wife, Bernice Kozlowski Jones...' When did he remarry?"

Margo grits her teeth. "Keep reading."

Missy does. "'...upon her death, any and all remaining properties will go to their two sons, Ashton and Bryson.' When did he have kids?"

"Keep reading," she says one last time.

"'As you have been divorced for more than the time deemed appropriate by law, you are not entitled to receive additional remuneration.'" Missy is silent as she finishes reading the rest.

"Blah, blah, blah," Margo finally says. Missy is speechless. "We were going to name our son Ashton. Ashley if it was a girl." Margo doesn't know if she should cry or laugh. Missy doesn't either.

"What the fuck? Like seriously, WHAT. THE. ACTUAL. FUCK?" Missy blurts out, stunned.

"I didn't know. I didn't care. He was awful to me when we couldn't have kids. He hated that I asked for the divorce before he could. He hated paying me a pittance for spousal support. Turns out he's loaded. Has a wife and two boys. How does an asshole like that get so lucky?" she wonders.

Missy holds up the phone, waving it at Margo. "He was fifty-five years old. And now he's dead. I'm not sure that's so lucky either."

"Ugh. I know. But he got to have kids. He got to have our dream. Just with someone else. And I'm forced to accept I was the reason we couldn't."

They sit there in silence for a moment, sipping their bubbles, staring out over the ocean, watching as the sun's rays attempt a tired dance on the water. It's an unusually calm late fall afternoon.

"You really don't seem that upset," Missy finally breaks the silence.

"I'm not." Margo sighs. "I really, truly hated him. I know I was never meant to have children, and I can't pretend to understand that someone else loved him and they got to have children. Feels a little like a slap in the face is all."

"Again, he's dead. Those kids don't have a dad anymore."

"Well, neither did I. I hope their mom is better than the one I got. The ones we got," she corrects herself. "Also, what's up with using the word 'remuneration'? Who says that? Just tell me I get nothing. To be honest, I never in my life have given a thought to what would happen when Russell died." She realizes she should have, at least early on, but Margo was financially stable without Russell's money.

She begins to laugh. "You know what I used to do with the money he paid me? I donated it. All of it. He hated giving money to charity. Thought it a racket. We never spoke once after the divorce was finalized. He stopped having to pay me years ago. Honestly, he could have just died. I didn't need to know."

Missy realizes that she and Cal will always be connected through their children. As much as she didn't want to be married to him anymore, she is grateful that he is alive and in his children's lives. Missy feels sadness for Russell's children.

"I wonder what they look like," Margo admits.

"The kids?" Missy asks.

"All of them. Her. The boys."

Missy pulls out her phone and types in the name 'Ashton Jones' on Facebook. There are fifteen search results. Then Bryson Jones. Ten. "What does the letter say his wife's name is?"

Margo looks. "Bernice Kozlowski Jones. God, that's an awful name."

"Yes, it is. But there is only one of her." They scroll through Bernice's pictures. They both admit that they looked happy. Bernice was plain. Russell was bald and fat. The boys looked like they'd won the genetic lottery, getting the good DNA not afforded either of their parents. Margo says flatly, "At least she isn't pretty."

"Wonder how he died," Missy says. The letter did not say. Bernice did not say even though she posted, "RIP, my love," and added a broken heart emoji.

"I'm guessing the same way his dad did," Margo muses. "Massive heart attack. Diabetes. They were a very unhealthy family."

Missy feels no bitterness in Margo's words. More than anything, she realizes her cousin is more human than she gives her credit for.

# Chapter 28

## *Ashes to Ashes, Dust to Dust*

As the pieces of Missy's life start to fit together like the pieces of a puzzle, she feels her spark growing. She feels it ignited inside her, roaring again. It hasn't been easy, she reminds herself. There is no guarantee moving forward. But she knows she can handle anything life throws at her. She's proven that. She doesn't want to be afraid of tomorrow. Of the potential for love and loss. Whether by lovers, friends, parents, or family, she recognizes being allowed to love is a gift.

Missy doesn't know if spending the weekend away with Zander has given her a renewed perspective on her relationship with Margo. Still, she feels something gnawing at her inside, like there are unresolved things between them. Who is she kidding? There is a lifetime of unresolved issues. The bigger question becomes how to address them.

As Missy feels herself come alive again, she actually hopes that Margo will follow her lead. *Just this once.* If Missy allows herself to hope at this age, then so should Margo. If she allows herself to love, then so should Margo. If she can be unapologetically herself, then so can Margo.

The day they plan to take the urns to the cemetery, Margo surprises Missy by asking if she can bring Adeline's, too.

"You still have her ashes?" Missy remarks. "It's been over twenty years."

"I didn't know what to do with them. Adeline just spread my dad's ashes in the backyard under his favorite tree. She left a bottle of whiskey and a cigar behind. The next morning, both were gone."

"That's creepy," Missy says. "I didn't know that."

Margo looks at Missy and starts to giggle. "I took them. I tried the whiskey, then poured it out where she put the ashes. I lit the cigar and took a puff. It was disgusting. I buried it in the dirt with his ashes. I was trying to connect with him on some level. Adeline said it was the devil that did it. I was okay with that." She gives a big sigh of relief. "God, it feels good to finally get that off my chest." Missy wishes she had known *that* Margo. She sounded fun.

"You're actually pretty funny, Margo," Missy says as they walk to the car, carrying three urns.

"I can be. Just no one ever sees me that way."

"I've always thought you were special, you know. I always wanted you to be happy. I wanted you to find a good man. I wished for you to have children. I hated those years when we lost our way."

"I slept with Cal. I get it," she says as she waits for Missy to unlock the car.

"Yeah. That was pretty bad."

"I've never said I'm sorry for that," she admits.

"Were you?" Missy asks.

Margo thinks about it as they carefully place the urns on the floor of the back seat, stuffing old towels between them to prevent them from shifting. Missy gets in the driver's seat, and Margo gets in the passenger seat. They buckle in, and then Margo finally speaks.

"I've asked myself that over the years. I wanted to be you. My whole life, I wished I was you. You had the perfect dad. You had the cute boys. You had the friends. You had Cal. And Macky and Kaid. You always had a light around you, Missy. Everywhere you went, you just shone. People always stopped and looked. And I felt like I was just your shadow. An afterthought." Margo feels a tear roll down her cheek. Missy hands her a tissue, then takes one for herself, leaving the car in park.

"God, Margo. If you only knew how hard it was for me to pull that off sometimes. I didn't always accept it either." She reaches across to her cousin and pulls her into an awkward car hug. "I had always hoped you'd share the light with me, not get lost in the shadows."

"You do cast a big shadow," she says, then blows her nose. "I was never sorry, though. I know that sounds awful."

"No, it sounds honest. Like you're allowing yourself to feel what you want to feel, not what everyone else makes you believe you should feel."

"I really wanted to hurt you. Because your life was perfect."

"You hurt me with the man I was divorcing. How was that perfect?" Missy wonders.

"Cal didn't want me for me. He wanted me to hurt you. It wasn't about me. It was about you. It didn't work. I knew that as soon as he left. You were too smart for that. And he used me. I was embarrassed. So I became a coldhearted bitch instead."

"Well, that we can agree on," Missy says, laughing. "I miss you, Margo. I really miss you. Our conversations. Our heart-to-hearts. Our birthdays. I want the old you back."

Missy tells her she wishes for them both to allow themselves to hope. To love. She hopes they can be unapologetically themselves.

"Let's make a pact. A sort of pinky promise," she says, thinking of Zander. "We old women of mid-fifty-something. We don't need to be precise," she declares. "We do hereby solemnly swear that we will find peace with all the parts and pieces of our lives. And that we will be there for each other 'til the end of time. And that, more than anything, we will not die crazy like our mothers."

Missy knows that version of Margo exists. Margo hopes she does. too. With Missy's encouragement, she believes she will. Somewhere behind the bitter walls of divorce, behind the sadness of not having a child she so wanted, tucked away behind the facade that she believed she wasn't worth loving is a Margo waiting to bloom into the most beautiful version of herself.

The cemetery in Sullivan's Island has long been a historical site, no longer burying or interring bodies. As high schoolers, they would sometimes dare each other to walk the tombstones. It was an eerie feeling, walking through, knowing bodies were buried under the ground that bore witness to history—the good, the bad, the ugly. Neither Missy nor Margo knew of any ancestors buried there, but several classmates would share stories of long-gone ancestors who had fought in the Civil War. "Of course, they fought against slavery," they would say. No one wanted to own their families' direct connection to supporting slavery, but it was hard to ignore. It was the South.

Her father had reserved their niche in the columbarium in a small cemetery just outside of Charleston. Dex's parents had both been buried there. Missy does not remember ever visiting them. There is much she does not recollect hearing about. When she was old enough to recognize that other children had grandparents, she asked if she had any. Dex said they had all died before she was born. They were never mentioned again.

They sing eighties songs on the way to the cemetery.

Madonna, Cindy Lauper, Men Without Hats, Prince, Duran Duran. They scream, "Don't you forget about me," as Simple Minds plays. They eye each other as if to say, *How appropriate.* "West End Girls" by the Pet Shop Boys begins as they pull into a parking spot. The first line about being better off dead, then thinking you're mad and unstable, leaves them in stitches. Missy looks over her shoulder. "Yup, they're dead. And two of them were mad and unstable."

Margo laughs even harder, then tries to speak. "We're sick."

"But not dead, mad, or unstable," Missy blurts out before she is consumed by uncontrollable laughter. Margo can't stop laughing either. The mirth between them is genuine, like it was when they were little girls.

They compose themselves, exit the car, and grab the urns. Missy has Dex under her right arm and Charlotte under her left. She is mildly fearful of dropping them, so she focuses intently on the path in front of her.

Margo holds Adeline in wrapped arms over her chest. She, too, doesn't want to drop her mother. Or maybe she's hugging the urn because she can. Hugging the urn feels like hugging Adeline might have felt if Adeline had allowed hugging. If she had, Margo figures, it would have been cold, stiff, and sterile. She can't remember her mother's touch. Only how she felt when she found her lifeless body. She was no colder in death than she had been in life, Margo remembers thinking.

"Do you know where we're going?" she asks Missy. "And why have we never been to the cemetery before?"

"Well, you buried your dad by a tree, and our other dead parents have been held hostage in these ridiculous-looking urns." Missy gawks at the ones in her arms. "How did my dad ever think these were nice? And why does Adeline have the same one?"

"Maybe they had a family special or a coupon," Margo speculates.

The cemetery feels large. It's unfamiliar to them. The trail leads to a small, white chapel that sits in the middle. It is so white it looks like it has been recently painted. It sits in stark contrast to the grays and blacks of the headstones placed at the front of the rectangular plots, perfectly spaced throughout. The geometric lines formed by the various grave plots align perfectly from one to the next, forward, backward, and sideways. It feels perfectly laid out, like a master-planned suburban community. All that's missing is a clubhouse and community pool.

"It is peaceful," Missy finally says as they approach the door of the chapel. Margo opens the door, and they walk in. An elderly woman greets them. She looks like she herself rose from the dead and momentarily frightens both Missy and Margo. In a quiet, quavering voice, she asks how she can help them. They simultaneously hold up the three urns.

"Here to put them to rest," Missy says.

"Oh, I see. Do you have an appointment?" the old lady asks in a monotone, unsympathetic voice.

"Did we need one? My dad has a plaque. The man on the phone said to stop here. It's space 490A. My mom just needed to die so they could be together." It sounds cold as Missy says it, but she wonders how else she's supposed to explain it. Is there proper etiquette for the non-burial of your parents' ashes?

The old woman, who looks many years beyond her own expiration date, now also looks irritated. "Well, normally you would need to make an appointment so we can get someone to open the compartment. We'd have a pastor, minister, priest, whichever you prefer. They'd say a blessing before."

"We drove from Sullivan's Island. They don't need the extra blessings. They're good," Missy says.

Over the tops of her glasses, her cloudy, cataractous eyes look them up and down, and then she lets out a harrumph. She walks to a desk and pulls out a large book. "What is the name?" she asks.

"Kinkaid. Dexter and Charlotte."

The old woman flips through several pages. "I see." Then she looks at Margo. "There are only two names listed for the columbarium. Who is the third?"

"This is my mother, Adeline. She was Charlotte's sister. They were very close," she lies. "She died suddenly but had requested they be together in death." She lies again.

The old woman proceeds to explain that it is against their policy to allow more than two urns in a niche. Missy digs deep into herself, portraying an emotionally damaged woman, deeply devastated by the passing of her kin. "Please, ma'am. Our mothers were more than sisters. They were tied together. They were *crazy* for each other. And my father really would have wanted it. Please," she begs with her emerald-green eyes. She tries for tears but is unsuccessful.

The old woman looks around. "I had a sister, too. I would have wanted us to be together, but I seem to have lived longer than anyone thought." She chuckles at herself. "I think that's very sweet. Do not mention this to anyone, please."

The cousins enthusiastically nod in agreement.

Her name, it turns out, is Agnes, and she has a heart that Missy and Margo have successfully weaseled their way into.

Agnes takes them to the Kinkaid family niche, opens it for them, and watches as Margo puts Adeline to the very back. "Bye, Mom. Rest in peace." She feels sadness at the finality of the act. It feels real, like having her ashes in that urn at home all these years made her death less tangible.

Missy pushes Charlotte's urn tightly next to Adeline's and then places her father's in front of both of theirs. Her hand lingers over her father's name: Dexter Bartholomew Kinkaid. His face flashes in front of her. His hand holding hers as a little girl. The smile when he held his grandchildren for the first time. The grin when she said she asked for a divorce. His whiskey glass. The

Sunday newspaper. His old Mercedes. "Thank you, Daddy, for loving me like you did. I was so lucky," she whispers. She says nothing to Charlotte, mostly because she doesn't feel Charlotte's done haunting her yet. They've had a lot of conversations since her death. But what do you say to a mother who never could love you anyway? *Thank you for not killing me?*

They gently close the door on the niche. On the outside, the plaque bears their names just as they were inscribed on the urns. Their lifespans are also listed. It's strange to Missy to think how much her father had planned it all so that she would have to do none of it. He took care of her even up to the end. "Maybe we can ask them to add Adeline," Missy says.

Margo looks at her and smiles softly. She says, "I think that would be beautiful."

Agnes says a small prayer. Missy and Margo mutter, "Amen."

"Take your time here. I know this is hard," Agnes says.

"Thank you, Agnes, for making an exception," Missy says. Agnes smiles at the women. She pities them. She does not know their stories.

Missy and Margo do not want to be pitied. They both survived their childhoods. They survived mothers who did not know how to love them. Their lives have been messy, there's no doubt about that, but Missy and Margo have each other.

They decide to walk through the cemetery. "Let's make up stories about the headstones," Margo says.

"Oh, I love that." They walk to the first one they see: Willamina Randolph McCarthy Price. Missy begins, "Wilma, as she was known, died of a broken heart when she was just"—she pauses to quickly do the math—"an old maid of five and forty. She bore no children despite being married twice. Her poor husbands could not handle her insatiable sexual appetite. She died from lack of orgasms."

They giggle and walk to the next one.

"Martin Gregory Smith," Margo intones. "Ah, yes, of the prestigious Smith family. There were only a thousand of them in 1845 when he passed at the tender young age of sixty-seven. His wife, Miranda Collins Smith, outlived him by another twenty years. Alas, she was twenty years younger than he. That bastard. They had twelve children who would carry on the Smith name because there were not enough of those already."

They giggle some more.

"We're good at this, you know?" Missy says. "Maybe we should consider working together again. I'll write. You paint. It could be fun. We can call ourselves M&M Books."

"I would really like that," Margo says.

They come upon one last grave, and it catches Missy's eye. It reads: "Here lies Dexter Bartholomew Kinkaid III and Melissa Jean Kinkaid." Their death date is the same. Margo does a double take. Missy looks as if she's seen a ghost.

"Did you know?" Margo asks.

"That I was named after my dead grandmother?" Missy swallows. "I didn't know I had a dead grandmother. He never said a word." She stares a long time at the grave, wondering what their story was. She begins to make it up. "Dex and Missy. They were madly in love. They had a son they named Dexter IV, apparently. They told each other every day that they loved one another, that they had found their forever person." Missy begins to cry. "And then they were killed in a car accident while their only son miraculously survived and would grow up to be the most amazing human that ever lived." She has difficulty finishing the words, her speech gutted as the tears begin to flow freely.

Missy has not cried real tears since her father first died. She wanted to be strong even in moments when she was alone. She needed to be the superwoman everyone expected her to be. She did not allow herself to truly mourn his death, even though she missed him every day. She saw him in her children. She saw him in her home. Of course she saw him there. It was his. There were things she would never change about the place because they were a part of him.

She looks at Margo, who is also crying.

"Why are you crying?" she blurts out, half laughing, like it's the most ridiculous thing that they're at a cemetery crying.

"Everyone is gone. Vance. Adeline. Dex. Charlotte."

"Alfie," Missy adds.

"Alexandra," Margo whispers.

They sit on the edge of Dexter III's grave, their knees almost hitting their chins. Missy puts her arms around Margo and pulls her in. "We're all we've got anymore," Missy says. "So no more fuck-ups, please." They laugh through their tears.

"No more fuck-ups, I promise."

Missy and Margo sit for a long moment. They cry side by side. Really cry. They cry for a lifetime of tears not shed. For a lifetime of believing their mothers couldn't love them. They cry for the lost moments, and they cry for the beautiful ones, too. In their silence and tears, they recognize that having each other is a gift their mothers gave to them. It's a beautiful gift, wrapped in crinkly paper with a ribbon tied too tight and tape that didn't quite stick. It's messy, unaesthetic, but once you cut the ribbon and ripped the paper, tear open the repurposed cardboard box, and throw out the recycled tissue paper, the gift of each other is precious.

"We've got each other," Missy says as she gets up.

"Always," Margo says.

They hold hands like the small girls they once were. Then they begin to skip. Their giggles echo off the gravestones as they leave the cemetery.

Margo asks to stay the night at Missy's. They order pizza. They drink wine. They dance to ABBA. They talk the night away and sleep on the sofa.

The next morning, Missy gives Margo the blue Moleskine

notebook. Margo opens it. In the front, Missy has written in her finest calligraphy, *M&M Books*.

"I know the first story," Margo says. "It's about two girls who grew into strong women."

Missy likes this idea. "I can work with that."

# Chapter 29

## *The Bridges That Connect Us*

"It is exactly one month before Scarlet's wedding and exactly three months since I started dating Zander," Missy announces as they meet for a drink before book club. It isn't their usual routine, but Scarlet wants to ensure the invite list is complete.

"I know it's silly, but is there anyone I'm supposed to invite that I didn't?" She hands the list to Missy. It has exactly fifty names on it.

"This is so short," she says.

"I didn't grow up here," Scarlet reminds her.

"But Beau did."

"It's mostly people he knows."

"I guess I didn't realize Beau was such a minimalist," Missy says.

"I like that about him. Neither of us has complicated friends."

Missy sees Abby's name on the invite list. "Did you add her or did Beau?"

Scarlet rolls her eyes. "We talked about it. I felt I had to because of the book club. She'd be the only one I didn't invite. He felt like it would be rubbing it in her face... so he was all for it." She laughs as she says this. Missy, Margo, and Amber do as well. "I sent an invite, and he talked to her about it. She hasn't RSVPed yet."

They wonder if Abby will show up. She and Scarlet will never be close. There will always be a wedge between them that Abby cannot look past.

"If it wasn't you stealing her husband, it would have been someone else," Margo says. "She will never own her place in that marriage ending. She will always be the victim."

It surprises them to hear Margo say something negative about Abby. Margo has become more reflective since she and Missy mended fences. They like this about her. Maybe an old dog can learn new tricks, Missy thinks.

* * *

The women are oddly excited about book club tonight. Maybe because it's the last one before Scarlet's wedding or perhaps because they're discussing a book they all loved. They recognize how easy it was to choose a book they, sans Amber, had read before, but there was something so intrinsically beautiful about *The Bridges of Madison County*. Even Audrey, who hesitantly agreed to have this be their book, admitted to its inherent beauty. "I have read this book three times now. I cry every time, even though I know how it ends."

They begin with Amber, the only member to be reading the novel for the first time. "I get why you all love this book so much. Her choices are so painful. I wanted Francesca to pick Robert so badly. My heart ached for her. But then it was only one weekend. So do you really throw away everything for one weekend?"

This is a loaded question. Every one of these women knows it.

They are divorced. They know the pain of choices. Of not being chosen. It is not an easy subject.

Audrey looks at Amber. "What would you have done in a lonely marriage?"

Amber surveys the room. She has only known these women for a year. Most are a solid decade older than she is, but some were married as long as she was.

Amber was married to Mitchell for exactly eleven years and 364 days. She could no longer bear another day wishing for him to love her as he once did. Twelve years was not a number she could celebrate with him. Twelve years was one day too many. She knew that when she had the affair. She knew that when she told him one day before their twelfth wedding anniversary that she could no longer be married to him. He was married to his job. To his money. To his houses, cars, and homes. But he was not married to her. And Amber knew she was worth being married to—not because she was pretty, but because she was an intelligent, interesting woman who just happened to be pretty. She liked that part. But that wasn't the part she wanted Mitchell to see. She did not want to be a mere piece of eye candy stuck to him.

Mitchell acted stunned when she asked for the divorce. "But I have something amazing planned for tomorrow night," he said.

"Awesome. You go. Imagine me there. Because that's what it would have been like anyway. You center stage. You smiling at me because I wore the glitzy, glamorous, sequined dress I saw hanging in the closet, with the four-inch Jimmy Choo heels. I always wonder how Heather knows exactly what I like. Doesn't matter. Creepy to think she might be going through my closet. Creepy to think you pay her to shop for you. Just creepy, Mitch."

Mitch had never been at a loss for words before. He owned major businesses. No one questioned him. But his wife did. Mitch did not know of Amber's affair. Amber had been lonely in her marriage. Much like Francesca had been lonely in hers.

"I get the loneliness," Amber says, her words directed to the book club though her gaze drifts past them, lost in rumination. "I was married to a handsome man with more money than most of us know what to do with. But he didn't know how to be present. So when someone like Robert walks into your life, brings you back to life by how he looks at you, by talking to you, and then by reminding you what it feels like to be touched, to really be touched like you're the most beautiful creature on this earth, even when you're old, God, you take Robert and you let him love you."

The women are quiet. The speech feels oddly personal, like Amber is reflecting on something. And she is. She could never explain what drew her to Christian. Not until she read this book. He was all the things Robert had been to Francesca, and like Robert, Christian left because she could not go with him. She had tried after the divorce to find him, but she could not. All she had was a first name and a country of origin: Greece.

"You don't look Greek," she remembers telling him.

"My mother is Swedish." That explained the blond curls and light blue eyes set against his olive skin. He looked like a Greek god—delicious. He asked her to go with him. She thought it silly. They had only spent a weekend together, a nonstop weekend of sexual exploration. Christian reminded her what a man could do to a woman, and she remembered what it felt like to find pleasure in pleasing a man.

"Amber, come back with me. Come see what it's like in Greece," he asked her as he stood in front of his Lyft, waiting to go to the airport. "What have you got to lose?"

She thought to herself, *Everything*, but she did not say it. She stared at him, taking in every part of the most beautiful man she had ever seen. How was it as simple as him asking her for directions in a hotel lobby? How was it that they were in New York City at precisely that moment? How was it that Mitchell had cancelled on her at the last minute, telling her to go without him, that she should go to the shows they had tickets for, use the reservations to the fancy restaurants he had made, treat herself to beautiful clothes at Bergdorf Goodman, and stop by Tiffany's to pick up the necklace he had ordered for her? She didn't want to go alone, but she did.

Christian went with her to Bergdorf Goodman and helped her pick out a sexy negligée, which he later traced his hands over, moving his fingers gently along her breasts, down her tummy, and between her legs. He helped her try on the necklace, kissing her neck as he clasped it shut. They went to the shows, leaving at intermission to return to the hotel to take each other again. They ate at the fine restaurants, laughing as they tried to seductively eat fruit and vegetables, failing miserably.

"How does one eat a vegetable and make it sexy?" he asked.

She chomped down hard on a carrot and said, "Like this, luvah."

"That is not the least bit sexy," he said, then threw out an exaggerated "luvah" in his distinctively hot Greek accent.

If you could truly fall in love with a person in just a weekend, Amber did. As did Christian. So, in her mind, it didn't make it implausible that Francesca and Robert could fall in love with each other in a weekend, too. Amber finishes her thoughts on the book by saying, "I wish she would have gone with Christian." They look at her, confused, and she realizes her error. "I mean Robert." She remains silent as the rest of the book club members start to chatter in small groups, and Amber is left to wonder if there will ever be a way to find Christian again.

Audrey takes back control of the club. "It's an interesting question, isn't it? We're all older women. Most of us are a little older than Francesca. And, of course, we're all divorced. But do you think Francesca made the right decision to stay with her husband?"

Abby is the first to scoff. Scarlet and Missy both roll their eyes.

"One weekend? Really? How can anyone know after one weekend?" she says.

"I knew with my first husband," Dahlia says. Several of the other women also confess that they knew within a few days. It feels silly when they think about it now.

"I think when we're young, we want to believe in love. We are so open to the possibilities," Margo says. "Some of us are eager to believe that."

"I get it when we're young. We're naive. Stupid. All sorts of things," Sandra says, which is something of a shock because Sandra never says anything. She's a meek woman, and because of her shyness, no one is entirely sure what her story is. Or if she's ever said a word at book club before tonight. But she has been a part of the group longer than anyone other than the original four.

"I was eighteen. One weekend with Sam and I was gone." She stops for a second. "And knocked up. I know. Shocker. But I really did think he was the one. And he was for twenty years." She doesn't stop long enough for anyone to say anything. "I would have chosen Robert. I would have gone with him and taken whatever time we could have had together."

Most of the women agree with her, even if they are stunned by her dual confessions. Only Abby feels the need to defend Francesca's decision to stay. "It would have fizzled out. Like all love does."

Scarlet thinks it's no wonder Beau and Abby didn't work out in the end. Being with a negative person all the time, someone who only sees dark when it's light, is toxic. Beau is a light. Scarlet is a light. They both make their lives brighter. They make their world complete.

"You're like the frosting on a cake," Scarlet often says to him.

"Sweet?" he asks.

"Well, there is that. But the cake's already whole without the frosting. It's the frosting that makes the cake better." She had borrowed that from one of the self-help books she read after her divorce, but she believed it to be true.

Scarlet doesn't share her thoughts with the group. The women agree that finding love later in life is challenging. "Everyone comes to the party a little damaged," Missy says. "I can see why Francesca decides to stay. Richard is reliable. Robert is exciting, but he's unpredictable. He's a risk. We all say, except you, Abby, that we would choose to go with Robert. But we're old. And broken. If we were still married and faced with that same question, I bet most of us wouldn't go." And she's probably right.

After some more back-and-forth, the women change the topic to Scarlet's upcoming wedding.

"We're just so excited for you," Audrey says. "I haven't been to a wedding in a very long time."

Even if the women aren't all close, they move in the same social circles, at least within one or two degrees of one another, and there have not been many weddings in those social circles in recent years. They could use COVID as an excuse, but that isn't the case. Some of their children are of marrying age but often choose intimate destination weddings. Some want to wait until they were financially stable. Others see the mistakes their parents made and swear they'll never get married.

The women never considered that one of their own might get married, not until Scarlet came to town a year and a half ago. She stirred things up, but she also reminded them that love can happen at any age. She represents hope—except to Abby, who will outwardly never like Scarlet. Even if she secretly does, she would never admit it.

Scarlet says the wedding isn't going to be anything fancy. "Feels silly since it's the second time for both of us." She admits to being both excited and nervous. They already live together and have made his home their own.

Missy is thrilled to see that. She knows from her time with

Travis that moving into a home you didn't purchase together means one of you has more at stake in the property. Beau is sweet with Scarlet, finding ways to integrate parts of her life with his. Theirs is a truly blended home. It helps that Beau doesn't have many opinions about art, furniture, or colors. He speaks up if he hates a recommendation or if he likes something more subtle, but otherwise he lets Scarlet's creativity run wild. Scarlet is grateful for that.

"It's not silly. It's adorable," Audrey says. Audrey has focused for so long on her children that she has forgotten what it means to be loved by anyone else. In her mind, she knows that perhaps she has never truly known love. She isn't pretty like Scarlet. Or athletic. Or artistic. If she keeps going down that list, she worries she'd find no reason anyone could love her. This makes her sad. Audrey is the same age as Scarlet. *Fifty-six isn't old*, she tells herself. *There are enough years left in me to love someone and enough of me to love back.* In that moment, she resolves to seek guidance on how to meet an appropriate man. Scarlet is probably busy with her upcoming wedding, so she'll ask Missy. Because Missy always knows best.

Missy is grateful for her small circle of friends. It's hard to escape drama in Sullivan's Island. She knows everyone and is vigilant about who she lets in. When she was younger, she might have worried she'd be made fun of for having a mom in the loony bin. As she got older, though, she felt good in her own skin and didn't need that questioned. Life was complicated enough without the potential for toxic outside relationships. She liked having a balanced life.

Friendship, Missy realizes, has become the cornerstone of her existence. The women in her small circle of friends are the most important people in her life outside of her children, of course. Her relationship with Margo is on solid footing again, no longer overtly tainted by the poor decisions her cousin made in the past. She wonders if anyone ever believed Margo's story about Cal. Maybe they didn't. She wonders in what world anyone believed Cal to be an upstanding man and Missy the villain, even if she was the one who ultimately cheated and left him. She knew there was no room for an outgoing, fun-loving wife in his life. The more she tried to be herself, the more repressed he made her feel. She knows she could have allowed herself to be the victim. She could have believed his behavior toward her was earned, but she knew better. She knew she was more. She was worth seeing—and not just in sexy lingerie. She was smart. She was quick. She was Melissa Jean Kinkaid. She was proud to be a Kinkaid, crazy mother and all. Dropping Sutton from her name was the ultimate declaration of her emancipation.

# Chapter 30

---

## *The Ties That Bind*

The time leading up to Scarlet's wedding blurs together as one week passes to the next. Scarlet's Harlots still meet weekly. They talk about wedding preparations. They wonder how Scarlet stays so relaxed.

"Easy. Missy has taken care of everything," she says.

They offer a collective "ahh" to which Missy replies, "It only made sense."

Missy updates the women on Zander. She shares that she thinks she's in love with him, but they already all know that. She's been glowing. Radiating.

Margo tells them about Russell dying and that he had two children and a wife named Bernice. They are stunned by the news. "And we buried our parents," she chirps. "The crazy Goodwin sisters and Dex are sitting in a concrete box with their trophy urns. I kind of feel bad for Dex, stuck with our mothers for all eternity."

She laughs at her own joke. Missy giggles with her because she knows Margo's right. Dex has his hands full.

Amber is one weekend and four dates into her relationship with Tyson. In a rare moment of doubt, her insecurities begin to

258

surface. "I'm just afraid he's going to realize I have an old lady body and freak out. He's barely over thirty, and we haven't even talked about kids. Oh my god, what if he wants kids? See, this is why I can't."

"Stop!" Missy commands. "You are barely in your forties. You have never birthed a child. All of your parts are still in pristine condition. Keep fucking him. Please."

Amber is horrified, but the others can't stop laughing. "This isn't funny!" she says.

"Amber, I love how you don't know how perfect you are. It's endearing. Truly. But, honey, if you don't take this for the fun it is, you're just being stupid," Missy says. "Seriously. The last of us to have hooked up with a younger man was—"

"Don't go there," Scarlet says, cutting her off. They all briefly remind themselves of Scarlet's hot sex with Ben when she first arrived.

"I can't wait to meet Ben," Amber says, grinning as Scarlet cuts her a look. "Will he be at the wedding?"

* * *

"The haunted mansion on the water's edge has a name," Scarlet announces. "It's the Rutherford Residence. So formal."

"I could have told you that," Missy confesses.

"You only ever called it the haunted house!"

"It is. If you grow up here, that's what you know it as."

"And here I thought I was being so clever," Scarlet says. "Anyway, Beau knows someone who knows someone, and they are allowing us to use it for the wedding!" She shrieks with excitement, expecting the others to join in, so she is surprised when she is met with silence.

"Why would you want to get married in a haunted house?" Amber asks.

"Because it's the most beautiful building on the island. And I don't want a church wedding," Scarlet says. "Besides, it's kind of special to both of us. You'll know when you see it."

Amber accepts that answer, then asks, "Why is it haunted?"

Margo and Missy share a look. "Rumor has it that one hundred years ago, the daughter of the original Rutherfords hanged herself from the giant chandelier because her father forbade her from marrying some commoner. So now she haunts the halls. Sometimes they say you can even hear her say his name, Victor."

Margo bursts out laughing as soon as Missy finishes her tale.

"That's horrible," Amber breathes.

"It's also total bullshit," Missy admits. "It's an old house. It just feels haunted, so we made stuff up as kids."

"Oh, thank god," Amber replies.

The Rutherford Residence is the perfect venue. It stands tall and proud in its hallmark antebellum design, with perfect symmetry and a stone exterior. Guests are treated to the beautiful chandelier hanging in the foyer, catching glimpses of the glamorous dual staircases and pristine marble statues methodically placed in the foyer. The home is regal, distinguished, with a reserved but charming air.

The wedding takes place shortly before sunset. It is a perfect day, with only a splattering of clouds in the sky, deflecting the sun's rays as they reach for the ocean's surface. Fall brings subtle winds that dance with the leaves on the ground and challenge the waves to a duel. It is Mother Nature at her finest.

The guests arrive in semiformal attire. They admire each other, telling one another how wonderful they look. They ask if they've lost weight or done something new with their hair. They agree they should make plans to see each other more often. *Why does it always take a special occasion to bring us together?* They wonder aloud repeatedly.

Dahlia has saved the entire second row for the Divorced Women's Book Club. She figures they are all practically family. The women are synchronized in dress. Three of them wear varying degrees of emerald; three wear brown in shades of chestnut, taupe, and bronze; and three wear blue: one baby blue, one navy blue, and one in slate.

The final three members of the club in attendance are Missy, Amber, and Margo. They consider themselves the unofficial bridesmaids and decide to wear dresses in the same shade of scarlet red. Missy hates how it clashes with her hair, so she chooses to wear it up in a ballerina bun. She is satisfied with how it looks.

Margo feels plump in the form-fitting, off-the-shoulder dress she chose. Alterations make the dress's slit go halfway up her thigh. She's uncomfortable with this much skin exposed in public, but as she stops at the mirror for one final inspection, she smirks just a little, admitting to herself she feels kind of sexy.

Amber, meanwhile, stuns in her dress. Her perfectly symmetrical, *I've never breastfed* breasts are firmly in place; her flat middle makes a straight line down to her long legs. "No bumps other than her boobs," Missy whispers to Margo. Amber is nearly as tall as Missy, and they stand in stark contrast to Margo's short stature. Margo feels like the tiny storage shed between two skyscrapers. She is thankful they don't actually have a role in the wedding and will be seated.

The wedding guests are seated in the giant ballroom, the room where Beau knew he loved Scarlet for the first time. The room that could have been a disaster. In the end, in this moment, the room is the most beautiful place in all of Sullivan's Island. The giant windows open to the ocean and allow perfectly measured light to enter. The crushed red velvet cushioned chairs are perfectly spaced. Pink and white flowers are spread throughout the room.

Guests fill the room with excited chatter. A piano begins to play softly, and they fall silent. The giant double doors separating the ballroom from the rest of the mansion open, and they all stand.

On this crisp November evening, Scarlet walks down the long, black carpet runner that is exactly three feet wide and separates the guests on either side of the aisle. The simple yet beautiful crepe-draped U-neck column dress in ivory with the buttons down the back that she selected looks nothing like it did in the shop. It looks somehow more elegant and sophisticated. She elects not to wear a veil, thinking it feels too young, too virginal. Her hair, lightly curled, hangs loosely over her shoulders. She wears only enough makeup to be the center of attention. Her smile never ceases. She holds a small bouquet of pink roses. Pink has always been her favorite color. It should have been a shade of red to match her name, but it isn't. She left scarlet to her Harlots.

Beau stands in the front of the room, his profile illuminated by the setting sun, wearing a simple linen suit in an off-white shade. "They call it sand," he said to Scarlet when describing it. His shirt is white with the top button undone. He looks the dreamiest Scarlet has ever seen him.

Emily and Henry walk Scarlet down the aisle. It makes sense to her. They are her children. They are her everything. They beam with pride, overjoyed for their mother.

As Scarlet walks down the aisle past their friends, past strangers, past faces she doesn't recognize but knows she should, she beams. She doesn't let the memory of what happened here interfere. It's the place where she first realized she completely loved this man, and he her. She forgets the part where Abby attempted to destroy them.

Henry's wife, Hanna, is pregnant with their first baby. She is barely showing but cradles her tummy in her hands. Scarlet smiles as she passes her, admiring how tiny her belly looks, remembering how huge she was with both her children. "It's a girl," she whispers to Henry as they pass Hanna.

"You keep saying that. We'll see," he whispers back.

Scarlet has so much to look forward to.

Ben stands by Beau's side. It is no longer hard for her to see them side by side. It has been part of her journey. Ben has brought his new girlfriend to the wedding. She looks older than he does. *He has a type*, Scarlet lets herself think briefly. Beau's daughter, Bella, is weeks away from delivering baby number four. She rests her arms on her giant belly. Her husband stands smiling by her side. They are both happy, and Scarlet imagines it's because they left the kids with his parents for the weekend. Scarlet loves his children almost as much as her own.

Emily brought her new boyfriend, too, a man she had met playing adult league soccer. He has a beautiful British accent and awful teeth, but he makes Emily laugh, which brings Scarlet joy. Her only wish for her children is their happiness. It always came before hers. Today, though, on her special day, she feels they have all found a place of joy. A mother could not wish for more.

Beau beams as he takes Scarlet from her children. He tells her she looks beautiful. She feels beautiful. She feels lucky. Like she's living a dream. As they share vows and commit to their remaining years together, she thinks, *I never want to wake up.*

"There really aren't that many left, are there?" Beau will sometimes joke. It makes her sad, but she knows they'll love each other until they no longer exist. She will take every moment she can get with him. Cherish him. Love him. Want him. Nurse him. Bury him. But inside, she hopes he buries her first. She can't imagine a life without him.

Missy and Amber are in tears as the ceremony progresses. Zander gently grabs Missy's free hand as she blots her eyes, careful not to smudge her mascara. Four months into their relationship, and he is still there. Four months into their relationship, he whispers into her ear, "I love you."

She looks at him with her big, watery eyes. "Now? Really?" she says, half joking.

"You've honestly never looked more alive," he whispers to her. "Like I just needed to say those words to you because I fucking love you, Missy."

She wants to laugh. She wants to cry even more. It's Scarlet's day, but it's also the day Missy will remember that she felt all the flame. All the fire. Like she knew she was totally, completely alive again.

She tells him she loves him, too. He pulls her in tightly to his side as they watch Scarlet and Beau exchange vows. Scarlet winks at Missy as she walks past her on the way out. Missy mouths, "He loves me." To which Scarlet replies, "I know." Missy supposes she knew, too, but those are the most beautiful three syllables she has ever heard uttered.

* * *

Tabitha, now a famous photographer, shoots the wedding at Missy's behest. She admits the piece on Missy was partially responsible for her climb, so she feels that she owes her one. Scarlet and Beau take only a few family portraits: alone, together, and with their children. Bella feels like a whale and does her best not to throw a hormone-induced tantrum during the portrait session. Hanna does her best to hold in the tears she feels compelled to uncontrollably shed every few minutes. Scarlet and Beau are oblivious to any drama. Tabitha takes a candid shot of them standing to the side in a private moment, gently touching hands, sweetly kissing. It becomes their favorite photo, and Scarlet puts it on their mantel.

The guests are served appetizers and drinks on the outside

deck of the house. They watch as the sun sets quietly in the distance, leaving dusk to bid farewell briefly before the darkness comes. The lights switch on as if by magic. Missy jokes that maybe it was the Rutherford ghost in action. Zander looks confused, so she says she'll explain later, when they're alone. He could tell her he loves her all over again.

An hour later, the guests are led back inside. The grand ballroom where Scarlet and Beau wed has been dramatically transformed into a dining room. The velvet chairs are arranged around eight giant tables. Scarlet and Beau sit toward the front. As they take their places, Scarlet realizes how small their wedding really is. The room feels massive in contrast to the tiny space the guests take up. Funny how she didn't notice this as she walked down the aisle.

Scarlet doesn't remember eating the chicken cutlet or slicing into the asparagus spears. Or eating the rice pilaf she so adamantly demanded having as one of their sides. She remembers buttering a roll, but she doesn't remember eating it. She drinks red wine, careful not to let any get on her dress. She loves her dress. It makes her feel like a princess. An old princess, so maybe she should feel like a queen instead, but she likes the idea of a princess much better.

Scarlet knows she will always remember the cake. She'll remember how she and Beau stood in front of the three tiers flaked with white chocolate shavings. There is a rustic, heart-shaped cake topper. It is simple but perfect. They cut the bottom tier, hand in hand. Beau sweetly put some frosting, her favorite part, on his finger and puts it in her mouth. She licks it slowly. Beau then takes a small piece of cake. He does not push the cake in her face like younger couples do. Instead, he gently puts the bite in her mouth, brushes his thumb on her lips, stares at her, and then pulls her into a deep kiss. Everyone cheers.

The cake. The kiss. They are testaments to their love. This man is hers, and she is his. How different it feels to be married this time. How few expectations she has. She knows it won't always be easy. There will be trying times. They are getting older, and there will more than likely be health issues. But in this moment, she knows that whatever happens, they will be there together. It's nice, they will later admit, to have had the experiences they did so that together they can be better.

"So cliché," she will say.

"Sometimes the clichés just work," Beau will respond.

Margo shares a table with Missy and Zander. Amber does not bring Tyson, and no one asks her why not. She looks happy, and they think nothing more of it.

Margo sits next to a man at the wedding reception whom she does not know. He says he is a friend of Beau's from their early firefighting days. His name is Drake. He is talkative. He asks questions about her. Compliments her. They make each other laugh, and then he asks her to dance. On the dance floor, he asks if she's married. She asks if he is. They smile warmly at each other. She feels herself drawn to him. It has been a long time since she felt anything inside her stir.

So when Margo mutters out loud, "God, that was romantic," as Beau takes Scarlet in that cake kiss, she is surprised when Drake smiles and then excuses himself from the festivities. Margo is beside herself. Is she that much of a turnoff to a man? She realizes it has been a long time since she's found herself in any sort of situation involving one, so maybe she misread Drake's cues. She holds on to her confused feelings throughout the night. *It doesn't matter,* she thinks. *I felt good for a little while.*

The reception ends at ten. One of the benefits of being old is that no one expects the party to go all night. Even their children find it an acceptable time to end. Thank goodness for the pregnant women, they think. Young, single adults can go all night. Alcohol acts like meth, shooting through their veins, giving them an artificial high. Or, more likely, it's the possibility of a one-night stand that drives them. There are no one-night stands at this wedding. And all are relieved.

Despite the darkness, the wedding guests stand on the stairs in front of the Rutherford Residence. Scarlet and Beau say their goodbyes and walk toward the BMW X3 she arrived in from California. It symbolizes her journey and is much preferred to his refurbished yet unreliable VW van in cherry red.

"But it's a classic," he had pitched previously, as they discussed their get-away car.

"It is," Scarlet agreed, "but I'd like to make it to the airport and know when we land, we'll still have reliable transportation home."

"We could just Uber."

"Okay. I admit it feels kind of symbolic to me. Like I made the journey here. It got me here safely."

Beau appreciated her honesty. "Okay. You win. Plus, I'd rather not have people write all over my cherished *Brigitte Bardot*."

"The van has a name?"

"Of course she does. Doesn't every classic car have a name?"

Scarlet laughed, remembering the first car she bought. She called her nondescript shade of green VW Scirocco Kaiser Willie. She wonders why she never named another car after that. It just made sense at the time, she told herself.

Missy, Margo, and Amber have written *Just Married* on the BMW's back window and painted hearts around the message. They tied old cans on a string to the trailer hitch. For an added touch, they placed artificial roses wound with wired stems on the door handles. It was cheesy, they thought, and weddings still needed a little cheesiness.

Wedding guests throw small handfuls of Rice Krispies at the newlyweds. It makes Missy laugh. At least no birds will be harmed. And the sentiment of showering the new couple with well wishes is duly received. Zander wonders why Missy giggles as they throw the cereal.

"Inside joke," she says.

Scarlet stands at the passenger door while Beau opens it. She smiles warmly at her friends as their faces are illuminated under the bright lights lining the steps to the car. She feels their love, their friendship, their hope. She feels lucky to be living this life. To have found Beau. To have weathered life's stormy seas. To have her children by her side. To be accepted by Beau's. To have the craziness of Ben behind her. (She skips over Abby.) She knows second chances are real.

Before Scarlet gets in the car, she stops. She does not look back. She simply takes the bouquet of pink flowers and tosses them backward over her head. Everyone cheers as she does this. Beau beams as he watches his happy bride, knowing he is the luckiest man in the world to be her husband.

Several of the book club women surge toward the flying flowers. Missy, Amber, Audrey, and Dahlia almost fall over each other as they half laugh, half fight to claim their future, but a wind blows, changing the bouquet's trajectory. The flowers land squarely in the surprised hands of Margo. The other women stop, compose themselves, and then cheer with everyone else. Scarlet winks as she sees this. Missy thinks maybe it will be Margo's time after all.

"Come on, husband," Scarlet says to Beau as she climbs into the car. "We don't have forever."

He likes how the word "husband" flows so easily from her lips. "Yes, wife," he teases back, then whispers in her ear, "But you're wrong. We do have forever."

This makes Scarlet smile.

They wave as they drive away, cans clattering behind them.

# Chapter 31

## *Happily Ever Day After*

The day after the wedding, Margo finds herself at the park. She tries to forget Drake. She wants to beat herself up for imagining any extra moments with him. She's resigned herself to a life as Sullivan's Island's perennial spinster, and she should be content with it. She knows the others talk about her like that. At least she imagines they do. They must, she convinces herself. Why else would they stop talking when she enters the room? Why do they talk about mundane things when she's there? Do they really think she's incapable of discussing their husbands, lovers, boyfriends, or children? She knows they do. She's trying to be better. Missy makes her see that she's more than a shadow. She needs to own her light. She let herself believe for a brief moment that Drake could see that light.

"Silly, stupid Margo. You never change," she chastises herself.

She sits on the park bench a half mile from her home. She likes coming here to think. She likes watching the children play. She can see her own children playing here. She imagines Skyler and Jacob, her twins, as they scream with joy. She tells them to be careful. Skyler is bigger than Jacob when they're little, but Jacob passes his sister when they're teenagers. Margo tucks the fantasy away. Even after losing Alexandra. Even after learning about Russell's two sons. She just changes the names now. She's never shared that with anyone. She imagines even Missy would have thought it stupid; that she was torturing herself. But she knows Missy never wished anything bad upon her, even when she deserved it.

Margo watches as a little boy falls. A man scoops him up from behind. "It's okay," the man says. The boy looks confused, unsure whether to cry. The man kisses his knee. "See? All better," he says. The boy giggles and jumps out of the man's arms. The man chuckles, tells the little boy to slow down, then turns toward the bench where Margo sits. His eyes light up when he sees her.

"Margo? Is that you?"

She smiles cautiously as she recognizes Drake. He walks toward her and sits down. She's surprised by this. Didn't he make it clear last night that he wasn't interested?

She takes inventory of Drake. He looks older than he did at the wedding reception. She guesses he's in his mid-sixties. His hair is thinning, and he cuts it to minimize the look of a receding hairline. He looks handsome this way. His eyes are an off shade of brown. Or maybe hazel. She gets confused by hazel sometimes. They dance, though, just like they danced last night. He's wearing black Vuori sweatpants and a grey Henley shirt. He looks fit. How did she not notice how fit he looked last night? She knows she is not fit. She suddenly feels fat. And very short without her heels.

He apologizes for leaving the wedding early. "I got an urgent text saying Caleb wasn't feeling well."

"Caleb?" she asks.

"My grandson." He points to the little towhead whose knee he kissed earlier. "He's my world." He holds back tears as he says this.

Margo feels herself get choked up watching him. She says, "He seems sweet."

"His dad—that's my son—and his mom were killed in an accident a year ago. I'm all he knows. I retired to take care of him. I suppose we're each other's world."

Margo shares that she never had children, though that was not by choice. She realizes that the pain of not having children cannot compete with the pain of losing a child. She watches Drake smiling and waving at Caleb.

Caleb runs up to him. "Pop-Pop, I'm hungry."

Margo feels saddened. It has been wonderful sitting next to this man, watching him, realizing she was not why he left last night.

"Walk with us?" he asks her as Caleb grabs his hand, pulling him up from his seat. She laughs at the sight of a small child using all his strength to pull Drake up.

As Margo walks with them, she and Drake talk. Drake tells her he lives just over the bridge in Mount Pleasant. She asks if there's a Mrs. Drake. "There was once a Mrs. Hollis." He looks at her with a smirk. "You do know Drake is my first name?"

She smiles. "Of course. I never caught a last name."

"Her name was Stephanie. And she passed away during COVID, but not from it. It's complicated. How about you? No Mr. Margo?"

She likes his sense of humor.

"No. I'm a Harper. I was once a Jones. We divorced a long time ago. He did just recently die, though." She says this way too perkily, to the point that Drake gives her a questioning glance. "He was not the nicest man. At least, not to me."

He watches her not with pity, which is the look she is used to getting. Instead, his gaze is one of opportunity. "You believe in fate?" he asks.

This is a loaded question for Margo. If she believes in it, then it means her life has been fated to be a disaster. "I try not to," she confesses. "I had an alcoholic father. An absent mother. I couldn't have children. Love hasn't been in the cards for me." She slows as she says those words, realizing she has said too much. "What is it the kids say these days? TMI?"

He laughs at this. "Not TMI. I think honesty, candor, and the ability to own how we got here are refreshing. So many people make excuses, lament things they couldn't control. When Stephanie died, it felt like a cruel joke, but I wasn't laughing. I forgot how to laugh for a long time. Then my son died, and I really couldn't believe the cruelty of that on so many levels. But then I stopped. I looked at Caleb. I saw all the flowers around him, and I just started to smell the air. Life is a gift. It is not guaranteed. So I'm enjoying every day to the best of my ability. So go to dinner with me, Margo. I think fate might have something to do here. And I'm going with it."

This makes her smile. Then she laughs like a giddy schoolgirl. It feels so good to laugh like this, she thinks. Drake impresses her. He looks at her like she's beautiful without saying the words.

"Is that a yes?" he asks.

"Yes. That's a yes."

"So only one problem," he says, and Margo's heart sinks. "I don't have a babysitter. Never needed one before."

Margo is suddenly relieved. "I think I can take care of that."

Margo thinks of Macky, but it is Missy who winds up watching Caleb. She squeezes Margo's hand as she and Drake head out the door.

"Have fun on your date," she says, and she truly seems to mean it.

A date? Margo is going on a date with a man she met at a wedding. She doesn't allow herself more than the moment to revel in that fact, but she finds she can't stop smiling. Neither can Drake.

"You look beautiful, Margo," he says as they walk to the car. "I'd like to kiss you if that's okay."

Margo's heart flutters. Her stomach churns. They stop, and he leans in and sweetly kisses her lips. It is a lingering peck. It feels like she imagines a real first kiss should feel. Not like the leftovers she devoured in high school.

"That was nice," she says as he pulls away, grinning from ear to ear. He has one crooked tooth in his otherwise perfect mouth. She likes it. It makes him feel real.

Missy gently pulls the curtain aside to afford herself a glance. She sees the kiss, and her heart melts for Margo. Little Caleb tugs at her arm in that moment, begging her to build a fort. She stares at Caleb and can't help but think he'll be the luckiest little boy in the world if he gets to grow up with Margo in his life.

For over fifty years, Margo has tried to be like someone else. Now that she has finally allowed herself to come out of Missy's shadow and be her own, true, authentic self, she has blossomed into a mesmerizing, confident woman. Drake saw that immediately. Missy knows Drake will love Margo in all the ways she never knew she could be loved.

"Missy always loved me," Margo will tell Drake. "Even when I didn't make it easy for her."

When they are old, Drake and Margo will sit on their porch and say, "Maybe it was fate after all."

The day after the wedding, Missy wakes up tangled in Zander's limbs. His arm rests across her chest; his leg is bent against her thigh. His weight feels like a firm pressure against her body. On her other side, Enzo snores loudly. It makes her happy sharing the bed with the two of them. She is stuck between two perfect creatures. She represses the tiny part of her that feels claustrophobic in the moment. Zander snorts like he forgot to breathe, gasping for that missed air. She wants to giggle at how perfect it sounds. She closes her eyes and allows herself to hold on to this moment.

Missy knows she can't predict what will happen in the future with Zander. She knows she does not need a man to define her. She is, after all, Missy Kinkaid. She stands strong and resilient on her own two feet. But it is Zander who has made her come alive, made her remember what it was to feel like a sensual woman.

Missy takes a long, deep breath, feeling the oxygen penetrate her lungs, filling them. Her chest rises, and still Zander does not move.

She had fire once before Cal, and she had it in the beginning with Travis. She hadn't realized how deprived of oxygen her lungs had been. She reflects on the past few years, the ones she has spent navigating life alone, on her terms. The flame was extinguished in her darkest moments.

As she lies next to Zander, she realizes it isn't him—or any other man, for that matter—that makes her fire roar. It's her children. It's Margo. Her friendships. Even those damn book club women. They are the ones who helped her spark light. Her circle of life, the people she would go to the ends of the earth for, are the ones who brought her back from the ashes and truly made her fire burn.

She recalls her seventh-grade science teacher explaining that fire needs oxygen, fuel, and heat. She often lacked enough air, but now she breathes deeply, her fire burning brightly once more. She glows, content in the moment.

# Chapter 32

## *Life Is Like a Box of Cereal*

Life in Sullivan's Island settles back into its routines after the wedding. The Divorced Women's Book Club resumes their meetings on the third Thursday of the month. The group grows to fourteen women. This frazzles Audrey only a little. Inside, though, it makes her feel like the popular girl. Scarlet's Harlots continue with their weekly w(h)ine sessions. They relish their place in each other's lives. Margo and Missy begin writing books together.

Months later, Missy runs into Travis at a fundraiser. Chemo has aged him, but he is in remission and doing well. "They caught it early enough," he says. She is genuinely happy to hear it. Comet helped him get through his active cancer treatment, he said, and passed away shortly after.

"Alfie's gone, too. I hope they find each other," she says. It makes her feel lighter thinking about their dogs being reunited in heaven. She tells Travis she is happy, splitting time between Sullivan's Island and Charleston without telling him specifics. He says he is, too. His blues eyes sparkle with a familiar light, but they no longer dance like they used to. He laughs. Hearing it reminds her how delightful it used to sound against her ear. She forces herself to repress the memory. "You were a beautiful love, Travis," she tells him as she releases him from a farewell embrace. He doesn't have the words to say letting her go has been his one regret.

* * *

Missy and Zander find joy in simple day-to-day things. They enjoy morning coffee together. He cooks dinner. She offers moral support. "You only love me for my cooking," he teases. He knows this isn't true. She tells him daily all the reasons she feels like the luckiest woman in the world, and he tells her daily he loves her. It feels right. Just like it should.

They even shop for groceries together. Today, Missy decides to walk down the cereal aisle. Charlotte's cryptic messages have grown further apart since she and Margo placed her urn in the columbarium. She momentarily wonders if she dreamed it all, but she knows she hasn't. Life has been very real, and Charlotte, some-how, was very much a part of it in death. *The irony*, Missy muses.

She stops in the cereal aisle and thinks back to that fateful day in early summer. She mentally scans the boxes. Was he there? Obviously, he could not have been. He hadn't been a part of her past. But she sees him. He was the leprechaun on the box of Lucky Charms, the only box on the shelves that didn't have a photo. Zander was the box of Lucky Charms. She smiles as she comes to that conclusion.

Missy does not think of herself as an overly sentimental person. She prides herself on her strength and conviction. She was confronted by heartbreak and sadness that forced a deeper exami-nation of the woman she knew she was. She would be lying if she hadn't thought of running away, disappearing, hiding under the covers and never awakening. There were dark moments in those years. There were secrets and stories that came together to create the canvas of her life.

She realizes she didn't see herself amongst the boxes of cereal that day. Maybe she was the milk. She was what made the dry cereal palatable, easier to chew. She gave it added nutritional value. Sometimes the cereal would get soggy, and it would get tossed. Other times there wasn't enough milk left in the container, making it hard to chew. But there were those cereals she knew she had given just the right amount of milk to. She had loved Cal. She had loved Travis. And she has just enough milk left to love Zander. She isn't a cow with an endless supply, after all. Missy laughs at herself for getting carried away with the whole milk analogy. All she knows is that she has given love, had it taken away, but in the end she has stood strong enough to welcome it again.

Zander rounds the corner, exasperated, his arms full of groceries. "I forgot a cart. Good thing you've got one." As he releases the items into the cart, he notices it's empty. "What's up?"

Missy puts her arm through his and gently kisses his cheek, staring at him for an extra-long moment. He would not understand the story of her life in cereal boxes. She's not sure she would have either. She looks up to the heavens she knows are beyond the newly replaced ceiling tiles, and mouths the words, "I love you, Mom," sensing the gift of reflection her death has given.

As they walk down the cereal aisle, Missy smiles. She grabs the box of Lucky Charms and puts it in the basket. Zander looks baffled.

"A happy memory," she says.

He smiles and grabs a box of Frosted Flakes.

And, of course, they will stop for milk.

# About the Author

Kirsten Pursell is a best selling and award winning author known for engaging narratives that often blend romance with deeper emotional themes.

Outside of writing, she is an avid swimmer who enjoys training and competing in open water and pool events near and far. She is fluent in German, loves to channel her inner mermaid through SCUBA adventures, and will travel just about anywhere given the opportunity. Time with her now adult children is her favorite (a nonfat latte a strong second). She lives in Southern California. Visit www.kirstenpursell.com to learn more about her books.

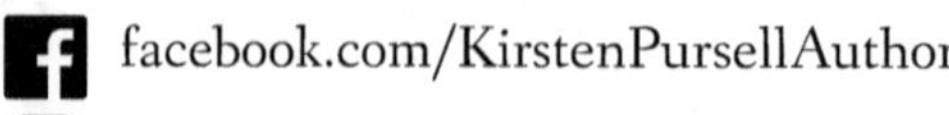 facebook.com/KirstenPursellAuthor

instagram.com/kirstenpursell

# Also by Kirsten Pursell

Finding Scarlet

Long Enough to Love You

On Becoming Me: Memoir of an 80's Teenager

Harvard

Company Clown: The rise and fall of a corporate icon

www.ingramcontent.com/pod-product-compliance
Lightning Source LLC
Chambersburg PA
CBHW071458110726
47908CB00003B/656